JONATHAN BROOK is tw[...]
born in Los Angeles, Calif[...]
family relocated to Leed[...]
soon installed in the loc[...]
nothing of particular note except learn to play the
guitar and skank. As a member of an almost-known
Ska outfit he toured the UK for a number of years,
finding time to write reviews and music articles along
the way. Moving to London in the late Eighties
Jonathan did more of the same including studio work
and US/Japanese tours for many an Acid Jazz band
including the Night Trains and the Humble Souls. The
closest he has ever come to any sort of stability was
his three years' work with rocksteady superhero
Desmond Dekker. HERBSMAN is Jonathan's third
Backstreets novel, his first two being SLACKNESS, and
the clubland classic, BIG UP!

BACKSTREETS

HERBSMAN
JONATHAN BROOK

B☘XTREE

First published in the UK in 1995 by
Boxtree Limited
Broadwall House
21 Broadwall
London SE1 9PL

10 9 8 7 6 5 4 3 2 1

Cover Art – Eddie Otchere
Cover Design – Martin Lovelock
Series Editor – Jake Lingwood

Phototypeset by SX Composing Limited, Rayleigh, Essex
Printed and bound in Great Britain by
Cox and Wyman Ltd, Reading, Berkshire

ISBN 0 7522 0622 2

A CIP catalogue record for this book is available
from the British Library

For Pinewood and he who sails within

One

Wednesday

I gave him a chance to prevent all this. He could have nodded his head, muttered something about talking it through later and gone back to his newspaper. I would have smiled and waited patiently for our little chat in the evening, the sober advice and parental slap on the back as he talked, father and son coming together. That's what I wanted to happen. I've always been a law-abiding citizen, working hard at school, didn't cheat, lie or steal at any point. I've played it straight down the line and for all that honesty over the sixteen years and ten months of my life I was expecting a positive result.

"Dad, you know I'm close to seventeen."

"I do know how old you are."

"Well, seeing as I'm getting close to the test – driving, yeah – will you buy me a car?"

"No way."

Newspaper. Mother arrives with his coffee cup, places it by his elbow on the table and stands next to him with her arms crossed in full support.

"What's wrong with you using our car?"

"About a thousand things."

"Go on."

"It's old and tired, painted the *worst* shade of brown, he takes it to work every day so when could I use it to practise? It doesn't go over fifty . . ."

"How do you know that then?" His voice booms across the table, changing from the breakfast drawl to a shout in an instant. "You expect us to trust you with a car when you can't even respect the speed limit?"

"I was only saying it was slow."

"Reckless talk, boy, that's what it is. All you're thinking about is how fast you can go."

I have lost. They have something to moan about now, the shield of a parental gripe, so I abandon any hope of bringing the conversation back to my justifiable need of a car. I stare down at the floor. There is a moment of silence. He puts the paper on the table, stands and kisses my mother, then walks through to the hall where he collects his coat. That should be it, next comes the slam of the door. But instead he returns, stomps back into the kitchen. I can see he feels foolish to have lost his temper but is too proud to calm down.

"You have to learn first, you know?"

"Yeah, I need something to learn with though, don't I? A few lessons and lots of practice in my own car, innit?"

"Stop talking like Trevor all the time."

Now my mother has charged in because there was a bit of a London twang. I have to flick my head over to where she stands, like I'm watching a game of tennis – keeping up with the conversation.

"Everyone talks like I do."

This is almost true. It's only when Trev goes into bits of patois that there's much difference in the way we sound. Back to the old man.

"You think you've passed already, don't you? Who's going to sit with you for all this practice anyway?"

"Dominic said he'd take me out."

"Your brother, drive our car?"

It was a mistake to mention my brother.

"No, he can just sit next to me while I do it. I'll have the provisional licence, all legal an' everything."

"Listen Charles! You can practise in my car only when I'm sitting in it with you. Then, after the test – no, if you *pass* the test, of which I have grave doubts – " At this point his finger is raised and begins to hover an inch from my nose – "then we can see how you do for a few months and then, maybe then, we will talk about getting you a car, a very old and cheap car that you can afford to insure and everything else. Okay?"

It was quite a speech.

"I understand."

"Good, then I'll be going."

When I heard the familiar door slam and the clapped-out motor of his car bark into life I felt a surge of relief. He had made the decision for me. I could get on with my plan. I had been thinking about it for a while but would have dropped the idea altogether if he'd been more open-minded about my request.

I finished my breakfast and went up to my room. There I opened the top drawer in a cabinet that stands by my bed and took out the one hundred and thirty-eight pounds, fifty-seven pence that I have saved from all my efforts – working in a shop on Saturday mornings for the last year, carting telephone directories from door to door, saving my change, preserving every bruised five pound note that I was ever given by the relatives at Christmas or on my birthday. I jammed the money into the pocket of my hand-down leather jacket (which is the only hand-down from Dominic that is remotely wearable because of the way leather can still look criss as it ages) and went round to see Trevor on my Muddy Fox. This machine I got for my last birthday, sweet sixteen, second hand with scraped paint and a mix of parts on the frame but I gave it a massive re-haul and painted it a wild red. It looks pretty good.

I live on the west side of the park, a small estate of three-flight maisonettes. Trevor lives in a block one street down from mine and I could have walked, but I was travelling on after his so I rode around, pulled the bike up the stairs to his flat and hammered on the door. The only difference between his flat and mine is that his parents don't own theirs. They still pay rent to the council. This is a big deal for my parents but I can't see it myself. Whether you own it or not it's still a broken-down council flat. Down in the courtyard you have a stinking dumper bin covered in spray-can sprawl. Round the edges of the concrete square are some tired flower beds with more crisp packets and drink cans than flowers. A dog pads past looking for scraps or someone to bite and a few ancient cars like the one my father owns are parked in the corners.

Trev opens the door and as usual he's in all his smooth gear, some smart cords and a silky shirt. Half-past nine in the morning, I know he's not going anywhere but that's just Trev. His aftershave wafts out to me on the landing over all the other smells from the flat. I hear the TV blasting out a cartoon in the front room to keep his kid sister interested. He's looking after her over the holidays.

"Charles, man."

He wanted to chat but I was in a hurry so I cut it short. When I make up my mind to do something I want it done now, no hanging around. I offered him thirty for the weekly hire of his mobile and he agreed. He only got the mobile because he thought it would make him look cool and soon discovered that no-one wanted to waste their money ringing him. He's always at home anyway, 'cept the evenings sometimes and then he's out with all the people that might want to ring him. He wants to know why I need it but I hand over the notes and tell him I'm rushing.

I got all the gear off him – the charger, code and number – tucked it all in my jacket and jumped on the bike. Then I steamed round to see Freddy. I go through at a missing section in the railings and pick up one of the paths.

Freddy is an old hippy dealer my brother Dominic buys his draw from. He lives over the other side of the park. I met him last week when I was over at Dominic's yard, an almshouse bedsit he's living in. We went out for a walk, which I found strange at the time because my brother is so lazy he hates walking anywhere. We cut across the park, past the lake with the odd sad duck floating by and came out into a money street – 'Palace Avenue' type of place I've only whizzed by on the bike, Saabs and Mercs parked up and down. Dominic wanted me to wait outside but I insisted on coming in. I'm pushy like that. It's the only way to get ahead, learn anything. I'm the guy hanging around after class, hassling the teacher about some point they made in the lesson – not because I'm sucking up or anything though. I'm just thirsty for knowledge. Wisdom makes you free.

I went in with Dominic and met the guy and it was clear he sells big time because all the gear and apparatus was there – slabs of resin, tightly-wrapped cling-film of bush in a pile on the floor, an electronic scale I've only seen in physics lessons at school and fresh bank bags lying around. I would have thought he'd be more cautious but Dominic later told me that Freddy 'believed in human trust', whatever that means, in London, in the nineties.

They were chatting away for a while then Dominic asked for a sixteenth. I knew he was a smoker but it still made me feel strange seeing him with his dealer, different from watching him light up in his flat, real casual. It made me think back on the other Dominic, when he was still living at home and working. Sitting there on the sofa, surrounded by all the blow and scales and everything I just couldn't put the two pictures of him together. Maybe it was Freddy. I'd never met a proper dealer before. He didn't even bother to weigh it, just took out a handful, dropped it in a bag and handed it over. It was like they were old friends and I was interrupting things with my memories.

As well as the selling stuff, Freddy had a collection of smoke pipes, rolling papers, mild cigarettes, food wrappers all scattered around – heaped over stacks of records and books that covered the floor. The air stank of grass. Underneath all the trash though, I could see the flat was mint-cream carpets, soft white walls, brass fittings, massive kitchen full of gleaming white machines and chrome everywhere – the kind of place I'll be looking for in a couple of years. The only furniture he'd moved in was the sofa I was sitting on, right in the middle of the room, and a large TV against the opposite wall. Dominic and Freddy both sat on the floor. Studying the contents of the room I decided that he didn't know what to do with the place, it was too smart for him and all his mess was a struggle to make it look like a home. But Freddy and his room were poles apart, like a tramp eating in the Ritz. He's one of those old-time, stoner white guys with a bushy beard, the jumper and jeans brigade – brains a bit scrambled I reckon. Must be loaded to live on that street.

He was friendly when I met him with my brother and when I turned up on my own, panting a little from the ride across the park, he opened the door and gave me a big smile. There was a towel wrapped round his waist and he was busy rubbing his eyes.

"Freddy, didn't mean to get you out of bed. Sorry, man. Can I come in?"

"Feel free."

I walked past him into the living room, leaving the bike in the hall.

"Want a cup of coffee?"

"Nah, just had my breakfast."

He went into the kitchen and started messing with a fancy coffee machine. I followed, leaned against the wall by the archway that separates the two rooms. When he'd fixed the paper filter and spooned out some coffee he turned to face me, crossed his arms and smiled again.

"And how can I be of service at this rather novel hour of the morning?"

"What do I get for a hundred?"

That's how to do it, be direct with people. It was that simple. Freddy gave me a wide smile and an ounce of Colombian gold, which I thought was very generous – but he said we'd be doing a lot more trade.

Wednesday

That was a week ago. I've been back three times. Now I'm lying on my bed, it's about eleven in the morning and the phone rings.

"Yes, Charles. It Clark. How long?"

"Twenty minutes alright for you?"

"I see you then, my friend."

I am a mobile weed-selling industry, a modern pony express service. The bike can get me round this part of London faster than any other mode of transport, except maybe a jet-pack. I know the roads, the alleys, the estates, the park cut-throughs, the dead industrial estates round the river. Back from when I was a kid I remember roaming these streets. I know them as only a kid can do, when there is nothing else to do but stroll around, chat, take the air, learn the short cuts home when you know you're late and the long, summer evening light is starting to fade. When a call comes in I can judge the delivery time in a second, give them an answer, no matter how many drops I've got to do. I've always been time motivated anyway, I value my time. I have a lot to accomplish.

The first few days it had been slow. Call one, and I jumped for the mobile – but it was only Trevor checking me.

"Wha' go on then?"

"A business thing, innit?"

"Wha' business? Hey, call me back, this costin'."

I sensed that he knew what I was up to. It amused me that he was calling his own phone.

"You know you payin' fo' this two time, Trev?"

"You wha'?"

"Well, it your bill. You still wan' me to bell you?"

"Pass by later, yeah."

I lay on my bed and waited, thought about the business. Trade and commerce is a science and I made my calculations. I've never been a big smoker, just a few times at a party maybe, the odd smoke with Trev. I don't like my thinking getting foggy, so, rule one, I wouldn't be smoking my profits. At the same time I knew that most of my friends smoked – rule two, demand was good. I was sure I'd get calls because I told Spence I was selling the very same day I got the ounce and he knows everyone. He also talks to everyone which is weird 'cause Spence is a thief and you would think it would be sensible for him to be a quiet type but the opposite is true. Spence is the king of gossip. Maybe that is why he is so unsuccessful in crime and is always ending up with useless junk that no-one wants to buy. Anyway, I knew word would get around and I knew how popular blow was so, rule three, I had free advertising.

My plan seemed flawless.

I just had to sell small. A sixteenth would cost me six twenty-five and I could charge ten, maybe fifteen on each sale. Figures were flying round my head. That was one-forty profit on an ounce. I'd good with numbers. I wasn't worried too much about the police 'cause they rarely bother anyone for draw, even when people smoke it in front of them. I've seen that plenty of times. They know it's not worth the hassle. I would cruise around selling until I had a couple of grand and then cut it. I roll up in the wheels the day of my seventeenth, after making some cunning plans to explain me having it. My parents won't pay too much attention. Dominic was always their favourite and they don't get too close to what I'm doing since he left.

I like the Fox, always been trusty, but it's time to move on. Getting wheels is part of the maturing process and I can't afford to hang around waiting for it to happen. This is the way I see life. You decide what you want and you go out and get it. Nothing to do with the eighties greed thing, I'm just a nineties realist making things happen. Everyone knows you have to make your own luck these days. Helps if you've got brains of course, which naturally I do. I'm way up at the top in most of my classes, ready to eat up the exams next summer – then I'm off. I've got it all mapped out.

I watch my father going to work every morning, an order clerk at a parcel depot. He's been doing the same job for years, missed out on a promotion last year because a younger guy had taken the time to study, had some certificate to his name. You can't just keep working for one company and move up the ladder like you used to do. That's all changed. Now he's just happy to have the job. My mother was teaching part-time but she hated it and quit. It was giving her a 'nervous condition' apparently. I've seen the teachers at my school piling into the local every Friday afternoon to get smashed and I can see they're all half crazy, even the young ones. She was too delicate to cope with it. Dominic became the answer to all their frustration and when he. . . Well, that's another story.

I'm taking a different track, making myself a future. I'm not fencing myself in yet though, that would be stupid. First I get through the exams, then the business course. After that I'll take a few subsidiary subjects and then I can specialise. By the time I'm Dominic's age I'll be a finance king.

I'm always thinking as I move. This is all running through my head as I burn down Battersea High, weaving through the cars and jumping the pavement when I get to a traffic light so I can cut round it. This is my main street. I know the shops, the bars, where it's cool to go drinking, where you might get hassle. I know the faces here, run into one of the crew from time to time and shout my hello but I keep moving, always moving. It's the mid-morning rush, a final cough of traffic before lunch. From here I have to cut up the hill and across the Common, then sail down to Balham. It's a muggy day, even the breeze is hot. People are saying we're getting smog like they have in the States but I don't go for the mask idea or anything. I try and stay with the breaks of grass that make up the Park and the Common and that must kill a lot of the pollution fogging up my lungs. I fly by the other riders with the dumb paper cups over their noses.

Ten minutes and I'm at the top of Balham High. Clark lives off in the backstreets. This is my third visit in as many days and he must be selling on a little but it doesn't surprise me. He needs the money.

Clark was my main friend at school. It was always Trev and him and me in a circle but Clark was tops. He had everything going for him, everyone liked him. And that turned out to be the problem 'cause Clark got it together with the number one looking girl at our school, Indigo. It was the school romance, the perfect couple, like a soap opera with daily check-ups and gossip flying round the school yard. The beautiful twosome were in love, big time. Then real life sneaks in and things go wrong. Indigo was pregnant, the parents blew up, Clark quit school to get a job. There was a touch of excitement with them setting up home together and the baby arriving – but it didn't last.

I pull the Fox up the path that leads round to the back of the houses in their street. There's a little square of a backyard. Their flat is up some shaky iron steps. Two dark rooms and a cupboard bathroom stuck up in the attic of the house. I hitch the bike over my shoulder, climb the steps and bang on the door, looking down at the patch below as I waited for Clark to arrive – litter and rusty bikes, weeds poking through the trash.

"Morning to you."

He's in a T-shirt and jeans, no socks or shoes on yet.

"Yeah. Boy, you look rough." I can see he is tired, the baby keeping him up all night.

"You've got no idea."

"You could try sleeping."

"Thanks for the advice."

We go into the kitchen. I wheel the Fox in and lean it against the door. Clark wanders off to the far end of the room and fiddles with some matches, lighting the gas under a pan of water. The kitchen is also the living room, very thin with a little table at the far end by a dirty window. Behind me is a door with two steps leading up to the bedroom. The carpet on the step is frayed. In the kitchen it's linoleum, stained and curling, worn through round the base of the work surfaces to show the dark wood underneath. A bare bulb hangs in the middle of the room. Even in full daylight this room is dark. Almshouse flats are always dark.

"What you been up to then?"

"Nothin' much. How's things with you and Indigo?"

"Hello, Charles. I'm fine, thank you."

She's behind me, on the steps that lead to the bedroom, wearing a towel dressing gown. Despite the strain of the child and living here, scrabbling for money all the time and growing up early, she looks young, as pretty as she was at school. I move back to let her pass.

"Oh man, do I have a headache, Clark, make me a cup will you?"

He stoops and kisses her forehead. "I'll bring it in to you. Charles and I are talking."

"Really. Don't talk too long, will you. I have to go round Sonja's remember, so you're looking after him." She scowls at him and pads back to the steps, brushing past me. "I leave you to your man talk then. See you, Charles."

It seems a decade since she rushed past me in the corridors, laughing and shouting at the end of the day. I hear her close the door and then the murmur of a child crying starts up.

"Have a seat."

I yank the end of the Fox steering handle and work the grip free. This is my stash. I can stuff an ounce into the hollow bars. I pull a plastic bag out and walk over to where he sits at the table.

"Things not going too smooth with her then?"

"Oh, she's just like that in the mornings. It's taking it out of her."

Six months ago I would have been stunned to hear them talk like that, almost like brother and sister their words were so flat, passionless.

"She's not working then?"

Indigo had been working as an office temp the last time I saw her. That was nearly a month ago. It was usually Clark on his own with the kid when I went round.

"For that money it made more sense for her to claim. Anyway she was sick one day, left early and they told her not to come in again. It was nothin' money anyway."

"Yeah, I know. Who wants to work for three pounds an hour?"

"But if we're here all the time together we only get on each other's nerves. You can't win." I am unwrapping the plastic on the table. He reaches over and helps me. "Never pictured you as a herbs man you know, Charles."

"It's got limits, boy, all under control. I do it till I get what I'm after, that all. Maybe you should think of it yourself. Come in on it."

It almost sounds like an insult but to my relief he smiles. He doesn't need my money suggestions, Indigo probably takes care of that. If Clark would take my help I would offer it but I know he wouldn't accept. Whether it is a strength or a weakness I am not sure but he has always been proud, confident, even now when he is stuck in this situation.

"I'm getting by. Got some ideas about work, maybe even go back to studying."

I don't say anything even though I know he couldn't study and that his work prospects are slight. To study he'd have to get a grant and with a kid there's no way he could live on it. They can only get emergency benefits and, like he was saying, he'd be lucky to get three pounds an hour for pumping petrol or stacking shelves or whatever job he could get. However, Clark manages somehow to keep his nobility, like a ruined king down at the bottom, hanging on to his manners and grace.

"She's been getting a bit jumpy lately. Doin' my head in a bit."

He at least has the week to relax, with the respect of a few close friends for sticking it out with her. He was always mature for his age, independent, happy with his own company – and that's why people envied him, because of that strength. But I can imagine Indigo seeing her girlfriends cruising out with new and different guys, still wanting to look good and be a part of youth. Indigo was always the party queen.

"Maybe we could go out for a drink this week, get Trev along."

"Yeah, I'll bell you about it. Look, I should get back and see her before she blows her top."

"Safe, I'll get going."

He stands up from the table and fishes in his jeans for the notes. I finish the coffee, take the money from his outstretched hand and leave the bush pile on a piece of newspaper, then walk over to the Fox and open the door.

"Let's meet up then. We haven't had a drink up for months, man."

"Course. I'll call you, yeah?"

Then I struggle down the steps and walk through to the street. I check the handle grip is tight and wheel off towards the Common.

Kids. There is nothing so final. Except death, maybe. I think if you pick the right time there can be nothing better but if you have one in their circumstances, in the mid-teens and poor, then it's like running into a brick wall. I can't see how they can break out of it either, not until the kid is old enough that they can leave it with someone, and that's years away. I never go out with Clark these days, he rarely leaves his flat. Everything changed with the arrival of the baby. My friend and Indigo were bonded forever and not ready for it. The strain is showing already. Even so, he's coping and I have to respect it in a way. But it's not the way I'm going. Not in a million years.

The mobile shrieks as I reach the Common. I stop the bike straight, with my foot up on a bench to keep it steady.

"Hello."

"I was looking for something."

It's a girl's voice, one I don't recognise.

"How did you get this number?"

"A friend told me I might be able to get something from you, uh, I was hoping you could come round now-ish."

"Round where?"

"I'm in Chelsea." She gives me the address. I know it.

"Twenty-five minutes."

"Great."

I slip the phone back into its holster under my jacket and start off. Every time a cold call comes in my heart races but I have to ignore the fear and press on. People do pass on the number so I shouldn't be surprise to get strangers ringing. I have to remind myself that it's just a trade like any other and I need customers. Besides, I know her area, even though it's across the river. I like it. It's the type of place I'll be living in soon – restaurants, wine bars, fancy grocer shops, pubs with stripped-pine floors, pastel stonework on the front of the houses. She could be a useful contact, a good buyer. She could be anyone. All the potential risks and gains of the situation buzz around my head and I enjoy the ride down from the Common, winding round to the bridge. I feel a tingle of excitement as I reach the river.

Two

There's a lot of cool bullshit talked about Brixton but I don't see it myself. It's as though the people who live there have to keep convincing themselves the place is sweet or they'd all go crazy – and there are enough basket-cases there already, truth. They opened up the head hospital, shoved them back on to the streets, and now they wander up and down the main road, muttering in a private world. I can't deny the area has a vibe all of its own. There's a lot going on, every third person you meet is a musician or an artist, and this adds to the community feel of the

place that's so rare in London, everyone pulling together for a change. That's only one side of the deal
though. Head off the high street and you soon see the
down side – guys with crack bags hidden in their
mouths, coming over to give you a look at the shiny
white crystals resting on their tongues, rows of
trashed houses and empty stares making up the
scenery behind them. Then there's the mugging. A
few of my friends have been taken round there,
pressed up to a wall and robbed. There are no requirements on the choice of victim – male, female,
black, white, makes no difference. It's just desperate
people taking your money or bag or whatever they
can get. Of course, I'll get slagged for saying that
because Brixtonians say it's just a 'negative image' of
their area. I can't help what I see and hear though. It
goes on.

Maybe that adds to the energy of this place, a little
tension spicing things up. The club I'm in is buzzing –
lot of noise from a system in the other room, crowd of
people round the bar where there's a bit of light,
drinking tins and smoking. It's a small basement club
off the high street. The ceiling's low and the walls are
painted black, dance-floor partitioned from the bar
by a wire fence so the bodies are bunched in tight.
Everyone's talking loud. Trev's gone off to look for
some girl he recognised and left me on my stool, sipping my Brooklyn beer. Right now I'm feeling chill,
even though the doorman gave us a stare when we
came in, wondering if we were worth hassling about
our age. We stared him out, handed over the money
and breezed in. In other circumstances I might feel a

bit edgy about it but tonight I'm easy, leaning back on the stool and taking long sips. I'm completely relaxed, anaesthetised. This afternoon I went through an eighth of a bush with my new client.

When I got round there (bang on time I should add) I was expecting the girl who rang the mobile to answer the door. All the way across the bridge and up to the King's Road I was trying to guess what she'd be like. My imagination was being extremely flattering and by the time I got to the address she was a goddess. I think about girls a lot at the moment and it angers me because I know that any distraction is bad for my business – indeed, for all my future plans.

I was seeing a girl earlier this year but it fell apart. She wanted to see me all the time, started ringing up and hassling me every day. I didn't want to get dragged into anything too heavy. She wanted it to get serious before we jumped into bed, 'cause she hadn't been with a man before and was nervous. The thing was, I have to admit it, I haven't been the whole distance with a girl. This may strike you as weird so I should say that it's nothing to do with a lack of offers. On the contrary, I get the come-on signs all the time. No, it's a conscious decision on my part. After the last girl hassle I realised that I don't need it. My friends think it went all the way a while ago with another girl I was seeing but the truth is we did everything except 'final entry'. I have never felt the need to set them straight on this. There's a pressure on guys my age to jettison their virginity and they'd only tear into me if I told them. I haven't got a problem with it.

However, it's a chemical thing I can't always stop, so

when I ring her bell I'm getting that familiar cold rush and the skin tingle. Then the door opens and there's a guy standing there in a suit.

"Deals on wheels I take it?"

I have to smile. He brings me in, I park the bike in the hall and we walk into the living room. A girl stretched out on a sofa smiles up at me. I take in all the details.

"Hi. You're Charles, yeah?"

It's a bit like Freddy's place except they fit with the decor – he in the suit, neat hair and a Tag watch, she wearing leggings and a loose rave shirt that costs close to a hundred. Two wall windows open out on to a small garden.

"Yeah, Charles it is."

"Have a seat." She's almost as good as my fantasy.

"Thanks."

"Have a blast on that."

There's a stick burning in an ashtray that sits in the middle of the carpet. With first-time buyers I keep it sociable, so I lean down, pick it up and take a pull.

"What are you selling then?" He's next to her on the sofa, with a joker's grin on his face. He pulls at the tie round his neck and starts wriggling out of the suit jacket.

"Bush. Colombian Gold." My voice has lost its flat calm. Whatever is in the joint floods my system and I feel a high already. I twist the stick in my fingers, staring at it.

"What's in this? Not heroin I hope." I'm half-kidding but Dominic once told me that dealers sometimes mix a bit of smack in with resin, for an extra stone if the draw is low quality. You can see little white specks in it.

"No, it's oil. Nice clean hit."

Obviously, I've been smoking more than usual since I started the business. There are certain situations where it's very hard to refuse. The buyer may want to try a joint before handing over the cash. Then there is the whole 'social' thing with smoking. They often roll up as soon as I hand it over and that makes me feel obliged to hang around for a quick smoke. I've smoked more in the last week than I have in my whole life but up until meeting this guy I'd managed not to get too blasted. I always make my excuses and leave. But sitting in Chelsea, after the first pull I could feel it washing over me and I knew I was heading for a real stone. It wasn't just the oil that was carrying me, though I know it's dangerous. I'd only heard tales about it. They distil the resin into alcohol or something, make it a liquid, then you soak the papers in it, for a concentrated high. No, there was something else. I liked their flat, the atmosphere. It felt like coming home.

"I'm Theo and this is Julia."

Must remember this is business. Go in with the sell speech.

"Hello. It's fifteen a sixteenth. . . . This oil's kickin' man."

"Strong, I know. A 'man's' smoke." He puts on a mock-cowboy accent and I laugh.

"Can I skin some of yours up then?"

"Sure."

It's harder standing up from the chair than it should

be but I keep my footing. My legs feel rubbery as I walk over to the bike and take out the stash. I shuffle back. My eyes feel dry and a smile is setting on my face.

"Have to watch out for this stuff . . . bit trippy." He's toking on the joint, making the end glow and filling the room with smoke. The girl swings her legs off the sofa and reaches out for the joint. "Specially if you have to go back into work this afternoon."

"You're working?"

"Sadly . . . that is the case."

He pulls an album cover over and starts rolling some of the bush I've handed him. She's busy smoking the last inch of the joint and smiling but when he gives her a soft nudge she reaches for a cigarette packet on the floor and passes him one. I'm feeling trashed now. The idea of working after smoking the stuff he's got intrigues me. Julia gets up and walks over to my chair.

"Want a drink, Charles?"

"Yeah, thanks."

They are both relaxed, easy in the flat. She moves through to another room and I hear a cupboard door open.

"Can I see this oil?"

"On the shelf there."

I stand and step carefully over to a long shelf.

"Why you want bush when you've got this?" I'm fiddling with a small vial of black, greasy liquid. I hold it up to the light and can see it's actually a dark shade of brown, the same colour as resin.

"Different hit. I like variety."

"So what do you do, Theo – work-wise, I mean?"

"I'm a lawyer."

"No shit?"

"Would I lie?"

"That's part of the job, innit?"

Laugher. A lawyer. In a few years my friends will be lawyers or other professionals. I'd never thought of them as human before, in the flesh, as smokers. Meeting Theo I feel reassured about my ambitions. He seems happy, laid back. He has this flat, he has Julia.

"Well, I'm in music law, not quite as mean as the other branches of the family."

"Contracts and stuff, yeah?"

"That's right, yeah."

Julia is back with a tray. There are three tumblers of clear liquid on it. The glass is frosty as though made of ice.

"Theo boring you with his life story?"

"It's something I'm interested in myself."

"Really? Like how?"

She offers me a glass. It's so cold it burns my fingers. Theo passes me the bush joint which he's been toking, takes a shot from his glass and starts rolling another with the oil. I take a pull on the bush, then he speaks.

"How much is here?"

"An eighth."

"I'll take the lot if I may."

"Absolutely feel free to do so."

I blow out slowly but most of the smoke has been taken into my lungs. The rush hits me. Julia is staring at me, waiting for an answer, but I've forgotten what she said. She has black, bobbed hair and china-white skin and I'm staring back at her.

"Charles?"

"Uh. Yeah ... I'm gonna move into things ... along those kinda lines, you know?" Really feeling blasted now. The bush is the icing on the oiled cake.

"Right." Her smile widens and she moves back to the sofa. She knows I'm wrecked. I take a sip from the glass and have to suck in a mouthful of air.

"Wah, this is sharp, man."

"It's vodka, from the freezer ... with a squeeze of lime."

Theo looks up from his rolling. "Refreshing, don't you think?"

"I have to agree, yeah." Now my mouth is a mix of flavours, the spirit hits my throat hot but my cheeks are chilled. The stone is making the taste stronger, boosting my senses.

"Let's have some music." He lights the new oil joint and steps over to a pile of black boxes which I realise is the system. "This is a band I've been dealing with. They all give me copies of their CDs, the ones I do work for anyway."

The room fills with sound, a heavy drum beat and rock-style guitar. We have to shout.

"I'm not so into rock."

"It changes in a second. Here ..."

Now the music drops into a funk groove. Julia is nodding her head to it and passes on the joint. It comes over to me.

That's how it went. Time passed in the dope blur. Theo stood up after several more joints and said, "Fuck the job this afternoon."

Julia beamed at him. "You tell 'em." She was drunk. As we carried on smoking she filled our glasses now and again but hers was never empty. Or never full. Depends how you look at it.

"You gonna be able to ride back alright, Charles?" Her smile is loose and her eyes bleary. "Sure. I can ride in any state."

And we talked and smoked and drank on and on. It was my first proper stone session, with strangers, but I felt comfortable. The more I smoked, the more I wanted. The music came alive with the drug and Theo pulled out some dub and dance stuff. I usually liked fast house, jungle, beats but the slow dub carried me right out. The sounds made sense to me. I focused on the music, picked out what each different instrument was doing. The world closed in so it was just the room we sat in, the music and the draw. Then the homing instinct cut in.

"I should disappear, get back south."

I made it to my feet and smiled at them. It was dark outside. Theo stood up.

"How much do I owe you then?"

"Oh, forget it. We just smoked it, call it a friendly, yeah."

I couldn't ask him for any money. I'd smoked lots of the oil. Stoned, I don't feel bad about smoking the goods but I knew I would later. It was one of the rules and I'd broken it.

"Well, can you drop an ounce in tomorrow?"

"No problem Theo. Ring me, yeah."

Julia was asleep. She looked like a huge kitten, curled back in her original position on the sofa. Theo saw me to the door and we shook hands as I left. It was a wild ride home. I even stopped for a kebab on the way. It tasted better than anything I'd ever eaten before in my life.

I'm still smashed now, leaning back on the stool but it's mellowed down so my body feels loose and relaxed. Trev came round and hassled me into going out with him. I fancied a beer and just watching the dancers move it. Theo's taking an ounce so I'm still clearing profit on smoking the eighth. This afternoon was 'client attention' and I closed the deal. I see Trev pushing back along the bar and call out to him.

"You find her then?"

"Nah. Met an old friend of mine, well, of my brother really, been chatting to him, Clayton, you know him?"

"Don't think so."

"He's coming over in a minute. Want a drink?"

"A Brooklyn." He's looking pleased with himself, clicks his fingers at the barman. "You glad I got you over to Brixton then?"

"This place is alright, yeah, I have to agree."

"It's all women, pure gal. We should get out on the dance floor and mingle a bit, boy."

"I'll leave the dancing to you I think, Casanova."

He stands straight at the bar and takes gulps from a fresh can of Red Stripe. Tonight he's better groomed than I've seen him for a long time. Any money he ever gets is put into threads.

"There this girl I just met over with Clayton . . ."

He starts the familiar story and I drift off into the

land of nods and the occasional 'yes' or 'I know', not really listening. Girls are everything for Trevor. He's wearing a pair of cream slacks and a burgundy shirt – the seduction outfit. The hair is short and slick and I can smell his aftershave. He must apply it every few hours. His lines always strike me as clumsy and obvious but he has a high success rate with girls. The last few times we've been out he's wanted me to pair up with him on the chat but I invariably end up leaning on the bar and listening to the sounds, letting him get on with it. Trev's a bright guy, doing nearly as well as me with the study bit but he's just playing with it, doesn't take life seriously. He's into girls and clubbing, looking sharp and getting by. I don't think he's even thought about college. His story about the girl comes to an end and he gives me a fatherly look.

"Look to me like you been working too hard, Charles."

"I do feel a bit wrecked, yeah."

"You look it . . ."

For a moment I examine my slouching form on the stool. The baggy jeans could do with a wash, my sweat shirt is way past clean as well.

"Look like you been dead a few hours."

I don't mind him ribbing me but I rise to it anyway. "Listen, man, I just dress comfy, that all."

"Comfy? You a scruffy wretch man. I lend you some money and you can go dress yourself up a bit, yeah?" He makes a waving motion with his wallet which is still out on the bar top.

"Ya fuck. I've made more money today than you make in a month."

Trev works for his elder brother sometimes. He owns a video shop over at the Junction.

"Then why don't you use some a it an' stop dressing so trampy?"

"What? So you want me to look like a game show host like you do, yeah . . ."

"Huh?"

"With the silk shirt . . ."

"Not silk boy, fine cotton."

" . . . an the showy cords."

"If you had the sense, maybe."

"Listen, man, I was getting trashed with a lawyer this afternoon."

"You lie."

"No, no lie. He was in the suit and all the gear, some girl there straight out of a model line-up . . ."

"Nah."

"Yeah, no shit. And I was getting wasted with them on *high* grade ganja, boy . . ."

"Ganja! You saying that! Man, what the world comin' to?"

"Me an' the girl and the lawyer all sitting round blasted."

"Yeah?"

"An' that's the sort of company I'm keeping these days."

He looks puzzled, takes another sip and finished his can. "Get us a beer then, business man."

I pull a note from my jeans and drop it on the bar I've still got his attention so I carry on.

"Now I realise that at a certain point it will be necessary to dress up a bit, to further my business ambitions . . ."

"Man . . ."

"That's when the suit comes out, but until then I keep it casual."

"Too casual, you ask me."

I order the drinks.

Trev speaks again before I can respond. "This whole thing you've got in your head about respectable business, boy . . . all bullshit. You're just selling weed, that all. You think it a big deal to be wid the lawyer man there but there a world between you."

"Nah."

"Yes, man. You should look out for what you are a bit more. And right now you're selling weed, don't matter to who it is, selling weed . . ."

It's always friendly with Trev, even when we get into this kind of talk. We're both smiling, feeling a little drunk.

"Enterprise, Trevor . . ."

"Bollocks."

"And the ability to carry things through. My dress is irrelevant at the moment."

"You still stoned, aren't you? Stoned *and* scruffy, man."

"Ah, you don't understand, Trev . . ." I'm interrupted by the arrival of a huge guy with dredds. He pushes between us at the bar.

"Clayton, this is Charles.

We nod hello. He's wearing an olive-green, linen two-piece outfit with black trim. I put him a few years older than us.

"Trev say you might be able to set me up with something."

"Yeah?"

So, Trev has been spreading the word, getting respect for passing my name on.

"Just a bit, to tide me over, yeah." He's carrying a stack of flyers and he puts them down on the bar.

"Tide you over to what?"

"You know, just a drop."

"I can give you a sixteenth, fifteen quid."

I brought a wrap with me in case this happened. Be prepared.

"Ras expensive, boy."

"I'm not forcing you, am I?"

The club is booming now, full of people. I'm starting to feel a bit tranced, the lights from the stage end of the dance floor are playing games with my eyes. The alcohol is making the stone colourful.

"I get it to you through Trev, yeah. In a day or two."

"Don't do credit, man." It makes me feel in power, having something he wants.

"Well, just a couple of spliff then. I give you a ticket for this." He flashes one of the flyers in my face and backs it up with some more talk.

"Tenner a shot, man."

I take one of the flyers from his outstretched hand. On the front is all the usual stuff – 'spectacular', 'extravaganza'. It's just a jungle night at a club I know in town, on Friday. I flick it over and on the bar there is that photograph of the super-models, the one with them all naked, hugging each other. Sex sells. The club's called Two Foot Table. I smile.

"I don't know ... the age of bartering is long gone, you know.'

"You a businessman right? I give you two time ticket. Trev buy one from you, bound to. Can't say no to that."

"Well . . ."

"Have some compassion, man. I need it to soften up this girl I'm with tonight. Put a glow on the evening, yeah?"

"So I'm a dating agency then?"

"No, just to ease things down a bit. She a bit 'clampy'."

"That's a new one, 'clampy'."

"She's a friend of a friend, don't know her well. Bit cool, yeah? Come on, man. Wouldn't mind asking her back to my place if I had a little smoke."

Trev pipes in. "Girl criss, it's the truth."

"You come to this show then, Trev?"

"For a fiver maybe."

I give in. "Alright. For two of the tickets, yeah?"

"Deal."

I slide off the stool and start pushing through the crowd with Clayton following.

"Trev. Watch my seat, yeah?"

There was no-one else in the bathroom so we did it in the middle of the room. I didn't want to go in a cubicle with the guy. Trev would have ribbed me about that for weeks if he found out. Toilet humour. I pulled a bit of cling-film off one of the bags and dropped enough bush for two hefty sticks into it, then wrapped it up.

"That should do you for a magic wand or two."

"Come again?"

"Nothing, just an old joke. So, you promoting this

thing then?" I've taken my flyers and some tickets in the exchange.

"Nah, just get a few freebies and a bit of money for passing the flyers out for a friend. I'm a musician."

"Yeah? Reggae musician?"

"Why you think reggae? 'Cause I'm a black guy?"

"No, it's what I'm into, that's all. Best music, innit?"

"Fair 'nough."

"So what is it then?"

"Rock band I play with, called Radical."

"Radical?"

"Yeah. We just starting to gig around a bit. Fact, we might need some of your gear 'cause we going in a studio this week to do a little thing, recording a tune. Helps with the uh . . . inspiration to have something to burn."

"I can imagine. I'll give you my number then."

"Yeah. Look, I should get back and see this girl. Get your number from Trev."

"Alright."

"Everyone's running round after girls."

The club must be at capacity now and I'm glad Trev's been watching my seat. Bodies everywhere. Pushing through the crowd makes me feel a little wobbly, I'm still wrecked. They're all moving, talking, smoking, heading for the packed dance floor. I'm hemmed in, thick body scent in the air, getting a bit panicky and then there's a tap on my arm.

"Well, Charles. What you doin' here?"

It's Indigo, looking like she used to back at school. Her hair is up in a tight clump at the back of her head and she is wearing a skin-tight black dress. She looks young again, fifteen.

"Alright, Indigo. How are you?"

"Good, boy, you alright?" Her hand is fixed on my arm. I can feel the heat of her palm through my sweat-shirt.

"Yeah. Just a bit charged, that's all. Been at it all day."

"Oh yeah?" A sex humour smile. Indigo's eyes are gleaming.

"Smoking . . . that is."

"I know, I know. Charles, this Martin, say hello."

"Hello, Martin." There's a guy next to her, tall and well-dressed. I thought he was just in the throng of people and hadn't registered him. She puts her other hand on his arm so we're joined in a triangle.

"Hello, Charles."

We don't shake. He doesn't look at me but gazes off over the heads in the crowd. He's older than me, twenties. I turn back to her, notice her flushed face.

"You out dancin' then?"

"Yeah, takin' a break, you know?"

Now I see she looks a little uneasy and suddenly I feel uncomfortable, like I wasn't supposed to be here, bumping into her like this. She speaks first.

"Thought you never came down Brixton."

"Now and again."

There is a surge in the crowd and like people bob-bing in the sea we start to drift apart. Her hand leaves my arm.

"Catch you later, yeah?"

She smiles a good-bye then they move off. There

was something in the smile I didn't like but I'm too trashed to work it out. I pace off in the other direction, picking my way through the people, thinking more about not stepping on some bad boy's foot than about meeting up with Indigo.

When I get back to the stools at the bar Clayton's just ahead of me, but I can see Trev talking with someone who's perched on my resting place.

"Jump in my grave then?"

I think it's a guy but when she turns round I see it's a girl in her early twenties. Long brown hair and the same bright white skin like Julia. Beauty. She curls a tight little lip and speaks softly. "Sorry. I didn't know the seat was reserved."

Trev and Clayton both looked at me, like they're expecting me to stare back at them and nod in agreement ... yes, she is attractive, yes, she can do anything she wants. But I need to sit down.

"That's all right, long as I can take possession now I'm back."

I slide in, forcing her to step off. She looked a bit shocked.

"Manners slipping in south London then?" Fancy voice. Now she stands next to Trev and I can see him melt. Clayton steps in.

"I've got something for later. Why don't we move on?"

"No, I'm getting a taxi home. Thanks for taking me out."

She says this with a little shrug, then leans in, gives him a brush of a kiss on his cheek and walks off. Clayton and Trev watch her vanish in the blur of people. I speak to the back of their heads.

"What's all the noise about? She's OK I s'pose, nothin' special."

They both turn and give me a dull look. And that's how I first met Bond.

Clayton dropped me back at my house. He had a smashed up Mini with squeaky brakes. It was close to three in the morning.

"Sorry if I put the girl in a bad mood for you."

"No, it nothing. I wasn't getting anywhere anyway, real icy. I'll just have a spliff and team up with Mother Palm . . ."

"Give me a ring if you need sorting, yeah?"

"Sweet. Day or two."

I almost fell out of the car it was so close to the ground, then I waved him off. I was all over the place opening the front door but I finally slid in and closed it quietly behind me. Even though I was trashed I knew I had to keep to my business methods so when I was safely in my room I took out my little account book and entered the day's exchanges. I'm keeping the cash in the same cabinet by my bed that I've always used. My parents don't come near my room.

I've made five-sixty, minus the eighth profit that went up in smoke round at Theo's, so there's already a fat roll of notes, more than I've ever seen before. I need two grand. Strangely, I feel rather neutral about the cash. Maybe I'm getting used to the idea of having a lot lying around. Another three weeks and I'll be clear, two thousand and off looking for the wheels. My plan is working perfectly.

I kick off my trainers, slip off the jeans and the

sweat-shirt and lie back on the bed in boxers. I feel the muscles in my legs and arms relaxing, coming down from the stone now that I'm out of the club and the noise and lights. The air feels good, lapping my skin. For a long moment I consider rolling one up for a final chill before sleep and I remember how I caught Dominic smoking in the house once. He looked worried for a second as I poked my head round the door, then smiled when he saw it was me. Sometimes, when I think back on him living here, I start missing him badly. The two of us being around kept things more equal with the parents. I spent a lot of time with him. Now it's just me and them. But these things happen, have to accept them. I decide to drop by his place in the morning, see how he is.

I put the phone on the charger – it's been out for hours already, doesn't last long into the night-time. Then I go through to the bathroom, brush my teeth and get alarmed by the red eyes staring at me in the mirror. I make it back to my bed and collapse. Just before sleep comes rushing in my mind is buzzing – Theo, making it as a lawyer and still chill, still smoking; Julia stretched out like a cat on the sofa Radical; Bond and the jungle night tickets. It all feels good, all feels like things are working out.

Three

Dominic has a decrepit bedsit off the main road that runs down to Vauxhall Bridge. The sound of lorries and cars screaming past is a low rumble in his room so he keeps a radio on all the time to cover the noise. He says he'd go crazy otherwise. I sit on his bed whilst he pulls some clothes on.

"I heard what you're up to. S'pose you think I'm gonna give you a lecture for dealing blow?"

"Why should you? Nothing you wouldn't do, is it?"

"Don't know about that."

The room is a mess. It's too far gone to be neat,

even if he bothered to clean it from time to time. The wallpaper sags in places, the carpet is threadbare. His only furniture is the bed and a tired dresser. Apart from that there is a round mirror on the wall and a two-ring electric stove. I've never seen him use it. He buys sandwiches or take-aways when he's hungry.

"Want a tea?"

"I'll take you out for a coffee, yeah?"

"Woh, big spender?"

"Not that. It's your tea cups, Dom. You should throw them out an' get some new ones. Disgusting."

"Let's go."

That's the thing that gets to me about him, he just doesn't care. His appearance, the way he lives, his diet, his future, it's all a joke to my brother. He stomps out of the door and we leave his little box.

It's grey and windy today but still mild. I wheel the bike along the pavement as we talk.

"So you're rich then?"

"Saving for a car."

"What d'you want a car for? The bike's all you need."

I don't want to start him off on one of his rants so I say nothing.

"Getting it off Freddy?"

"Yeah."

"He's alright that guy, I like him. You should listen to what he tells you."

"What? You mean the hippie stuff he's always coming out with?"

Dominic smiles. "He can get a bit flowery . . . but he still talks sense."

I've already been round to see the dealer. Stuffed into the Fox handlebars are two ounces that he's given me. I hadn't stayed long but Freddy had been chatting, coming out with some of his mystic ideas. I hadn't been listening, felt sluggish from the night before.

"This place?" Dominic sounds disgusted.

I've stopped outside an up-market bar on the Wandsworth Road, the 'Mexican beer, candles on the table' type. Through the window I can see a waitress laying out ashtrays and wiping the tables.

"It's alright. I come here a lot an' it's cool."

"Well, I can have a cap-oo-chino then." He puts on a Chelsea voice to mock the coffee-drinking classes. He goes on. "I thought you meant a cafe. Think they'll let me smoke roll-ups in here?"

I chain the bike up and then we push against a heavy wooden door and go in.

"Hi. How are you this morning?" The waitress has the chirpy American twang to her voice. She gives us a big smile.

"Miserable actually."

"Oh, sorry to hear it. What can I get you?"

"We'd both like cap-oo-chinos." Dominic is livening up after escape from bedsit-land. She retreats to the bar. "Let's sit by the window so I can keep an eye on the bike."

Now the truth is that I've only been to this place once. I came here on a date (a double that Trev had arranged) thinking it was a 'sophisticated' choice. This part of London is being flooded with these bars. However, the girls thought we were paying and it was big

money just for a few bottles of beer and a plate of tor-
tilla chips. Out of my league at the time. We didn't get
anywhere with the girls that night either. Now though,
with my new-found wealth, I can afford to hang in
these places and not just pubs and greasy fast-food
dumps. I feel comfortable with the potted plants, art
posters and flash decor, suits my new status. Of
course Dominic spots this immediately.

"So've you've become a bit of a social climber
then? Always thought you'd end up making the
money in the family." He fiddles with some rolling
papers. The top flap of the packet has been ripped
off to make a roach.

"Nah, should have been you making it."

He is staring intently at the thin tube he is making
between his fingertips, chewing his lips in concentration. He is wearing a denim jacket, oily around the
cuffs and collar. An ancient T-shirt covers his chest.
Jeans are the only trousers he wears, the same pair all
the time I suspect.

"Dominic, I wanted to have a talk with you, see if
things are alright with you, yeah?"

He looks up in surprise. For a second he pauses
but then goes back to rolling the cigarette. The coffee
arrives as he lights it, using the paper-pack of
matches in the ashtray.

"Don't worry about me, Charles. I spend enough
time doing that myself."

"I just wanted to . . ."

"Fact is, right now I'm more worried 'bout you." He
blows a cloud of smoke across at me.

"Yeah?"

"That's right?"

'Why so?"

" 'Cause you're fucking with things you don't understand, people you don't even know about yet, boy."

"It's only a bit of blow."

"Now it is . . ."

"It'll never be anything more, I tell you."

"You can never be sure about that."

"Ah, you're just pissed off I've got it together. Jealous."

Now his shoulders hunch up and he pulls hard on the cigarette. He speaks slowly.

"I keep telling you to stop thinking about me . . ."

"Who says I am?"

"To stop comparing you with me all the time."

"I'm not."

"I know you're still a bit . . . unhappy about what's happened but you've got nothing to prove, you know?"

"Back off, Dominic."

"So stop thinking you've got it all sussed then."

"Well, I fucking have got it sussed."

I don't want him to go strange on me now, not here. I should say something to break the spell but his eyes are fixed on me, he talks as though there is nothing more important than what he is saying.

" 'Cause that's what I was thinking just before it happened. It all changes just like that, so easy, no reason, an' I got . . . well, I got fucked like, you know. One minute I was on top, then it's like, it just couldn't be worse – things changing so quickly and everything's upside down' yeah? Charles, you got to stop thinking it's all straight forward, take it one step at a time, yeah . . ."

He goes on but I'm not listening. I'm back in the corridor with my mother, under the strip lights, surrounded by sick people sitting on plastic chairs. There are tea machines in the corner and old, yellowing posters on the walls reminding you to do this or that to stay healthy. I'm in the hospital. Dominic is in the operating theatre. My father is rushing across town to get here, screaming at the car ahead of him to move over. Dominic may die.

What worries me more than this though, more than my mother sobbing and my brother lying there looking like a piece of meat, is that I suddenly know something. I know things will never be the same again for us. This is a time of change.

It wasn't his fault. It was a girl driving and she hit the kerb at sixty. The steering was power-assisted and when the wheel clipped the side her wrists snapped like twigs. The steering wheel flew round and the car flipped over, broke in two. She was already dead when we got to the hospital. Dominic was in the back with another girl. She died later on that evening. There was a guy in the front and he walked away from it, picked himself off the road and walked down to a nearby bar, called the ambulance. That would have been it. It was a bad crash. Two promising students had died driving from a party out in the country. The problem was that the police turned up before the ambulance did and they helped get my brother out of the crushed rear of the car. They found drugs on him.

He took all the blame. The other parents wanted him prosecuted, as though he had caused the crash, tarnished their daughters' reputations with a lump of blow and a small bag of amphetamine they found in his jacket.

He was in hospital for weeks but nothing shows now. He puts his lack of energy down to the accident sometimes but that's probably a mental thing I think. Once he got out, that's when it got bad. He was on his way for a first at college but they dumped him. It wasn't the sort of place that could accept it, just let him get on with his life and his studies. They had always thought he was above criticism. He was a brilliant student – charming, confident, hard-working. After the accident he was only a drug addict, a sore reminder that under the surface the perfect students were flawed, far from pure. He had to cope with the death of his friends, the expulsion, the court case, his injuries, our parents' shock at discovering the truth about their son. He flipped. It didn't work out when he came home. My mother tried but she was too disappointed in her son to pull it off. She had lost any respect for him and when that goes there's nothing you can do to get it back. They asked him to leave. He couldn't get a job, dressed badly, withdrew into himself and his friends deserted him. He got lost in his own depression, staying in bed all day smoking. He sat in his bedsit and did nothing.

That was nearly a year ago. He must be coming up to twenty-one and it still doesn't look as though things are improving. I can see he doesn't care about his appearance or his life style. I don't know how to help and even when I try he . . .

"Listen to me! Fucking listen' will you? I've learnt a lot in the last year, Charles. About people and about myself. It hasn't been easy. I'm not gonna give you the 'life' lecture. All I'm saying is . . . don't be too . . . rigid with your attitude. Don't get too high strung an' . . ."

"I know what I want to do."

"Yeah, but that don't always make you happy."

"It'll make me happy."

"Don't fence yourself in though. You're young, take it slow. And the drug thing . . ."

"So it is the lecture after all?"

"No . . . it's just that there are kids your age starting to get guns and growing up like that . . . selling for real."

"Bullshit. Total bullshit."

"These aren't games to some people, Charles."

"Dominic . . ."

"I think you should go back to your studies and relax over this summer . . ."

"Did you a lot of good."

"I got stressed out trying to do too much, trying to please everyone 'cept myself. But there's another side to that which is just as dumb, which is when you get too selfish, thinking about making it all the time . . ."

"Oh, words of wisdom here."

"I'm only saying . . ."

"Well don't." I get up from the table, take a five out from my pocket and drop it in the empty cup. "There. Don't suppose you've got enough for it, have you?"

"Charles, come back man."

"I'm walking for the door but I turn and speak.

"I came to see how *you* were, not to get hassled about what I'm up to."

"I wasn't telling you how to live . . ." Now he's all hunched over the table – scruffy, suddenly a bit desperate. "Charles."

"See you, Dom. Take it easy, yeah."

I go out and take the chain off the bike. He taps on the glass but I ignore it and ride off.

Spence is on the mobile by the time I hit Battersea High. I pull the bike up on to the pavement and tell him I'll be around in ten minutes. I'm still raging, muttering under my breath. Dominic had no right to get on my case like that. When I think how ruined he is – going nowhere and him telling me that I should be working it out? Crazy. It must be the drug connection he's thinking of but it's different with me. I'm just using it as a commodity, for set aims. I've got ambition, drive. He was into the lifestyle and besides, it was the speed that really got him. No-one minds about a bit of puff.

There's something about family. They get to know you so well but never seem to use that knowledge in the right way. It just ends up winding you up, putting you on edge. I push off into the traffic.

Spence lives in Clapham, down towards the Junction in the backstreets that run up to Clapham Common. He's got his own place on the dole, a couple of years older than me so he can claim benefit. I bang on his door.

"Easy."

The door opens a crack and he pops his head

round to see who it is. Spence is always worried about his visitors, about who might be sitting in a car watching, about everything. Spence is a thief and it makes him jumpy.

"Here, I have to bring the bike in."

"Watch the walls' man. Just decorated it."

He has the ground floor of a terrace – a large front room with blinds always drawn and some rooms in the back, down a thin corridor. I've never been back through there even though I've known him for years.

"Want a tea?"

"Sure. Hey, you got anything stronger?"

"You celebrating or something?"

He's stocky and short, balding already so he keeps his hair a bristle on top.

"Nah, the opposite. Just had a talk with Dominic."

"In that case you deserve a drink. How is he?"

"Same."

He leaves the room and returns with a bottle of cheap Scotch and two glasses.

"Can't understand it, after all that happened, but he is a bit of a waster, in't he?"

"Yeah. Say that again."

"Should get his act together."

"Of course."

He pours a small measure in each glass. We drink. Spence moves some of the junk from a sofa by the window and sits down. He's fat, the sofa creaks. Before speaking he fiddles with the glasses he always wears.

"Man, life's a bit of a shit, you know."

"Tell me about it."

"I mean, look at all this stuff in here."

The room is full of boxes, crates, plastic bin liners and shopping bags. This is his warehouse. I speak first.

"Before you start, I don't want anything you may have, alright..." He's always trying to sell to his friends.

"Course, I wouldn't give you the grief, Charles."

"What you been up to lately, getting I mean?"

"Music gear and I can't do nothin with it."

Spence is famous for being a terrible thief. Sometimes it's a comedy act when he tries to sell you something.

"Nobody wants it."

"What is it?"

"A music program – you know, the works..." He also talks in the comedy style sometimes, goes into the cockney bit.

The whisky tastes good and I decide to pep it up with a spliff. I roll as he talks, break a Silk Cut in and sprinkle, light it and sit back, trying to forget the row with my brother.

"You got all the cartridges, monitors and keyboards, the fucking lot, only there's a language problem, you know..."

"Hmm."

"Yeah, it's all in fuckin' Japanese, not a word of English. 'S cool till someone wants to see a manual or whatever 'cause then they know there's no way to understand it. I even got the thing running with Bruce..."

"How is Bruce?"

"Oh, sweet. He's down at the office all the time, working his balls off, coining it . . ."

"Yeah, I heard he had a job."

Bruce is another friend in our circle, a real computer freak. He moved on from arcade games to bootlegging, then to hacking and finally a job with a design company. He's seventeen.

"It's not a 'job', more a way of life, yeah? The guy is at it all the time. Anyway, he got the system running but when the screen came on an' everything . . . I mean I thought it was cool by then, you know . . . but all the words on the screen are fucking oriental too."

"Yeah?"

"Truth. I was crushed, Charles, I tell you."

I have to smile even though this rates as only a minor event in his inept criminal history.

"Well, I'm sure you'll find someone to take It."

"Nah, gonna dump it."

"Got anything else?"

"Just a few bits an' pieces. Oh, there was something. Thought you might do an exchange for a draw."

"I don't think so."

"Here."

He rummages in a pile of boxes by the far wall and lifts two wheels up into the air.

"Fuck. They're mint, man!"

"Yeah, I know. Got 'em from the shop itself."

"That's better than taking them from some guy in the street."

"Like you, yeah?"

"Yeah, like me."

"Ah, don't give me the morality bullshit. This is my career, there's a demand for people like me."

I've got up from my seat and am turning the bike wheels, admiring them. I speak without looking at him. "What you talking about?"

"Give us a blast on the doobry and I'll tell you."

I pass it over. He goes back to the sofa and sits down again, picks up a remote control that's lying on one of the cushions and hits some buttons. Spence has the best system out of all my friends, this is one thing he has managed to get right. Sky FM cuts in and he turns up the volume. A slow reggae tune starts shaking the room, no static, full base and bright treble. Spence is mad on it, the slow ragga beat stuff and dub. He gets back into his speech.

"See, without the criminal element – myself that is, you understand – the powers that be would find it hard to survive. I'm what keeps 'em all going."

"I'll give you a sixteenth for the wheels."

"I and others in the same position as myself . . ." Fiddling with his glasses, toking and slurping on the spirit. Mounds of stomach flab rippled under his grey sweater. He wears real boy-next-door clothes – grey jumpers, white shirts open at the collar, straight blue cotton trousers. Spence describes it as his 'anonymity disguise', looking so plain no-one would hassle him. Spence has a theory on everything, is always happy to sit back and chat for hours, long as there's some music and some smoke. I'm used to his speeches. " . . . yes, we are what is now known as 'the underclass'."

"Yeah, I heard about it. Old news."

"I mean, who the fuck can survive on the jobs around, man? The pay you get, I mean."

"Look at Bruce. He's doing all right you said."

"But he's skilled, in't he? No, I mean unskilled guys, don't I. You have to have a trade these days."

"Yeah, that's obvious. Anyone can see that."

"Never used to be like that though. I remember my old man, he never fucked around with exams. A man could work if he wanted to, when and wherever he wanted . . ." Spence looks a little blasted already. His voice is rising, thinning out. "Now you have to be tough, man. Get in there and start kicking and that's what everyone's doing. Even crooks aren't safe these days."

"Spence, don't talk shit, man."

"I mean it, Charles, no lie. I need a burglar alarm for this place. Have to go out and nick one soon, I'm tellin you. It's getting wild round here. All the youth . . ."

"Yeah?"

"Well, they're desperate man, bored and desperate. That's why they nick cars and rob and all that shit."

"Always been the same. That's just some new bullshit the press has put about to make it sound rough. Anyway, Spence, not as though you're pure or something, huh? You're out thieving all the time . . ."

The rocksteady tune on the radio cuts out and the DJ chimes in: "Message going out to Tony down there in Wandsworth, down the wing there – your brother'll see you tomorrow, alright. Keep the chin up, boy."

The music cuts in again, another old time tune. Spence is beaming.

"You see? It's growing and this is the thing I was getting round to, right . . ."

"Pass the wand, man."

"You see, it's on the surface now, out in the open, that's what's new, that's what I'm saying. It's us and them now, man, clear as fucking day. People have lost their respect for the Power. They'll be out in the streets soon. Riot time. Everyone knows the score."

"Bollocks, Spence. Oh, people were saying that in the seventies, been saying it for years, fair enough. Never happened though, the people are too crazy in this country. I don't go for all the political bullshit."

"No. It's different now. They're passing new laws every fucking day – just you have to be a crook to find out about it 'cause they're sneaky. And it's nearly all public hmm, public . . ."

"Public order."

"Yeah, crowd control basically. They know there are gonna be more and more demonstrations, yeah? 'Cause it's time for everyone to stand up and have their say about things, man. Getting closer, I tell you. What they're doing with the country you know, it's not fucking democratic, is it? I mean when was the last time there was a . . . shit a . . ."

"Referendum?"

"See, you know more about this than I do. Anyway, yeah, a vote basically. I'm telling you, I've felt the mood lately boy and it's gonna get nasty."

"Spence, you're scared about opening your own fuckin' door, let alone going out demonstrating. Besides, that's a guaranteed way to get your head bust wide open."

"Exactly. It's all happening now, boy. Police wilder now than ever."

I like debates but with the whisky and the joint I'm feeling sluggish so I bring it to a halt.

"So you want the sixteenth."

"Eighth would be better."

"No way, boy."

"Alright . . ."

"Taking the piss there. An eighth."

"I know, I know. Yeah, a sixteenth is cool. What you doing tonight? We should carry on this discussion in the great English tradition, which is sitting in the pub getting blasted."

I start up a bag for him.

"Don't know yet. Might see Trev."

"I'm into a beer or two, yeah. Why don't we go out?"

"I'll give you a ring then. And stop worrying about the 'Power' as you put it, before you lose your marbles."

"You don't know the half of it, boy."

"Bad as Dominic."

"Well, you're in the trade now, thought you might have a new angle on it, you know."

"What d'you mean?"

"Well you're not straight anymore, are you?"

"Hmmm. I guess not, not strictly anyway."

"One of *us* now, Charles."

He slaps me on my arm and takes the bag I've filled for him. I pick up the wheels and head for the door.

"But Spence, this is a short term thing for me, remember. I'm going into one of the professions – business, law, whatever, that's what I'll be doing. I told you, this is only for a month or something till I get a bit of money . . ."

"Or you get a taste for it." He smiles.

"No, Spence, you are talking to a future king of

commerce here, a pillar of industry, a budding millionaire."

"Well in that case you're not going straight, are you? 'Cause those guys are the biggest crooks around, boy."

Both my parents were out when I got back. I made a sandwich and wolfed it, then changed the wheels in the hall and admired the bike. It looked criss, the new wheels gave it that chunky feel, like putting alloys on a motor.

I'd stopped at my local shop on the way back from Spence's and picked up a couple of magazines – was planning on diving into bed for a few hours and chilling with them and my Walkman maybe. But just as I was moving up the stairs the phone burst into life down in the hallway.

"Yeah?"

"It's Dom."

"You're taking a chance, aren't you?"

"No. Well maybe, I don't know how it is with them these days."

I haven't heard him on the phone for a long time. My father just put the receiver back in its cradle last time he called. He told me that if he rang again he didn't want to know about it. They prefer to think he doesn't exist.

"So . . ."

"I'm sorry, Charles."

"Oh yeah?" He doesn't want to lose touch with me. I'm the last link to the family.

"Yeah, I am sorry. It's not down to me to preach, is

it? Just wanted you to know ... Hope it's cool between us."

"Yeah, course." It surprises me that I give in so
easily. He sounds a long way off on the phone. I can
hear the traffic, so he's probably ringing from outside
his flat, lorries flying past him. "It's cool."

"Well, let's get together then."

"Yeah, I'll call you. Listen, Dom, I'm gonna have to
go 'cause ..."

"No problem. Give us a bell."

He rings off.

I start up the stairs with the magazines under my
arm. When I get to my room I sit on the edge of the
bed for a while. It's been a hassle of a day already. I
always feel mixed up when it comes to Dominic, sad
and angry at the same time. I wish it was back to the
way it was before, without him stranded in that dirty
box he lives in. I pull off my trainers and slide into the
bed, flick the magazine open and start reading.

The mobile woke me up at seven. I was lying on the
bed, covered in magazines, chewing the Walkman
cable. It took me ten minutes to feel human again.
Then I was running around on the bike till nine. Trev
rang up and said a bunch were meeting up down at
Beautiful People and I said I'd see him there later. I
was thirsty. I'd been over to Streatham, some new guy
who wanted an eighth, then I had to drop all the way
over to Chelsea. It was brief with Theo. He was on his
way out so I just took the money in the hall and split.
Just as I was leaving he said he'd be in touch soon,
had a big party happening in a week's time and he'd
need to see me for some more bush. I got an invite as

well. The social calendar is booming and in all the right circles. All the riding around made me feel grubby so I got home for a quick shower, ducked the parents and walked round to the club.

"Charles, what you drinking?"

Beautiful People is a small place and basic, but it's local and there's a good vibe to it. Rough concrete floors and corrugated iron walls means the system bounces all over the space so you have to shout up to chat. At one end of the bar there's a thick cloth partition that hangs all the way across the domed room. If you push past the edge of it you're in the 'dance room'. There's no furniture, just the box cabinets and the DJ in a corner. It's so loud it makes your ears sing. I pace in to the first room and there's a crowd round the bar. I see Spence and he shouts the drink question. I mime a pint glass. Then I see Trev and a group over in some easy chairs they've pulled up against the tin wall.

"Trev, alright?"

"Charles, man. How's it going?"

"Good, good."

I mutter greetings to the others. There's Lenny, always well-dressed, flashing notes. He's a DJ. I don't know him that well. He makes his pennies doing deliveries to dance record shops and Trev told me he sells the odd bit of coke. He's with two girls I don't know, probably linked somehow with Trev 'cause he's all smiles and bright eyes this evening. Then there's a guy on the other side of the low table they're seated around – Ben. I like him but he's a bit wild. Older guy. He's never got any money, bums off the rest of us.

Spence comes back from the bar with a fistful of bottles.

"No draught."

"Shit, they used to do it."

"Make more money with bottles, don't they? Two quid a go."

So there's seven of us sitting there talking. Spence is quite drunk, been at the whisky all day he says but I know it doesn't take much to get him blasted. Trev begs enough for a spliff off me and I hand it out. We pass it round under the table. Then another one. Everyone's hustling up to the girls 'cept me. I sit there and scan the room.

It's the usual crew in the club. There are lots of girls from across the river, in their seventies gear so they look like schoolkids. There are some older guys in twos at the bar, in expensive leather and smoking Marlboro Lights. The music's thudding and the girl serving has to lean across the bar top to hear the orders. Her breasts are spilling out of a lycra thing and Spence goes over and keeps changing his order so she keeps coming back until she rumbles him and shouts an insult. People shuffle in and out from the dance room and it gets louder every time the curtains get lifted up.

" 'S all fucking house the geezer's playing, man. Sleepy time."

"We should have gone into town."

"You rich tonight?"

"So you work in a bank then?"

"Yeah, I'm a clerk, down the Junction."

"Get us a loan, can you?"

"Have to come in and see me, won't you?"

"You see Clark?"

"What? Clark here?"

"Yeah, he's pissed up bad, man. Out in the other room dancing like a cripple he's so drunk."

"Can't believe he's out of his house."

"Yeah, he rang me up. Was him who said we should come down here."

Then there's a hand on my shoulder and Clark's behind me. His face muscles are all loose, eyes bloodshot. He's in a lot of bother, sweating, got a tumbler in his hand.

"Charles . . . good to see you." He's almost slobbering. I've never seen him like this. Usually so cool, leaning on the bar and making the odd quip, drawing a card. "I need to . . . fuck . . ."

I stand up and I'm virtually propping him, he's all over the floor.

"Let's dance."

Then he's pushing for the curtain. Everyone's behind me, just staring at him. I follow him.

When the curtain goes up it hits me. The music is like a punch, a house track with a thumping drum pattern, mad vocal screaming and a wash of cymbals, bells – so sharp it hurts. 'To the beat of the drum . . .' The room is heaving, a mesh of bodies. Clark dives into the crowd. It's dark except for a cheap light rack that's shooting out some rays and I catch a glimpse of damp faces, wild eyes, hair thrown back in a flowing arc. It stinks of sweat and perfume, leather and tobacco. The music gets more intense as I follow him – over and over, pumping in my years. I push a girl out of the way – 'Hey, fucker, watch where you going!' – walking further into the mesh. The tune changes, bass beat on its own, then a cymbal. Man, I hate this jaded house, got no 'depth' to it. I push through two girls, rubbing up against their bodies, hot and firm, regular dancers with tight skin. It's all teens or early twenties in here, hands going up in the air. Can't see Clark, what the fuck is wrong with him?

Then I know and my chest goes tight. Indigo's bailed.

"Charles man, bitch has left me."

"Where's the kid?"

"Kid's alright. Got . . . my folks in looking after her but . . . she gone man, fucked me over."

I've found him. He's on my shoulder in the middle of the room. We're bumped by the other dancers and it must look like we're in on the dance but Clark is frozen, I'm carrying him.

"C'mon, get you back, yeah?"

I don't know whether I should tell him. It must be the guy I saw her with. I can't think with the noise in my head. I start pulling him back to the curtain.

"No, man, don't want to see them, all taking the piss."

"Nah, c'mon, you need some fresh air."

"Leave me here."

He breaks free from my hold and accidentally steps back into a guy dancing tight with a girl.

"Fuckin' problem?"

I break in. "Sorry, he's had too much, yeah?"

The guy gets cocky. He's standing straight, chest out, putting on a show for the girl.

"Fuckin' should be sorry."

Clark's not in the mood. "Yeah, big man, huh?"

"Take you, fucker."

"Really."

I don't want to look. It feels like it's out of my hands now. Clark drops his left hand in a fist. Even this drunk I don't fancy the other guy's chances. He sees the fist go down so he moves forward to block it with his right arm and lifts his own left. but Clark was waiting for this. Instead of doing anything with the left, his right fist comes up in a wild haymaker. It smashes into the guy's head and I can hear the thud above the music. He drops. I'm trying to hold Clark but he's pissed and angry. He lifts his foot and kicks the guy in the side of the jaw. He'll be eating yogurt for the next six months.

Now it's run away time. This isn't my scene. The girl is screaming, Clark's staggering all over the place, bumping into the other dancers, now stationary in a little clearing. I'm losing hope, feel the stone coming on from the spliffs I smoked earlier as my blood speed rockets. There's a guy rushing through the crowd, one of the mammoths that watch the door. It's all going wrong.

I'm a little wrecked so it's all in slow motion, playing out right in front of me. I can't fight for fuck so I try to stay out of it. It's a no-win game anyway. Funny, but the music's changed and I know the track, a Soul Power remix, and it's kicking. The fight has this as the backing music.

Clark throws a punch at the bouncer and it's pretty good. The guy pauses for a second and Clark hits him again. Both of them are trying not to step on the wounded dancer which strikes me as odd seeing as Clark beat the crap out of him a moment ago. The bouncer is stunned but grabs Clark in a bear hug and squeezes. Clark looks contained. Then I think – fair enough, it has to stop now. But suddenly there's another shape knocking people out of the way to get to the fight. There are shouts going up as he shoves through the crowd and he arrives, another mammoth. He doesn't hesitate. Clark's pinned anyway but the new guy rams a fist into his back and Clark lets out a sob. Then the attacker pulls his fist back for another one. The first bouncer is smiling, holding my friend.

It's too much. Clark shouldn't have hit the dancer but he doesn't need this. He's having a hard time at the moment. The Soul Power track has got me charged. I move up behind the mammoth, who's got his fist drawn back – like I said, it's all in slow motion with the blow – and I take the Silk Cut out of my mouth, stab the burning end down on the tight skin of his fist. I can smell it burn. They guy spins round and Clark kicks him in the ass so he comes flying at me and I manage to get a couple in before he whacks me and my nose feels like it's been torn off my face. He's big and heavy and he falls on me, trying to pin me down. I think, *This is it, Charles, you died helping a friend at least*. I can see Clark breaking out of the bear hug a few yards away from me but it's too late, the mammoth with the burnt hand is raising a fist like a brick over his head.

"Goodbye, you fuck."

I think he's angry. Anyway, I still feel a little trashed so I'm just watching this, rather nervous, and then this face appears next to the bouncer's. It's Spence. His glasses are all foggy.

"Bastard."

He's climbing on the guy's back, wrapping his arm round the neck, trying to strangle him. The guy staggers up and tries to shake him loose. Then I see Ben, looking wilder than ever, come flying through the crowd, actually *in the air* and his trainers thud into the guy's chest. Then the guys are everywhere, helping me up, prizing Clark free, kicking the mammoths all over the room, lifting us and dragging us out into the other room.

"I've called the police, you bastards."

The bar girl is screaming as we file past. Ben hops over the counter and gives her a kiss, grabs a fist of beers.

There's another guy still at the door. He blocks the exit and this one is king mammoth. His arms are crossed.

"You fuckers ain't leaving till t' police get here."

We all just stand there and look at him in surprise. The girls have gone. They must have split when the guys piled through. There's me, Spence, Ben, Trev, Lenny and a wilted Clark.

"Fuckin' death wish or somethin'?"

"I said you're not leaving."

Then Ben slipped back into the room and he comes crashing back in a charge. We all separate and he steams past holding one of the sofas we were sitting on earlier – must weigh a fucking ton – crashes back into the mammoth – waving arms, then we're all behind him, squashing the guy against the wall. We keep him pinned like that whilst we break, then we're out in the road, falling about laughing.

Clark is beginning to sober up by the time I get him into a mini-cab. He talks as the street lights flash by and we cross the park down to Balham.

"What a mess, man."

"Yeah, well, I can tell you that was well out of my character what went on back there. I'm worried they might know our faces."

"No, they used to getting smashed now and again. Probably enjoy it."

"You feeling alright?"

"Just a bit breathless. The guy nearly broke my ribs."

The car stops at the front of his house and he wants to go in alone but I insist on joining him. I pay the fare. After a moment's fumbling for the key he pushes the door open and we go in, clean up a bit at the sink. The flat is very quiet and dark. He sits down at the table.

"Can't see what I'm gonna do, Charles."

"She'll be back."

"I don't think so. We've never had a split before."

"But the kid . . ."

"That's the last thing she wants to face up to. She's gone all the way, wants a break."

I consider telling him about Martin but it seems like a bad idea. I can't be sure the guy was with Indigo in that way. Maybe they were friends. Clark looks worse than he did in the club – all the alcohol fire has left him.

'You get back."

"I'll stay if you want."

"No, I'm gonna sit up for a while and think things through. I've been drunk all day, need some time alone."

"Yeah, I never seen you so smashed."

"Thanks for getting me back home, Charles."

"Alright. I'll call round in a day or two."

"Yeah."

I'd told the cab to go when we got out, and Clark doesn't have a phone so I have to walk up Balham Hill to reach the nearest mini-cab office. It was a long, lonely trot through the night. Apart from the odd car whistling past there was no noise, a dead time. I get back and make straight for my room, fall on to my bed. It's close to three in the morning. My body aches, I have a massive bruise on my left cheek and the sour taste of beer is still on my lips. I leave the accounts for the morning and fall asleep, making a whispered promise to myself that I will never get stitched up that bad by a girl. Clark is cracking with the strain. There are other promises too. I'll have to slow things down a bit, lay off the smoke, maybe, check the accounts properly. The day has been frantic and I'm going to have to impose some control. Then it all calms down and I'm out. I'm too tired to dream.

Four

Friday

I wake up and it's eleven, a late start for me. My face is swollen and when I examine myself I find scratches and cuts on my hands, arms and shins. When the bull at the club fell on top of me I must have crashed down on the dance floor and thrashed about underneath him. The concrete mashed me up. I look a mess. The physical injury is only one part of it though, I feel drained of energy, grubby, ragged. I crawl out of bed and head for the bathroom.

Twenty minutes later I feel revitalised, pummelled by the shower. I covered myself in shower gel and went for it with a loofah, rubbing till it hurt. My face has come back to life, a normal shape again. I feel vibrant. I've got that post-shower tingle. I pull on some black jeans and a clean shirt, a button thing, push my hair back and head downstairs. The flat's empty. I prepare a huge breakfast – cereal to kick it in, toast, everything I can find in the fridge that belongs in a frying pan – eggs, bacon, mushrooms, some potato chunks left over from another meal that are longing to be fried, two sausages, a tomato chopped in two, onion and tobasco all over the top. I dump it on the cooker, full fire, and run upstairs for a magazine to read whilst I eat. By the time I get back it's ready and I devour it, flicking my eyes from the plate to some bullshit article about 'Plastic Jungle'. Some track they're slagging off for being too commercial. I haven't even heard it and I'm always checking the radio.

When I'm through with the meal I dump the plate in the sink and head back upstairs. Back to business. I spend nearly an hour working on the accounts, figuring my profit, the average weekly score required, all that stuff. It's just like the economics classes at college, 'cept this is real and not some dumb theoretical model. As long as you keep some discipline, it's easy. When I'm through with the calculations I put everything back in the drawer and roll a single skinner. I check my door is shut and the window's wide open before I light it up. Lying back on the bed I take a long pull and stretch my arm over and hit the radio switch. The accelerated beat of a jungle tune kicks in, which surprises me for a second. I take another blast on the band, remember the article I was reading. It must be hard for the DJs seeing a lot of their stuff being changed a little, re-packaged and then put out on more commercial airwaves. A few months ago this station wouldn't have gone near this track, now they're bigging it. But you have to move with the changes and it was obvious it would happen. Must be like that with anything underground. Once a major company gets involved then it can't truly be underground any longer. It's not hip to be popular.

I mull things around in my head, letting the bush carry me along, thinking about the music, life, money, girls, the car, cruising. I feel in control of my destiny, the choices are mine to make. Even though I've always been one of the team I was often considered a bit straight by the others, maybe 'cause I didn't smoke much, kept my head down and worked. Thinking about the last few days though I can see that has changed. I'm not on the outskirts now. It's me who's selling, making money, chilling.

The bush kicks in heavy and I let it rush round my body. I'm still thinking it through. This is only the first step. It all fits in. You act for yourself, and if you act properly then you get what you want. My philosophy has been proven so far. I'll go on with the long-term plan.

About twenty minutes into my charged mental meanderings I hear the front door click open and know my mother has just walked in.

"You still in bed? Charles, you here?" Our house is small enough to shout to anyone from any room.

"Yeah, I'm up here."

I give it another few seconds until she enters the kitchen then the next shout goes up. "Charles come down here!"

I'm a little blasted so it's almost funny. I have to wash up, with her checking each piece is clean and dry.

"Satisfied?"

"Just do it before I get home next time, will you?"

"Yeah. Where you been?"

"Just did a bit of shopping. Bought a lottery ticket."

"Oh yeah, dream on."

She sits down at the table and slowly relaxes her shoulders, turning her head in an effort to unwind. She learnt all that when she was a teacher. Tried everything – breathing exercises, stress busting techniques. None of it did any good. The real problem was that the kids she was teaching used to nick cars and crash them into the school gates, or assault the staff, or smoke blow in the toilets, or scream 'bitch' at her all the time. I'm glad she got out of it.

"What have you got planned today? Seeing Trevor or something?"

"I'm having a 'me' day."

"Sorry?"

"Personal attention. Just spending a bit of time in my room, listen to some music, tidy up. I don't want to strain myself."

"Don't think there's much risk of that."

"Well, the holidays don't last for ever."

"No, they don't. Well, I'm going to have a look at the lunch-time news, your wake-up call."

"That's not true. I've been up for hours."

"Oh, of course. You seen your brother lately?" She is casual with the question, her voice does not flutter. I'm not sure if she'll be happy or sad to know but I decide to be honest.

"The other day. I went round to his flat."

"The palace he lives in? You went round there? Hmm. Anyway, he rang for you last night."

"You spoke with him?"

I am amazed she sounds so calm about him ringing. A few months ago it would have produced tears.

"We had a chat, yes. We were . . . well, getting on better, I suppose. I still find it hard though." I don't like the tone to her voice.

"You sound as though it's Dominic who has to make all the apologies. It was you who asked him to leave."

"Not exactly, there was more to it than that. But I did . . . we had such hopes for Dominic, you know that. It was impossible to go back to how it was with him here. Something had to change."

"Well, what's the point of talking about it? You've made up your mind, haven't you?"

"Oh Charles, give me a chance to speak. You don't know everything I'm trying to say to you."

"I'm going upstairs."

It doesn't really upset me because I've been through it so many times. I brush it off. The time when it hurts is when I suddenly picture him at the kitchen table, or sitting in the lounge, joking with my father. It feels as though they have taken him away from me, and the gulf with him living all that distance away in his shabby bedsit is too great to be bridged. He's not the same any more. If they had accepted him again then I'd still have a brother and not some shadow I find it hard to be around.

Anyway, I don't get too sad 'cause I'm used to it. I go upstairs and roll another single. I tidy up my tapes and stuff all the clothes away in the cupboard. I stack my magazines at the foot of the bed in a neat pile. Then I do some more grooming, tend to my nails and stuff. After an hour I'm ready to go out for a spin on the bike down to Battersea High, turn the phone on and wait for some calls. I pick it off the charger and throw it on the bed, check my wallet and smoking equipment. I've got all the gear now – a fresh Clipper, some Cuts, a packet of double-decker Tops so I don't run out of papers, a plain circular stash tin. Then I hover by the mirror at the end of the room for a while, checking my chin. I had cut myself shaving in the bathroom that morning and I try to snatch off the dry blood.

When the mobile starts bleeping I have to dive for it across the bed. If my mother hears it she'll freak in a huge manner. So far, I've managed to keep it hidden. They never come into my room and I put it on charger as soon as I get in so it can't ring. I wasn't prepared for it to go off in the minute or so it takes me to leave the house.

"Yeah?"

"Charles, you sound a bit jumpy."

"Just speak, yeah?"

"It's Clayton. Can you pass by the studio we're in?"

"Where is it?"

"Over in Hackney."

"Hackney? Man, I don't know – that far, you know."

"Make it worth your while though."

"Alright then."

He gives me the address but I need some directions. I tell him I'll be there in under an hour. I won't take the tube. Even on a long trip across town the bike is quicker than anything else. I turn the phone off and stuff it in the back of my jeans, pull the brown leather on and cover it. Before leaving my room I yank a green baseball cap off a shelf, lay it on my head. I bought it a few days ago and it smells new. It's got the golden bush emblem on the front. Then I'm down the stairs, swinging past the front room, grabbing the Fox and yelling a quick goodbye to my mother. I'm out on the bridge in less than a minute.

Hackney. This is a land of brick, litter-strewn streets, low broke-down buildings that haven't been used for years, squats, bad pubs with desperate drinkers and carpets the same colour as dried blood, back-alleys and stray dogs. I hate it. I don't really like crossing the river. Going over to Chelsea is alright 'cause it feels close to home but once I'm far out of my patch I get edgy. I don't know the terrain in the north. The mood's different as well, a bit tougher. Hackney's got it bad. I had a friend living up here and some guy just kicked his door in, walked right in to the living room and took the TV, with my friend sitting there on the couch staring at him. The thief didn't give a fuck and my friend was wise enough to know not to try stopping him. There's a lot of powder freaks round in Hackney. They don't care what happens, long as they get a charge.

I cut up through the city to Old Street then out to Shoreditch, along to Hackney Road. This is the bottom part of the area. Hackney is massive, runs all the way up to Islington, Stoke Newington, places I rarely visit and I was glad I didn't have to go deep into it. It was quick on the bike. I got to the address in forty minutes – found a three-storey rehearsal place called Kick Ass. I rang a bell and pushed along a corridor piled high with box speakers and music gear. Clayton was sitting in a little coffee shop they had set up in the back. There was some acid jazz track playing from wall speakers but I could still hear rumbles and groans coming from above and below us. The building was full of bands.

"Herbsman, nice timing. I dig that hat."

"'S a clever psychological trick, you see. Too obvious to be worth a pull."

I pull up one of the tacky plastic chairs to his table and wave at a dull-looking girl who's leaning on the counter. "Cap-oo-chino."

Clayton laughs. "You're buzzy today."

"Yeah. The ride livened me up a bit. What you doing here then?"

I stretch out in my seat, wrap my hands round the back of my head and slide the cap back.

"Working with the band down here."

"For the record?"

"Yeah, but that's not here. This is where we practise, yeah? We get it right before we go into the studio 'cause it cost for the time there. Can't fuck around at forty an hour."

"See what you mean."

"Come up and see the band."

"Yeah, I'll just have the coffee."

The surly girl has made it over to the table. She wears a shapeless black top, skin-tight jeans and Caterpillars. So many girls wearing boots these days, they must see it as making a statement or something.

"Pound."

"You're welcome. You want something, C?"

"Nah."

We chat a little. He's into the music scene in a big way, talks about the band he's in and the problems they're having getting any press or gigs.

"People were supposed to be dealing with black guys playing rock yeah, but it never happened. All sewn up by middle-aged whitey fuckers, no offence."

"None taken."

"Plus we're not on the Livin Colour tip, yeah. We're using beats, bit like what they're doing with jungle, speeding them up, yeah, but then keeping the rock thing hitting man, hitting . . ." He has leaned forward and is slamming his fist into his open palm. "Not the ragga style bit. That's all DJs putting it together anyway, not musicians."

"Well the DJs are making records so that makes 'em musicians in my book, boy."

" 'S true. Some of them are doin' it but, well, you see the band anyway."

"I can't hang around too long."

I want to get back to Battersea and check Trev, get something sorted drink-wise for the evening. Besides, any calls coming in here puts me a long way from the next customer.

"No sweat. Come on, let's go up."

We have to push past some musicians on the stairs, all with pig-tails or shaved heads. I'm still stuck in the middle on that one. I admire Clayton's dredds bouncing as we take the stairs. He's in a new leather, long coat style, so he can't be too poor. Then we get to the landing and there's more musical junk everywhere and some doors leading off. I hear the thud of music behind them as he leads me up to the next set of stairs and we head up to the top of the house. I'm huffing and puffing by the time we walk into a big studio room. There are two AC units on the wall and it's quite cold – stings my face when I first go in. There's a little stage at one end with a drum kit spread out. Next to the kit is a huge box, a sampler I think. All around the walls (the colour scheme is brilliant white, so with that and the temperature it feels like walking into an igloo) are box speakers with shiny lights on the front. There are three guys standing talking in the middle of the room. They stare at me when I come in.

"This is the guy?"

"Yeah, this Charles."

"Alright Charles, come to help us out, yeah?"

We stand around shaking hands for a minute. They're all massive, like Clayton, all in their twenties I think.

"How much you after?"

"Was thinking . . . a quarter maybe. Depending on the price you have in mind, of course."

I think this guy must be the singer. He has the easy confidence you associate with someone who is happy standing up in front of a thousand people. He's got dredds and lots of gold.

"Well, Clayton knows the score. I knock a little off for you taking a quarter."

"Safe. Well, we take it then."

We talk for a while then I have to go back down to the bike to get another eighth I have stashed in the handle bars. When I get back two of the guys are fiddling with guitars, sounding the odd scraped note.

"Go on then. Give us a blast of Radical."

They were heavy. I huddled at the back of the room, making a polite nod now and again. I'm not into rock and the music sounded like one of the old beasts from the seventies. There was an opening riff, lots of guitar and a big drum beat. I was regretting making my request. But just before the singer stepped up the drummer threw his arm back and triggered a little round pad off to the side of his kit. Under the beat I heard a rumble, then a monster line came in, a weird vocal sample with lots of effects, followed by the fast beat style of jungle. They were mixing the two together and it worked. As the vocal came in he flicked the sample off, then hit it again for the next section. Clayton was rocking with it, throwing his head back and giving it the full rock'n roll bit. They went on with it for a few minutes then it all faded out, the band watching each other so that could time it right.

"Yeah. Yeah, I like it. Tough. You got anything coming up, a show or something?"

"Got a gig in a few days, yeah. On Sunday actually."

"I'll come down for that."

They leave their instruments and wander over as the singer and me do the deal. Then it's smoke time. I wasn't planning on staying too long so I roll one up, take a few drags then make my exit.

"Just bell me if you need a repeat."

"Sweet."

I go out into the hall and shut the door behind me. My ears are ringing from the music so I don't hear them on the stairs. I turn round and Bond is smiling at me.

"Hello again."

Lenny is behind her. He gives me a smile.

"Alright, Charles. Dig the hat. You making a statement?"

Bond almost giggles and I'm surprised to find myself blushing.

"Not that I know of."

Lenny has sharp eyes, looks sly. I think he's going to make another crack but then his face changes and he smiles again. "You been in with the band?"

"Yeah."

"I'm doing some mixing for them on stage."

"Yeah?" They said they had a show coming up."

"I better go in and see them. See you there then. No fighting this time though."

He laughs and goes in. I wait for Bond to move with him but she stays out on the stairs. Then she steps over to the door, almost pushing past me. When she speaks her voice has a flirtatious twist.

"Why don't you come along?"

"Said I might. You going with Lenny?"

"Maybe. I'm a free agent. Lenny's good for a kidder, that's all."

"Huh?"

"He keeps me amused."

"Lucky you."

I feel uncomfortable. She's very close.

"Well, I might see you there."

"Yeah."

Then she goes in and I pad down the stairs to the Fox. I've got the body tingle, can still smell the dry, almond scent she was wearing. I don't really kick the feeling until I'm out on the road and the air's rushing past me, waking me up.

I take a different route home. The traffic through the city and down the Embankment is so thick it slows me down, even on the bike, so I cut across Blackfriars Bridge and take the south-side way back, following the twists of the river. I keep pumping the pedals, trying to concentrate on the evening ahead, but my thoughts are betraying me. The girl has got to me.

I remember what she was wearing – a funky, seventies-style leather coat, a tight cotton top, leggings and a pair of those terrible trainers that are somehow creeping back into fashion. I think about her hair, the skin and I'm trying to stop it because this is the last thing I need right now. When I hit Waterloo roundabout I actually stop the bike and talk myself down, leaning a pedal on the kerb.

"Forget the fucking girl, man."

To punish myself I push the bike to its limits and I'm flying down the south side, running through the thin channels in the stationary cars. The traffic's bad on this side as well, getting bad everywhere.

She's still on my mind. The mobile goes.

"Is Trev. What you up to?"

"Ah, not much, over at Vauxhall."

"So we still going out?"

"What? To what? You wanna drink already?"

"No, man. Is the jungle thing, innit?"

"Huh?"

"Man, you dopey today. The free tickets you got . . ."

"Shit yeah. Yeah safe. I'll come round about ten."

"See you then."

That clears my head. Clayton's ticket had slipped my mind completely. They're back in my room in a shirt pocket. I decide to get blasted at the club tonight, feel a rush at the prospect of going out and everything's back to normal. I almost blow a breath of relief. Don't need the hassle.

If that wasn't enough to get me back to ground level then what happens next makes sure of it. I hitch the mobile back into its holster and get ready to push off. Just as I lift my head I see a car on the other side of the road. I can't explain it, it's like instinct I suppose. My head goes up and I look over at this blue Ford and my blood goes chill. The windows are up so I can't see the faces but it's two fat white guys. They're staring at me. For a second I'm still, then I push into the traffic. The car starts up and joins the stream behind me. I can feel them back there. We move down to Stockwell in file. I catch sight of them every few hundred yards. My heart races, I can actually hear it beating. Are they DS? Or is it some other seller? I try to play it cool and stop at some lights when they change so I can lean back and have a closer look. If they get out I can take off on the pavement. The car would be useless in this traffic. I stretch a foot down to the tarmac and swivel on the saddle. They have gone, must have turned off a few streets back.

When I get home I take a shower and lie out on my bed for a while. It was probably nothing. I've heard that if you smoke regularly then you get jumpy. It's just one of the symptoms of the stone. Freddy told me he had learnt to ignore it, because if you were ever going to get busted you wouldn't even know about it. It comes out of nowhere. I stare up at the ceiling and let my muscles go loose, try to ease down. As I relax, I allow myself the image of Bond, floating by my bed, smiling down at me. It takes my mind off everything else.

Five

Trev had roped a friend of his into the club idea, a guy he works with sometimes called Malcolm. I've only met him a couple of times. He has a car, a rotting Sierra. We're steaming up across Westminster at fifty and he's got a hard–house tune blasting. The bass is making my butt quiver it's so loud. It's just past eleven and all the suckers are piling out of the booz-ers, falling round in football T-shirts and dumb cottons. Time for them to go home. The centre of town is full of lights and noise, ripping up to Charing Cross Road. Now we're in the heart of the best, the money god. I'm feeling fresh, even made the effort to dress up a bit. There's a strong-smelling cloud of aftershave coming from the front, where Trev and Malcolm are trying to out-smart each other.

"You two smell tarty, boy."

"Fuck off an' skin up if it's bothering you. The smoke'll cover it."

I'm bouncing all around the back of the car but I manage to pull all the gear out. I've got a little bank bag of bush with me, not carrying anything more than that. I ditched the mobile back at the house as well. After my bit of panic this afternoon I decided there was no harm playing it smart. I'm sure it was just my imagination but I don't need the hassle of even think- ing about it. I just want to chill this evening.

"Hurry up, will ya? Almost there."

Now we're in the maze of latticed roads round Soho. People are sitting out drinking coffee and trying to look cool, strolling, spilling out of the midnight- extension pubs. We roll past a gay bar.

"Fruity round here, innit?"

"Live and let live, boy."

In my eyes, everything here has the kiss of money, class. The cars parked up make me feel embarrassed to be sitting in Malcolm's Sierra. We pull up at a little crossroads and a jeep full of girls flies past. They're all laughing, pretty, well-dressed. They slide round a corner, off in the night. Another world.

"Follow that car!"

"Man, check her!"

"Pass the joint, ya hog."

Malcolm turns the music up so it's impossible to

talk. The car is like a huge Walkman. We're getting looks as we cruise up past the Square. Trev answers them.

"Fuck you, sucker." A pinched-faced, middle-aged woman sitting out at a little bistro.

"You know, this is the only place in the city that stays awake after eleven."

"What? Can't hear you."

"Turn the track down a bit. Fucking loud, man."

Malcolm turns the dial to the left a millimetre. I'm still screaming. "I said this was the only part a London that's got any life after eleven."

"Bullshit."

"It's true."

"Nah, you just have to look under the surface. Just 'cause the pubs shut, that mean fuck all. You go down south there's loads going on."

"Well, the public's face, that's what I'm talking about."

"You mean the money face. 'S all restaurants or coffee shops round this area."

"That's what I mean."

"Well, that's not what I'm into. I'm only coming into town for this club, not to pose in a coffee shop and eat flash sandwiches." Trev sounded smashed. We bought a half bottle of Scotch before crossing the river and have been taking it in turns to slug on it. I can see the empty bottle shining on his lap. He goes on.

"Charles, you're not saying you wanna fit in with that crap, are you?"

"Parts of it appeal to me, yeah."

"Man."

"Pass the wand back, will you?"

" 'S gone."

"We got time for another?"

"Yeah, still a few minutes away."

"I'll assemble another mighty stick then."

"That last one was hard, boy."

"I don't roll mean, do I? Anyway, what was you saying, Trev?"

"Nothing. Just your aspirations – crack me up sometimes that's all. Sorry, your 'ambitions'." Even slightly drunk he's still trying to be articulate.

"What's wrong with them?"

I'm licking the papers, staring up in front. Trev breaks out of his easy mood sometimes and makes a crack. I know he can be sharp but it always surprises me when he gets serious. He turns round in his seat and faces me.

"Just all that money thing, status . . . 's bullshit."

"Have to have it to get by these days."

"Hard enough just takin' it a day at a time, you ask me."

"I'm easy too."

"Me know, most the time. Just wish this shit didn't impress you so easy, that all."

I don't know what to say to him, just sit there holding the half-built joint. What he said sounded like a father talking to his son. I don't know if he's right or wrong, and not wanting the silence to be my reply I resort to confusion tactics.

"Oh, relax Trev. Let's not go into any bullshit psychology, yeah? You don't know everything in my head."

"Don't have to, you tell me you're into it all the time."

"You calling me a snob or something then?"

The conversation has moved from the easy intimacy of friends to the beginnings of an argument. Trev hesitates before speaking and I finish the joint, light it up. Malcolm looks uncomfortable.

"No, of course not. Sorry if I wound you up."

I'm relieved it didn't fall into a row. I have to admit to myself that I have been mouthing off a lot lately. Why should anything be different just because I've got some money coming in? But maybe Trev and I have got different attitudes. The changes that money brings could be starting already. But that's what I want. If Trev can't cope with it then it's his loss.

"Look, Charles, whatever yeah? I'll always back you up, you know that."

I just nod my head.

"Why you two being so fucking down?" It's the first thing Malcolm's said since we crossed the river. Trev and I stare at him. "You're friends, alright, get with it then. Where's the smoke?"

And we all start talking and the tension is gone but I'm left with Trev's last words, wondering if all the inevitable changes in life will bust us up one day. What can you do about change? It has to be a good thing.

The club entrance is a tiny doorway that leads up to a thin staircase. I flash the tickets and we get frisked. Malcolm's already picked his ticket up from a record store in Brixton. Then we take the stairs and crash the club.

It's dark, the light positioned to help you see steps and different levels, murky shapes. From what I can see, the main room is square, with a pit for dancers, and there is a side room for a bar and slightly more mellow sounds. In the centre of the room is the throng – young, mixed. It's black, white, girl, boy, all crushed in a square, arms up in the air for a second, then a pool of movement to the music. It's intense. The beats are shaking my lungs they're so loud – bass slow and lazy for a second, crashing into the drums that are almost a whistle of speed. The place smells of sweat. We can just about talk at the bar but our voices are indistinguishable, blurred with the music and the DJ dropping words in.

"It's just a club. Wh'appen this show thing then?"

"There'll be a PA but that'll be it. Maybe a couple of them. It's just to pull people in, yeah. It'll run right through to six through."

"Wanna drink?"

"Yeah, yeah, get 'em, in and I'll get the next lot." It feels strange to be able to say that, to have some money to throw around.

"I'm gonna do a reccy, yeah?"

Trev slopes off with a big smile. He moves down to the dance floor and starts to slide a little with the music. I watch him for a moment, wondering if I'm together enough to join in. Malcolm hands me a beer.

"Coming down?"

"I'm gonna rest up here for a minute."

He nods and moves off to follow Trev. Even when I have made it into a club it takes alcohol to get me jumping. Tonight I may have overdone it on the spliff, feel the club noise getting to me. There's sweat on my brow, my stomach feels tight. I sit and watch the dancers, trying to ride it out, spot Trev and Malcolm chatting the edges of the dance square now and again. I'm close enough to see the light in their faces as they check the girls dancing, then then fade into the crowd. Feeling ragged again. Now the music is pumping so loud it feels as though my vision is being affected, the pupils are shaking in my head. I hang on to the bar, wildly stoned I realise. The drink and the pure adrenalin music is boosting the stone. Maybe I should get out, find a taxi. My breathing feels strained, getting hot rushes.

"You Charles, yeah?"

At first I think he must be one of the club bouncers because of his size, but then I'm hallucinating. My heart's skipping. He's massive, muscled in a money denim shirt and navy slacks that hug the roots of muscle in his legs. But that's nothing. What's freaking me is his arm. He is leaning on the bar just next to me and his arm is up by my head as I slouch on my stool. It is a mass of swirling colours and I follow the pattern up to where it disappears under his shirt. Then I trace it to his neck where it stops in a dead line just beneath his throat. I see the same line round his wrist, and sense is finally coming back to me after long seconds of thinking I've flipped. He is heavily tattooed. The lines round his neck and wrists allow him to wear a suit without showing his colours. But here in the club it is not hidden.

"Charles?"

Even confronted by a buy who could rip out my rib-cage without breaking sweat, I keep my cool. This is one of the rules – no matter what, you keep face.

"That's me, yeah. You got a name?"

"Friend of mine would like a word if possible." His voice has the polite savagery of an army boy – just a flat stare, a slight London accent.

"Alright. Where is he?"

I don't feel even a shiver of worry. It could be the scotch or the blow but I step off my stool, wave a hand to indicate I will follow and leave the bar. At the back of my mind I feel somehow important – maybe that's why I don't panic. It gives my ego a rush to know someone wants an audience with me. We walk through to the back of the chill room where the music is not so piercing. There are several low tables, groups of people laughing, chatting. I spot a group of youth out on a date, lots of leather and clipped hair. Next to them are two bored girls, here to say they were here more than to enjoy themselves. Seeing the people here fires me up a bit and I feel like getting back over to the dance floor. My energy is coming back.

The giant sits down at one of the tables and smiles, starts talking to a girl who has obviously been waiting for him. She's blonde, tanned, twenties. There is an-other girl who stares up to me, cigarette between her lips, and next to her is a black guy who extends his hand up to me. I shake it.

"Hi Charles. Pull up a chair."

I slide a seat out from under the table and sit. I can't see how much of the guy's face because he's wearing a huge wide-brim hat – burgundy or puce, I'm not sure in this light, but it looks real pimpy anyway. I almost giggle. He's in his thirties I think.

"So, who the fuck are you?"

The other three are chatting, ignoring us. The giant has become human in the presence of the girls, laughing and smiling. The hatted man speaks.

"My name's Deacon, on account a the hat."

"No kidding."

"No lie. I know it's a stupid name to give someone but you don't pick your own, do you? Wore the hat one day and got named."

" 'Cause a deacon wears a hat?"

"Something like that. You want a drink?" There is a bottle on the table, amidst crumpled cigarette packs and lighters, torn flyers and empty glasses.

"Yeah, thanks."

"Wanna go to the bar then?" He reaches out, tips the bottle up and shakes it to show it's dry.

The giant sees this and turns round. "You're a lazy bastard, Deacon."

"I'm paying, boy. Money can be lazy."

I cut in. "I don't mind going." I wanted some champagne.

Giant rests a paw on my shoulder. "I was only going to the crapper and he's got me running errands for him, picking you up. Let him go."

I had thought the giant was working for the guy but they talk equally, it's casual. They're both laughing. Deacon pulls a note from his jacket.

"Alright, Allen, watch me now, this is me going to the bar, alright?"

"Bout fucking time."

Deacon squeezes past me and heads for the bar. I accept a cigarette from the girl opposite me and almost choke when I taste the menthol. She has a slack, easy smile, lazy eyes. Both girls are in the typical clubber gear – fake seventies stuff, skin-tight. Both of them are bony, no fat on their bodies.

"Here you go, Charles."

Deacon drops a bottle in the middle of the table and slides back on to his seat. He's wearing a white shirt, leather jacket and black cords. Allen fills the glasses. We all take one. Deacon makes the toast.

"Here's to hooking up again."

"You're on."

The two men clip their glasses down the liquid. I take a sip. Now I see they're old friends, easy with one another and it's me crashing a private party. Then I remember Trev and the dance floor.

"Yeah, like, what was it you wanted to discuss with me?"

"Oh, sorry Charles. I wouldn't normally bring business into a social meeting like this but I saw you at the bar and, well . . ."

"We haven't met before."

"Oh, I know most of the people you're selling to. I've seen you around. See I'm a Battersea boy myself – well, almost." He leans forward and takes a cigarette out from one of the packets.

I'm getting a little bored. Champagne doesn't last that long. "So what then?"

"So I know you're peddling."

"Peddling my bike yeah, that what you mean?"

"Don't fuck me about, Charles." His voice has been quiet up until now, smooth tones said through a smile, but now he turns the style easily. Without raising the volume he sounds dangerous.

"I don't see what . . ."

"I said, don't fuck. Think I'm an idiot. I wanted to sit down, be adult – business, you understand?"

"Of course."

"Now, I don't mind you selling 'cause it ain't my deal, jus' wanted a word with you. We can do it on the street if you prefer."

"What is it you want to say?"

"Thought you might want to work for me."

"Huh?"

"Doing a bit of running for me. I've got a crew, need some more workers and I thought you might be eager. You look the eager type."

"Selling, a course. Look, I'm easy. Long as no-one fuck with me then I'm easy so you go about your thing if you want. Just thought you might want to take something more than the piss money you getting now. You have to progress . . . to stay fresh."

I know he means selling powder.

"Nah, I'm a happy man."

"Cool. Only keep out of my deal, that all. Don't fuck with me or my crew, OK?"

"No problem."

"Sweet, that's it. I was thinking you might have some vision but I was wrong. Now I haven't seen Allen for some time and we have these ladies to entertain so, at this juncture I'll have to say farewell, Charles. Should you reconsider, then you can find me easily enough. I know your score."

"Freddy?"

"Sure."

My head's buzzing but I keep it cool.

"Thanks for the drink."

It scares me that he knows me, that he knows my seller. I had been thinking I was out on my own, that his market was a different level from my own. Now I see the scene shrinking, our paths crossing. I know it's just a different drug he's selling, that it's trade, business, but it still frightens me. I'm not prepared for this escalation. Underneath my fear is something else: surprise. I didn't think I'd react like this to such an offer, thought I'd grab the chance.

"See you, Charles."

"Yeah."

I get up to go but my way is barred by a man standing firm behind me. He's another Allen, huge. My heart's leaping. Deacon's gonna take me outside and turn me into paste on the pavement for turning him down. I flash back to look at him but can see no sign of recognition, so what does this guy want?

"My friend. Picture man."

He's dark-skinned, Mediterranean maybe. His hair is shaved, jet-black at the tiny roots. He leans over past me and shakes Allen.

"I want a show down."

Allen turns his head slowly and stares up at the man. A cigarette is stuck in his lips, making him screw his eyes up against the smoke. His face muscles are taught, drawing heavily on the tobacco stick.

"Yeah. See the chest then."

Now Allen kicks away his stool, brings himself to his

feet and straightens his back. The shirt is tight as he flexes. The guy next to me steps to one side and slips off the T-shirt he's wearing. Even with the dark skin I see the same spirals and colours that Allen has on his arms. Every millimetre of the arrival's chest, stomach and flank is covered in dye.

"Nice."

Now allen tugs at the bottom on his denim and pulls the shirt off. The girls are laughing wildly, Deacon stands up and roars. "G'wan Allen, see him off there, boy."

It's a tattoo showdown. The new guy steps out of his trousers. A little crowd is gathering. I'm caught in the event, feeling frazzled, Deacon screaming for Allen, me still charged, still panicky about the earlier conversation. The contender is down to wearing a tiny slip. Allen is the same. Both ladies are solid paint apart from the little white socks of feet, hands and faces that are still bare skin. The men move at the same time to strip away the final covering and I turn away, but I hear one of the girls scream . . .

"Allen! There as well? You dog. Was it painful."

He is the victor. The other guy looks shattered by the experience and walks into the crowd, carrying the little bundle of his clothes. Allen dresses and orders another bottle which I am invited to share but decline. I'm feeling tense, really jumpy, and flee to the bar. Trev and Malcolm are there, sucking on Brooklyn beers.

"You wouldn't fucking believe what's been going on."

"Tell us on the way back. Gonna dig up, yeah?"

"Nah, got a party to go on to . . ."

"Yeah?"

"Out east. Make this place look like the joke it is, fancy club nothin' else."

"I might head back . . ."

"Come on, live young, Charles."

I start feeling better with the car window down and the air blowing round the back, waking me up, cutting through the stone. I stare out at all the million lights of the city, trying to think about Deacon, the threat, the business, but it's difficult. There are two girls rammed in next to me on the back seat, screaming through to Trev, laughing and squealing and giving directions. I keep staring at their naked legs.

The girls were the result of Trev's foraging expedition round the dance-floor. I don't catch their names. Trev thought he was set up but when we got to the venue they were out of the car in seconds, hammering on an iron door that led through to the dance. Once inside they dived into the crowd and I didn't see them again. There was no option but to be into it. It was wild.

It must have been an old workshop or factory building, like the ones they used for raves way back. There was little light, no bar, brick walls and a black ceiling. Apart from that there were people everywhere, a crush. I had to dance. I forgot the meet with Deacon after a few minutes of the beat. My head was pounding with jungle. Trev found some tins for sale and we were drinking and spliffing, falling around in the dance. There was some cool dress but the atmosphere was sweet, no pretence, no hard-man bullshit, just girls in leather shorts or leggings, stroking the floor with their asses in the dick swirl and the guys looking on or getting into their own thing, chilling.

I tried talking with some girls but no-one was there for that, it was a dance scene and I retreated into the stone, the moves. The music soaked through to my brain, sent me into a trance. Even though I was dripping sweat I was relaxed, easy. When Trev started introducing me as a seller I just smiled and nodded my head. I must have had at least ten requests for a score. In other circumstances I might have been angry with Trev. He was using me as a ticket to impress but I just laughed 'cause I wasn't carrying and all I could do was pass my mobile number over. Still, it made me feel good, made me feel in control, important, part of the picture. Fuck Deacon. I had a little ring of people round me begging for a smoke and I rolled slow, watched the faces watching me.

It was everything I needed. Jungle's a body solution, the feel expression. All the rave crap has been filtered through, charged with the right vibe. Ragga crashed into rave. It's a lot of other things but I don't go with all the philosophy about it – music is music, that's the deal. Once you start hyping something, calling it things its not, that's when it begins to die.

I just chilled to the sound. We were there for hours, taking it in.

Six

Saturday

I open my eyes and the radio clock shows eleven fifty-nine. Next thing I check is the daylight and the grey lump in my head realises it's noon. After the club Trev came back and we scurried round my room getting blasted till way past dawn, quiet as mice in the sleeping house. I prop myself up on a pillow and stare at the room. It looks like an opium den. I jump out of bed an clean up in a hurry, bagging the roaches, papers, cigarette butts with their little twists of white paper, the tobacco shards, stinking ash-tray, four cans of lager we must have picked up from the local take-away – place never shuts, dodgy beer sales under the counter. I'd forgotten about them.

Trev and I made up about the row over the course of the session. If there was any stress caused by our talk in the car it's gone now. He left at six a.m. with a big smile on his face. After the dance it was impossible not to feel good.

Saturdays are usually slack days. I lie around, maybe bike down to Battersea High and check out Trek Records, call in on a friend. The afternoon drifts past and then I'll slip into a pub or a club. Lazy days. That's all changed since I started selling.

I freshen up in the bathroom, get dressed then grab the mobile. On the way out I shout that I'll be gone for the day to whoever's in the front room, probably my father recovering from a morning out shopping.

Then I'm out on the street, waking up, heading for the park. I'll cruise till I get a call. The meet with Deacon freaked me at first, then I was chill at the dance and forgot about it – but I'm sober now. I start thinking it through in the back of my mind. Maybe the guy's right. I'm not going to jump right away, there's lots to consider, but his offer has some appeal. It's the business game that matters, not the dumb morality about what you're selling. Everyone knows that's rammed into you just to keep you in line. Anyway, I have to think about it some more, look into a few things, ask some questions. However, that's no reason to stop pushing the blow. I didn't check the accounts this morning but I know the figure is building up. Then I start thinking about what will happen when I reach the two grand target. I mean, am I just going to stop like that, kill it dead? There are the studies to complete but maybe I'm on the point of by-passing that toil and moving straight into success. This is my thinking as I circle the park, waiting for the phone to bark.

It was a busy afternoon. I was over in Streatham again with an eighth. That guy's creepy – ancient, dirty fingernails and a bedsit like Dominic's. I got out of there quick. Then I was round with Spence who was trying to swap me a box of luxury ice-cream for a sixteenth. Only Spence would rob thirty boxes of ice-cream and forget he doesn't have a very large freezer cabinet in his fridge. Him and a friend just hopped in the cab when the driver was in a shop doing a delivery.

"It's Ben and Jerry, boy, top gear."

"It's fucking melted, Spence. What flavours you got?

I gave him a draw on tick for one tub of New York Super Fudge Chunk. He suggested we go out to his local tonight and I said I'd check with Trev. I tried drinking the ice-cream when I got out on the street but it was like sweet soup and I dumped it.

Then I had to bike over to the other side of Clapham and drop some in for a friend of Malcolm's who'd just got my number. He was in a rush to go out and wanted an eighth. We did the deal in his hallway, not even a quick smoke. That cleaned me out except for a single skinner which I fired up as I crossed the Common on my way over to see Freddy.

I wanted to ask him a few things but knew I should play it tight to my chest. Freddy comes over as all hippy-dippy but he must have brains hidden under that mane of hair to be such a major seller. I pull the bike up to his door and chain it.

It takes him a while to answer and when he does he just walks back into the hall, doesn't say anything to me as though in a trance. I drag the bike in and close the door behind me. In the living room he's sitting with his legs crossed, eyes shut.

"Rest yourself, Charles. The usual?"

"Yeah, thanks."

Not opening his eyes, he begins to fiddle with a brown bag that lies in front of him. All his equipment is in a rough circle around him and I watch him pile the weed on to his metric scale. When he reaches the right weight a thin tone sounds from the machine.

"Is everything well with you, Charles?"

"Great, yeah. Had a few things I wanted to talk with you about actually."

"At this moment I am afraid this is ... like, impossible."

"Really?"

"Yes, ab-sol-ootum, not gonna happen today. I ... perhaps unwisely ... took acid two hours ago and am presently operating in alternative existences to your own. I can handle this transaction ..." He is pushing the grass into a square of cling-film. ... but conversation is potentially very ... disruptive to my state."

"Sure, no problem. I'll leave you to it."

I pass him the notes and he tucks them inside his shirt.

"Mucho apology due baby, but pass by tomorrow and ... I'll be able to give you my full ... attention. Safe journey to you, Charles."

"Take it easy, Freddy."

I split. What little I know about the drug is enough to tell me there is nothing to be gained from talking with him now. It's never appealed to me but he looked very relaxed, at peace with it. His face was somehow focused.

I'm out on the street when the phone goes and Trevor's asking me to pass by. I decide to take it easy for the rest of the day, dump the gear and have a few beers. I say I'll be at his in a few minutes. On the way home I'm still thinking about Deacon's proposition, the tripping hippy I should talk with and my own feelings about the idea. It's been with me all day.

However, every businessman has to have rest periods, so I decide to put off worrying about it until morning when I an speak with Freddy. I walk round to Trev's, thinking how lucky I am to have all these choices to make.

"This pub's pure boozerama, boy."

"I know, wall to wall."

"Check the DJ."

He's mixing around with a tune that was in the house charts a while back.

"It'll be Abba next."

"Prefer to check the girls."

"So, who wants some ice-cream then? A pint gets you two tubs."

"Spence, you that fucking desperate?"

The bar is packed, full of the Clapham gang. Spence has got some of his friends in and one of them goes off to get him a drink. The pub's a mix – some of the off-road vehicle gang looking nervous in their flash casuals, a few bus-driver types on their own at the bar, surrounded by youth, holding on to the idea that this is still their local. We've got a table in the back room, bunched up against a pool table. The DJ's in the corner, trying to make an impact.

"That Bruce?"

"Yeah."

"Give him a shout."

I haven't seen him for a while. He's looking very straight – suede jacket and office trousers. He does the round of the table then finds a seat next to me.

"How you doing, Bruce? Been hiding yourself?"

"Yeah, no I'm well, doing alright."

He was always shy, lost in the computer screen at school in the breaks. It surprised me that he quit after the first exams and took the job but now I'm starting to understand. He jumped a stage. He looks nervy, pinches his ear lobe with one hand and takes sips from his glass, held by the shaky left.

"How's the firm?"

"That's alright. The same." He's sipping at the long glass.

"Given up on beer?"

"Fills me up too quick."

"So what's that, lemonade?"

"Vodka. I'm a bit stressed an' everything."

"You working too hard. I can chill you out with something if you want."

"Yeah, Spence told me. I don't smoke though. Wish I did."

"So how you relax?"

He rummages at his waist and pulls a thin paperback book from his jacket. "I've started reading a lot."

I'm puzzled. "Don't you work out on the computer too much to be busy reading anything?"

"I used to. But the machine has kinda taken me back to it . . . if you can understand that."

"Not really."

"No, not many people can but . . . it's gone full circle."

"Wanna drink, Charles?" Trev leans in and slaps Bruce on the shoulder. "Alright Bruce?"

"Hi Trev."

"Have a beer Trev, thanks."

He swings off to the bar.

"As I was saying . . . the whole thing about the computer . . ."

"Oh yeah, your reading habits."

"Well, I got in so deep, thought it was the only thing, you know? I was going deep into programming and there's tremendous pressure on you to . . . focus solely on the binary form . . ."

"You mean a computer?"

"Yeah, the computer thinks in that way. And I started looking at the source material and . . . well, I've decided books have it."

"Come again?"

"Books contain everything I was looking for in a much more approachable format and . . . I'm hooked. I started with manuals, then shifted to the classics, then the contemporary stuff and . . . I can't stop reading. All the computer thing is supposed to be the new frontier but there are very few people actually . . . saying anything with it. It's all gimmicks and trickery, all been hyped so they can sell the units and software. I walked into a book shop one day, never really scanned one before and started flicking through a shelf. At first it was the same, just another information system, but when I started reading one or two of them I got sucked in. These are writers with ideas, that's the think, not . . . just input you understand. They're artists, a totally separate league to programming, which is all about making things quicker, or look better . . ."

"Wild."

"Yeah, I may quit the job and . . ."

"What?"

"Well, I'm not sure yet, still thinking about it."

Trev's back with my pint. He takes a seat next to us.

"How's Brucy then?"

"Fine thanks, Trev."

"Still seeing Miss Balham?"

I cut in as Bruce hesitates. "Oh yeah. Who's she?"

"That's my girlfriend."

"Nicest gal in Balham, boy. Criss. Charles, you wanna play some?" He points to an empty pool table on the other side of the room.

"Yeah."

Bruce turns and starts talking with Spence. Even though they're poles apart they get on, old friends from school, and Bruce starts chatting away like he's happy, human again, not the nervous gush I got from him. I join Trev at the table where he's racking up.

"Weird. Bruce said he might quit his job."

"Yeah, Spence said he was 'finding himself'. Doubt if he'll pack the job in though, just moaning."

"Yeah, probably."

Trev beat me with ease. My concentration was going with the alcohol. When we strolled back to the table the crowd was thick around it. Indigo was sitting on the stool I'd been on. She was smiling, talking loud, looking good with crimson lipstick and a club outfit. She was with two other girls.

"Hi Charles, Trev. How are you?"

They were passing by to meet another friend before moving on to a club.

Everyone was getting drunk, shouting, laughing. I wanted to ask about Clark and it made me feel bad because no-one seemed concerned by his absence. I should see him. Things have been so frantic since Beautiful People though, there hasn't been time to pass round and he's not on the phone. It's clearly not a problem for Indigo. She looks happier than ever, glowing with it. It seems petty to bring it up so I decide to say nothing. My own guilt plays a part in this choice. The alcohol convinces me it's a good idea to ignore the whole issue.

"You wanna come down Swamp?" Trev is by my side, smashed. There is a move being planned.

"Nah. I'll head back if everyone's off down there."

"Not like you to say no."

"I'm tired man, had a long day."

"Alright, well I'll see you tomorrow probably."

"Yeah."

The girls have changed the atmosphere, altered the night's progress with their sex. Spence and Trev are walking out with Indigo and her friends, the other guys tag along behind. I put my glass down and make for the street, watch them all cross the road and walk down to the minicab office in a noisy group.

This happens to me sometimes. I can feel very alone, distant from them all. I think Dominic leaving may have produced the mood, made me isolate myself now and again. It's best just to head for bed when I feel this way, shut my eyes and wait for the new light of another day. As I stride off I see Bruce waiting at a bus stop on the other side of the road. His face is inches away from a book. Even though it's dark he's still reading. I shout hello but he doesn't respond. I leave him to it.

Seven

Sunday

Freddy looks straight when he pulls the door open.

"Charles baby."

So he's speaking today. We go through to his living room.

"How's it going, Freddy?"

"Not bad at all. I came through yesterday quite admirably. Nearly lost it a couple of times but I rode it out. Stronger than I thought. Anyway . . . this is a bit soon for you. Thought you'd be gone a day or two at least."

"I wanted a chat remember?"

"A chat? I'll make some coffee then."

I lean back on the sofa as he walks to the kitchen. It's around two in the afternoon but the curtains are drawn. Time doesn't dictate them being open. His flat looks tidy, not the usual debris round the sofa and TV.

"Had a clean up?"

"Yeah, I found it very calming last night. Menial tasks are soothing to the spirit." He's in a check shirt and jeans, smarter than usual. "And I have got a date this evening."

"Yeah? Romance looming is it?"

"Hope so. Been a while since I got carnal."

He's back with a small tray for the coffee. There are some plain biscuits on a white plate, a little jug of yellowing cream and two cups of black, steaming liquid.

"White?"

"Thanks."

"When he pours the jug nothing happens. He goes to the kitchen, comes back with a spoon and drops a dollop in each cup.

"It's fresh, just very cold."

"I trust you."

"So what's our talk about then? Birds and the bees?"

I hesitate for a moment, thinking I should bring it in slowly but I've always believed it's best to be direct, so I crash in. "You know Deacon?"

"I do."

"I had a talk with him the other night, he said he knew you."

"So?" He doesn't sound fazed by the mention of the man, sips at his coffee and looks relaxed.

"He kind of offered me a job."

"You gonna take it?"

"Thought I'd get the word from you first."

He says nothing.

"What do you think?"

"You want my advice?"

"I guess that's what I'm talking about." I feel irritated, a little stupid. I hadn't really thought what I should ask him.

Freddy sighs and stands up from the sofa. "Deacon's alright. You know what he sells?"

"Yeah."

"Well, if you feel it's not a problem then go with it."

"Is that it?"

"There's not much I can say, is there? Personally, I think it's bad shit and it'll rub off on you once you're in there. Drugs are drugs sure but it's a question of the market and the buyers. C's not friendly like blow. Starters, Deacon doesn't have a particularly smiley-smiley approach to competition. He knows I don't go near C, so it's cool, but I've known a few people who he's had words with. Don't be taken in by the charm. The guy's evil. Then there's the selling. The people buying off me are generally well-balanced individuals . . ." I've never heard him talk like this. He has abandoned the hippy drawl and speaks in a light, educated tone. ". . . like yourself and Dominic. With C you get maniacs in the game. And the legality angle. With cannabis you're not running much of a risk. I suppose you've thought about all this anyway but my advice would be to stick out your own selling scene for a while longer. You've met Deacon but you never know what other offers might come your way in the future. Don't be tempted too easily."

It was a bit of a sermon. However, I like Freddy, even when he goes off on the vocal hippy trail. This is another side to him, business-like almost. Rational.

"I hope that's of some help."

He places our cups back on the tray. That's the signal for me to leave. I stand.

"I think you're right, Freddy. Not often I waste time with decisions but I wasn't sure, but . . . well, I'm doing good as it is. I can always think it through again later if things change.

"Exactly. Don't rush things. I know you're . . . determined, but it's a question of channelling that drive with your self-regard . . ." We're back in the sixties again. I nod respectfully. "Doing the right thing to ensure self-regard, that's the best path. It can be difficult."

"Absolutely. I'll get going anyway. Hope the date goes well."

"Yeah, stay in touch there, Charles."

I go out on to the street and push off towards Clapham. Deacon's still in my thoughts but Freddy was right. I can play it cool for a while. I've nearly got enough for the car. After that I'll think again.

Radical are playing tonight at Pharaoh's, a club that starts up after ten. That gave me plenty of time to finish the day's business. I dropped by on Spence first to collect the money he owes. He was still blitzed from the night before and claimed to be broke.

"I'll get you some more bike gear' Charles."

"Rather have the cash, Spence."

He walks round the front room, fiddling with his glasses and yawning.

"Indigo was going for it last night."

"Don't change the subject, Spence." I'm sitting on the sofa staring up at him. I want to complete the accounts before I go out. Don't want a lingering debt.

"Yeah, well I'm down for some myself. I might be able to get it by tonight. Could see you later."

"You want to see a band?"

I tell him about the show. At first he pretends to be sickened by the idea of drinking but I know he'll come round to it. Spence hates staying in, must get lonely I guess. He smiles and speaks.

"Talked me into it. I'll see you there then."

"Yeah, come down with Trev if he's into it."

"Trev's broke."

"Everybody's fucking broke. Can always stretch to a few beers."

"You're right. Look, I'm gonna have a bath and stuff . . ."

"Sure. Catch you later."

I leave him to it and head over to see Clark. He hasn't rung me since the Beautiful People night. Spence's mention of Indigo angered me. Everyone's talking about her and forgetting Clark, including me. I'd never seen him look so rough as that night when he told me she'd gone. I should be there to help but it's difficult. There's a lot going on at the moment and what can I say anyway? This shit just happens, like a change in the weather. Indigo seems to be dealing with it.

I climb the stairs to his flat and pound the door. The back yard looks more decrepit than ever, trash and weeds everywhere. There is no sound from within. I think about banging again but change my mind and dig up. Maybe he's gone to stay with his folks or something, but what really scares me is I might knock three times and Clark would be sitting in his bedroom, staring at the ceiling, and finally decide to answer the door. If he's that bad then it would be a nightmare to see him, to try and talk with him. If he is there then he probably wants to be alone. I ride away and I feel rotten inside. The situation's depressing me, spreading out and affecting the people close to it. I feel down till I get over the Common and back to Battersea.

Pharaoh's is a dive. I haven't been along to it since a rap outfit played there. I knew one of the rappers from school. They were massive smokers, always too stoned to get anything together. There were five people there for the show. I don't think they played again after that. Pharaoh's was the final kiss-off.

The management have tried to smarten it up since then with some black sheet wall-hangings and a cheap light rig but you can see the tacky pub decor everywhere. Even the carpets are swirly and battered, covered in black circles from stubbed out cigarettes.

The club consists of two function rooms over a pub on the high street, right by the tube station. I swear you can hear the trains rumbling underneath your feet. To get upstairs you have to go through the lower bar and it's full of labourers and beat professionals – scruffy accountants and lawyers with drink problems, bad coughs from decades of office cigarettes. There are couples who have nothing to say to each other and a small group of men on stools talking about football. I glide swiftly through and take the stairs.

After doing the accounts and stashing everything (except my emergency bank bag with some choice cuts from the latest ounce) I made the effort to change into a shirt and a fresh pair of black jeans. The leather accompanies me as ever and the baseball cap fits snugly over my forehead. There's a bored girl sitting at a little table by the top of the stairs.

"Three quid."

I give her a twenty. As she counts out the change I try and look into the main room through a piece of dirty glass that is set into the top door. I can hear the thud of music but can't really see anything. It's only about ten-thirty so I guess the place is dead.

When I go in I realise why I couldn't see anything. There's a giant at the door. He steps aside to let me in and I walk past, brushing his chest with the baseball cap. Noise hits me, a thick jungle beat, low, dub bass. It's blasting. The place is packed. I try to squeeze through to the back room but get caught up in a wave of dancers. It's a young crowd, leathers and lots of skin-tight gear. I have to struggle to work my way round to the bar. It's five deep with people trying to get liquids.

"Fucking wild, innit?"

Spence is suddenly by my shoulder. I'm breathing in nothing but hot, sticky air and tobacco smoke, can feel the sweat on my back already. The club's so small I swear there are drops on the ceiling from the vapour in the air.

"Have to agree with you on that."

"Get the drinks in then, Charles."

"What is it?"

"Beer for me and same for Trev."

"Oh, is he here?"

It's a crush. There's an elbow at my face, a leather jacket pushing into my left arm. Spence is being swept away.

"Yeah, in the back. See you there in a minute."

He vanishes. I stand there waiting to be served for a decade.

Trev and Spence are in the back room, lurking by a group of girls. I have to laugh. Trev is in his usual casuals, neatly pressed cords and a slinky long-sleeved T-shirt, but Spence is wearing the same scruffy jumper and ancient blue cottons I saw him in a few hours ago.

"What's new, Charles?"

"How you doing, Trev?"

Spence is looking woolfishly at the girls.

"Give it up, Spence. You look like a dustman."

"Fuck you."

"You seen Clayton?"

"A while ago. They're going on in a minute. That's Lenny spinning right now."

"Yeah. He told me he was doing something for them."

We stand there chatting for a while, sipping the beer. I'm impressed by Lenny's choice of music – all the right sounds, got the place swinging. Spence suddenly hands me some notes. He does it in the low handshake movement that's suppose to look innocent but with Spence everything looks shady. I count out the money and shove it into my pocket.

"It's only some cash, Spence. Relax. Not counterfeit is it?"

"Never know who's looking, do you?" He taps his nose and Trev and I start laughing. "It's the code boy."

"Yeah."

The crowd in the front room has spilled into the back and we're getting hemmed in by people. Then there's a break in the music and I can hear band sounds – a drumkit coming across the PA system, a dirty guitar. Trev finishes his beer and slides the empty bottle on to a table.

"I'm gonna try moving up to see the band."

"It's too busy, man."

"Nah. Paid my money, haven't I? Heard they're good."

"I'll catch you up."

Spence gulps the last of his beer and joins Trev, pushing through the crowd. After a second or two I realise that I don't want to be left on my own so I pace after them.

Radical are spread all over the stage behind ranks of

equipment. Only the singer is out in the open. I can just see Clayton checking something on his guitar, making adjustments. The crowd is pushed right up to the front of the stage, staring up, expectant. Radical look cool, as though they haven't noticed the throng before them. Then the lights come on and we can see the whole stage in detail under a bright red glow.

The band are all dressed in black. They look criss – the drummer in a mint T-shirt and black basketball shorts, Clayton in a suit with a shirt open at the top, the bassist in black denims. It's the singer who stands out though. His dredds are falling over a neat black shirt. The shirt collar is a ring of ivory white an inch thick. He looks like he's just stepped out of a church, a rasta vicar. There are shouts from the crowd.

"Preacher man!"

He screams into the microphone. "Radical preaching to the masses!"

Then it's mayhem. I don't see the drummer move but a massive beat crashes in. It's so fast the crowd freak for a second, then there's a shudder and the ranks of people burst into life. Another second and the guitar comes in. This isn't the same rock thing I heard at the rehearsal room. Clayton is playing a funk chop on top of the beat. He struts to the front of the stage. The drummer bulldozes in with a mighty thwack to his snare drum and the bass comes in. Now the audience is shaking to it, the singer sees his moment and his arm shoots up in a blur. The music stops dead.

"Rock ya fuck!"

Then they're back and it gradually moves off into

rock. I try to follow the lyrics but my ears are ringing. There are bodies all around me pressing in – bare flesh of a midriff sailing past, Trev trying to do a reggae groove to it, Spence looking up open-mouthed, glasses misting.

"These guys are really fucking saying it."

I can tell the singer's on a wild ego rant, catch the odd word about the 'system' and other similar, broken slogans. But this crowd wants to dance and that's what they do. They don't care about the lyrics, they want the beat. It's a weird atmosphere for the area – everyone going for it, hands in the air, all that stuff. A real party vibe. It feels more like a West End club. I go with it, manage to skin one up even though there are arms, hands, hair, leather flying everywhere.

The jungle feel is cutting over the band's music and the crowd picks up the tempo so we're all popping. There's a thump of a bass and my feet are shaking on the floor. I flare the joint and the rush is incredible. It was pure bud, my special cuts. The top of my head is opening slowly like it's on a hinge. I'm moving now, the drug's in my blood. The light rig is flashing and I can almost feel the signals bouncing off the back of my retina. Room's swirling, crash from the band ... the mad vicar preaching.

After another stick I'm through. I've never been a big dancer, prefer to hang at the bar. I need to chill. It takes me nearly two songs to work my way back to the other room.

Most of the audience are crushed up to the front so

I can sneak round the side of the bar and get a Brooklyn. It's still busy but I find a space to lean. My brow is covered in sweat and I'm charged, eyes feel dry and huge with the stone. I'm staggering a bit with all the heat and noise.

"Hello."

She sounds like a cat purring. I'm only inches from the face but it takes me a moment to realise who it is.

"Hello, Bond."

I had buried her out of sight in my memory, forgotten she might be here. The last time I saw her I allowed myself to fantasise but that was a one-off, not preventable. I knew it was dangerous and I was right. Standing next to her I feel nervous. I'm getting the tingle again.

"You alright?" She thinks I'm sick. How embarrassing.

"No, I'm fine. Never better."

"Don't look it."

"Just a bit hard to breathe in here for me. I like a bit more space, you know." What? Talk sense, Charles. Can't concentrate. Now she thinks I want to be a farmer or something. My usually easy mood is being eroded by her presence.

"I know, it's terrible. The band's good though."

I'm finding it hard not to look at her body. She's in some cream leggings and what I can only describe as a bra, though there must be another style word for it. It's the same colour as her skin. She has a suede jacket hung across one shoulder. Her eyes are bright, checking the room then shining back at me, fresh skin. Perfection. I feel a strong urge to say something to her but my mouth doesn't want to co-operate. I force myself to speak, mutter a bit as I try to shape a sentence, then it all comes out in a frantic rush.

"I keep bumping into you but we never really get the chance to talk, do we?"

She doesn't look surprised but it strikes me as one of the stupid things I've ever said. I know nothing about her, so what's to talk about? This is what I can't deal with when it comes to females. I don't feel relaxed, have lost my confidence. When I find a girl like Bond it always reduces me to a mindless jerk, just when I need all my mental faculties the most. On top of that I'm sweating so much there must be a little pool of water round my trainers. In an effort to regain my cool I offer her a cigarette and she leans to take the light. My hand holding the Clipper is shaking. I imagine brushing my fingers against her hair, pulling her up to me. Something about her fires me up. Losing control like this frustrates me. I feel more trashed than I did back on the dance floor.

She smiles and speaks. "Well, maybe we should go out then?"

"Yeah."

Shock. Before I can speak another girl appears at her side – tall, blonde, the Chelsea look. You only get that from growing up with money, the silver spoon. She's holding some car keys, looking impatient.

"You ready?"

"Yeah."

Bond turns back to me.

"I have to get going. Nice seeing you again, Charles."

"Yeah."

She strides off with the other girl, both of them walking with the straight-legged confidence of models on the catwalk. Before taking the stairs she turns and gives me a little wave. Then she's gone.

"Shit, man. That the girl from Brixton? Bond, yeah?"

Trevor is standing next to me, almost squealing with surprise. His eyes are fixed on the empty doorway Bond was waving from a few seconds ago.

"She's criminal attractive, boy. You in with her?"

"I don't know." I'm still feeling traumatised by the encounter. My voice is weak.

"Too fucking criss, man."

"That I do know."

"Ah well." He spins round to the bar, breaks out of the spell. "Want a Brooklyn?"

"Huh?"

"Charles boy? Planet London calling C, come in please."

"Yeah, a beer. Brooklyn. Shit, sorry Trev, just thrown me a bit meeting her here."

"You should be happy. She looked well into you."

"Nah." I'm trying to recover but Trev can see the effect she has had on me.

"I saw her, all interested, boy. Charles you rascal."

"Well . . ."

"Here." He hands me a bottle.

"You a dark horse, boy. Have to watch you. Serious."

We drink. The band has finished and people are filing back to the bar. Spence arrives, huffing and puffing, wet with sweat.

"Kicking band, Charles."

"Yeah, wicked."

"Charles wasn't really watching, was you C?"

Spence lights up instantly. "Oh yeah?"

"Just met a girl for a minute. I saw most of it though." I don't want this turning into a men's group discussion.

Trev is not so eager to let me drop it. "He was wrapped with her boy, serious."

Spence pushes between us and asks for three beers. "So who is she?"

Trev cuts in again. "You know that gal Bond? Hangs round with Lenny sometimes."

Spence's face lights up. "Her? You dirty dog, Charles. Going for some high class, huh?"

"It's nothing. Nothing happened. Just said we might meet up . . ."

Trev cuts in. "A date?"

Spence goes on as I nod to Trev. "She is extremely good looking but . . ." Spence gulps at his beer. The sweat is trickling down his fat neck. He knows I'm listening for the rest of his words and is making me wait. Spence values information.

"But what?"

"I heard some things about her, that's all."

"You hear things 'bout everyone, Spence."

"Nah. I heard she's a bit wild. Lenny told me she only hangs around with him 'cause she gets the odd bit of snort from him. Her family don't give her any money, even though they're loaded."

"So what?"

"Nothin'. That's what I heard."

"Big fucking deal. I don't see anything in that."

"I wasn't saying anything, Charles. Didn't realise you were so touchy."

They're both smiling at me and I suddenly realise it must be a wind up.

"You two are just piss-takers, boy."

"Settle down,Charles."

"Taking the piss."

"Ah relax."

The three of us are laughing, drinking. Clayton pushes into our little circle by the bar.

"How 'bout a drink for a hard working musician?"

Trev ordered some more bottles.

"Was a good show, Clayton. You went down really well with the crowd."

"Oh, I had some problems with my equipment . . ."

"Go see a doctor then."

"Funny man. Nah, my amp was moaning at me a bit."

"You got some more shows coming up?"

"Yeah. We just got a manager so the work should be coming in now."

"I check you out again."

Another guy from the band walks over with two girls. We go back into the other room and I skin one up under a table. The crowd is thinning out now the band has finished and it's quiet enough to talk. There is some analysis of their show and some flirting with the girls but I'm not concentrating. The drug is settling me, making me seep into the wall-sofa I'm on.

"Hiya Charles, so you show up?" It's Lenny, sitting

down next to me, tugging at his shirt to try and free it from his wet skin. "Hot back there."

"Yeah, I heard you. Was good."

Then silence. He turns and starts chatting with Trev. It feels difficult to talk with him because of his link with Bond. I'm still thinking about her. I want to ask him about her but at the same time it annoys me that he knows things I don't. On top of that, I've never felt comfortable with the guy. He's slippy, too confident.

After ten minutes of the others chatting I decide to make a move for home.

"Trev, you want to share a cab?"

"Sure."

We nod our goodbyes. Spence gets up to come with us. Clayton lifts a finger.

"Might need you tomorrow, Charles."

"Sure. Well you know the number."

"Safe."

As we file out I stare back at Lenny but he's leaning in close to one of the girls, a fat smile on his face. She looks nervous but interested. Lenny's laying the 'I'm a DJ' crap on her. I start down the stairs.

The street should have been empty but there are people everywhere, faces flashing in the orange streetlight. It's way past midnight. Spence has his head tilted back.

"Check the sky spy."

There are two helicopters droning in the sky above us. I can't see them but the noise of their blades in the air and long spotlight beams trailing down to the ground show their position. There are cars tailing down the high street and my eyes follow them up to the traffic lights. Two police on bikes are blocking the road, pointing for the traffic to take Clapham Park Road. Horns are sounding.

"What's happening?"

"Must be a shooting."

In the last three weeks there have been four shootings in my area, all drug related. I've got used to seeing the old-fashioned yellow signs with the 'Murder – Can You Help?' message on them. Despite all the sophisticated technology at their service, the police still rely on notice boards for information. It's becoming normal – the gun play. A lot of it's spilling out of Brixton into Clapham. A guy was shot coming on to the high street last week, brains all over the pavement.

"Let's go have a peek."

"Nah, I wanna get home."

I start across the street to the cab office. There is a little crowd on the island trying to look past the police line. The High Street rises slightly past the lights. I can see the streets beyond it are dead, no traffic or walkers, just black shops. It's a shove to cross over to the cab firm.

"Hold up, Charles."

Trev runs up behind me.

"No way to get any closer."

"Yeah, I know. That's why I'm here."

I feel tired and stoned but not in an easy way. The police blocking the road and the hungry crowd are the last thing I need right now. Feel stressed enough as it is. What are these people hoping to see? Would it make their day to see a couple of limp bodies?

"Come on then."

I walk up to the end of the cab hallway. It's bright yellow paint and peeling linoleum are horribly vibrant under a bare strip-light in the ceiling. This cab firm doesn't even have the bit of glass you have to speak through. There is a rusty intercom box set into the wall and I yell into it.

"Cab to Battersea!"

"Ten minutes."

We pace back to the road. The crowd is getting thicker on the island. A patrol car flashes past with the blue lights going.

"Must be a shooting, innit?"

"Yeah."

The helicopters are still sending their white beams down from the sky. We stand and watch until the car comes.

Eight

Monday

I remember that man in an old rock song saying, 'No way to delay that trouble coming every day'. That sums up my feelings to what's going on in the street. I grew up in this town so I'm used to it. You have to live with it. Like the cab office for instance. They are anticipating violence because it is an everyday reality, so they have their office on a separate floor from the public. Security. I have to speak into a nasty metal box and wait out in the cold till they send a car. Cause and effect of the market.

They still get robbed. Two guys broke the door

down with hammers a few months ago and ripped off the till. They probably got no more than a few hundred pounds. That's how desperate these people are. They just stop caring. If you can't find work and you've got no money you get to a stage where nothing they can do to you is going to put you off. For robbery you get years inside, sometimes more than you do for killing someone. Spence told me that's because the State values property more than the public. Any sucker can see that. So you have to be way past caring when you start ripping off taxi firms. And the state keeps making people poorer so they get more desperate and you get more crime. All this Government can come up with as an answer is to build more prisons. Well, that's very fucking smart, I don't think so. They caused the problem and now they don't know what to do. People are getting killed all the time. But that's how it is these days. The politicians are all the same anyway. None of them have an answer, they just come out with the usual bullshit and people sigh and shake their heads in despair.

I lie on my bed and listen to the radio.

'A man was shot dead last night in a street running off Clapham High Street. Police are not releasing his name or details of the incident but it is believed that the man was in his seventies and a known criminal. He was shot four times.'

That's all he rated on the news, 'known criminal'. Some guys get in an argument and the guns come out so easy and then he's dead. That's the problem with guns – people always get killed. They're spreading into everything. I don't mind having to shout into an intercom box to order a cab but I can't get used to bodies turning up on the street every few days. That's another thing altogether. With all the bravado and show of the drug trade, they get in a row and then the guns come out. It's big money. A lot of the dealers know the risks and just accept it – and they're the dangerous ones. They want money and the good times and don't think too much about getting past thirty. I know this. Steaming round the patch, knowing the people I do, I hear stories.

Four times he was shot. Must have been messy.

What Freddy said made sense. I'm not cut out for that stuff, got my own plans. I'm making with herb and it's a cool buying circle. I'll have enough for the car soon and then it's back to the studies. That's where the real power comes in. Not blasting away with a gun on a street corner but making the rules from within, running the business.

I swing out of bed and get dressed. It's eleven. I check myself in the mirror, grab the mobile and go down to the bike.

"Charles?"

She's in the kitchen. I turn the phone off, tuck it in the back of my jeans under my jacket and walk through.

"Morning."

"Don't you want some breakfast. . ?" She makes a big play of looking at her watch. "Actually, lunch would be more accurate, wouldn't it?"

"No, I'll pick something up. Is that all you wanted?"

"Well, no, just wanted to remember I had a son living here."

"So you didn't want anything?"

"Dominic rang again. Just an hour ago."

"Ah . . ."

"Didn't speak to him then?"

"No. I'll drop round now and see him."

"Well, send him my love."

"Sure."

"See you."

I go out to the street and saddle up. She sounded different about Dominic, voice was more relaxed than usual when she motioned him. Maybe with him ringing me they've had a chance to talk. I cut over the park and join the traffic moving towards Vauxhall.

Dominic's yard is looking more ragged than ever. As I move up his street I notice the rusting cars, trash in the gutter, a stray dog yapping at me lazily. The paint is peeling off the window frames of his house, even the brickwork looks as though its flaking. I hit his bell. After a moment I hear his feet on the stairs. The door swings back.

"Oh, Charles, come in." He looks relieved to see me.

We go up to his room. "Dom man! You've gotta do something about this."

The floor is covered in this tangled clothes, tin-foil trays from a take-away, cheap beer tins and other junk. Spence's place looks like this sometimes, must be something to do with a guy living on his own.

"Yeah, bit of a mess."

I find a space on his bed, start flicking through a copy of *Deadline* that lies open on the sheets. The radio is rattling on a shelf above me.

"So what was it then?"

"Oh, me ringing you mean? Just wanted to meet up, you know. Thought I could buy you that coffee back."

"Don't worry about it."

"How's it going? Everything alright?"

He paces the room, trying to tidy up. I speak without looking up from the comic.

"Yeah sure, why all the concern?" Then I stare up at him and he's looking back at me with a weak smile on his lips, embarrassed. I suddenly realise why he rang this morning and it makes me feel cold, like I've swallowed a lump of ice and it's sunk deep into my gut. "You thought that was me up in Clapham, didn't you?"

"Nah."

"Man, you did. Thought that was me?"

"I just heard a bit of it on the radio and . . . I don't know."

"Don't know if I appreciate your concern, Dom. Got no intention of getting shot, I can promise you."

"It's tough out there. Things can go off."

"Well, don't worry too much."

It scares me that he could have imagined it, that he thinks of me as a potential stain on the street, but then I see the other side, that he was concerned.

"Yeah, relax Dom. But you should watch out. I mean I don't want Mum getting wound up if you ring all . . ."

"I was cool. We had a polite little chat. She said you were still in bed so . . ."

"You didn't need to wake me up, yeah. Well . . . it's the holidays."

He offers me a roll-up.

"Nah. Think you'd better take me out and buy me that coffee."

"Um . . . actually."

"Broke? I'll buy the coffee then. I'll even get you a cap-oo-chino in reward for your brotherly devotion."

He laughs, grabs his jacket and we make for the stairs.

I'm not sure if it's because I want to rub it in that he was worrying about me but I lead us up towards Clapham. Maybe it's because I'm curious myself. We walk up to the Wandsworth Road then cut through to the side-roads that trail off Clapham High Street. After ten minutes we're out by Clapham North. All the time we've been chatting away. He's in good spirits today, says he's feeling 'positive'. That fades a little as we approach a taped-off street by the drive-through burger place. A line of blue-and-white plastic blocks the street and a fat-faced police stands just beyond it.

"You see anything?"

"Nah, that road bends right round, could be anywhere up there."

"They probably cleaned it up anyway."

"If it was police then there'd be something to see."

"Huh?"

"Flowers. I saw it when two of them got shot and the place was decked out with bouquets an' reefs, the lot. Like a florist's."

We cross the road and start up the highstreet. Between here and the other tube station it's busy. The killing hasn't put anyone off. A line of cars shuffles

along, early traffic. People are shopping for the start
of the week, poking around in the greengrocer's display boxes and lining up outside a butcher's.
Clapham's still got a solid community keeping the
little shops open, but there are signs of money coming in, stripping that all away. The Range Rover gang
want delicatessens and restaurants.

"Where d'you want to go then?"

"Let's go in there, yeah?" Dominic points across
the street to a baked potato take-away where you pay
twenty pence extra to sit at a plastic table.

"Man, it's full of tramps. There are loads of coffee
places round here. Let's go down the old town."

"I fancy a potato."

He looks determined.

"Alright Dom, get you a potato."

We move between two stationary cars in the traffic.
I have to watch the bike because it's a thin gap. I'm
concentrating on that and the cars coming down the
other side. Then there's a wild screech and I flick my
head round. A three-series BMW has scraped to a
stop a few feet from us. They must have been flying
down the outside to get round the traffic. The glass is
tinted so I can't see in but the passenger door opens
and a black guy sticks his head out.

"You wanna get off the fuckin' road?"

I stand there staring at him. It was close, they nearly
hit us and I've got that rush you get from the unex-
pected charging me up.

"Think you're supposed to be in the other lane, you
fuck."

Dominic flashes a frightened stare at me. He takes

my arm and pulls me towards the pavement. The guy in the car look surprised.

"What that?"

Dominic is tugging now. "Leave it, Charles."

"Why? They almost ran us down."

The car is nudging forward.

"Move, ya fuck."

I'm feeling angry now. Why is Dominic just backing down? He's dragging my bike from me now. He's made it to the other kerb. Then the car pushes forward a bit more so it's almost touching my shin.

"Fuck you."

I step away and it cruises past, but I'm not taking it. Just 'cause they're in the car they think they can push it. I lift my leg up and kick deep into the side of the rear door. It crumples under my foot. The car was moving off but they hit the brakes and this time both doors open.

There's just enough time for me to make it to the pavement and hop on the bike before they're out of the car. I'm laughing.

"C'mon Dom, leg it."

"Are you fucking crazy or something?"

"See you in the Moon, yeah?"

There are two of them, in their twenties. Both of them are in the cheap gangster gear, cuts in their hair. The driver is close enough for me to get a good look. The face is thin, with sharp cheek bones and a long chin. His eyes are sick-looking, yellow like a tobacco stain where it should be white. They come steaming across the street.

Dominic's not stupid. He knows they won't give him

a quick pat on the back and say it was nothing to do with him. He's sprinting down Manor Street with me next to him on the bike. I can hear them padding after us.

"Come here, you little fuckers."

Then we're round a corner and there's a long road that runs parallel with the high street. I pick up speed on the bike. Dominic's starting to huff and puff. I'm still laughing.

"Too many roll-ups, Dom."

"Fuck you."

They're falling back. A few extra years make a lot of difference to the body. Dom and I are still in the last flush of fitness before alcohol and smoke flood the system out. We get round another corner and take a little alley that runs down to the Old Town. They've gone now, given up on the chase. Dominic stops, leans forward on a low wall and breathes hard.

"What you do that for?"

" 'Cause I don't take that shit, that's why."

"Oh, you a bad man now?"

"Let's get in the Moon. They might be cruising around."

"You better take the bike in with you so they don't see it."

"Come on then."

"All I wanted was a potato and you're pulling the 'don't mess with me' bullshit. Jesus."

The Moon is on the corner of the Old Town. We pace in and I drag the bike up against the beer garden wall, out of sight from the road.

"Here, an chill out a bit, will ya?"

I hand him a bottle.

"Maniac."

I catch a little smile so I know he's alright about it.

"They do food here?"

I come to the Moon in the evenings sometimes but have never been here in the daytime. There is one large central room and a smaller room in the back. It's done out in pastel colours, tangerine and turquoise with lots of mirrors and strange artifacts on the walls.

"This place is pseudo, man. Real Sloaney."

I stand up and walk over to the bar. There are only two other drinkers in the room, deep in conversation by the far wall. Some seventies funk track is playing and the barman is nodding along to it as he reads a paper.

"Hey, you do food?"

"Pizza." He doesn't look up at me.

Dominic was right about the place being too stylish for its own good. In the evenings it's suits or club casuals, a money crowd. Even the staff are stuck up. But that's the way money goes so it doesn't bother me too much.

"Dom, you want some pizza?"

"Yeah – sausage."

I shout down to the barman again. "You got any pepperoni?"

"Sure."

"Two, yeah."

He fold his paper carefully and walks over to a glass cabinet. "I'll bring them over."

Dominic has done half the beer already.

"Serious, Charles. You shouldn't be taking people on like that."

"What? You mean I should have just let them run us over?"

"Bad idea to get yourself enemies like that."

"This is London, man. I'll prob'ly never see those guys again."

"My nerves aren't up to it. Don't do that again when I'm around, that's all." He takes a massive gulp of his beer and finishes the bottle.

"I'll get you another."

"Thanks."

The pizza arrives and I go back with the guy for the beer. When I get back Dominic has almost finished.

"Any good?"

"Alright."

The mobile goes. Dominic nearly falls off his stool.

"Easy, Dom."

He's jumpy, fiddles with the rim of his beer, looks around the bar. Funny how some people never know what to do when the phone starts ringing. I slip it out of my jeans and punch the button.

"Clark."

"Alright man, been trying to see you."

"Yeah. How long then?"

"I'm with Dom. Be half an hour or something."

"See you then." He rings off.

I shove the phone back in my jeans and start on the pizza. Dominic looks as though he wants to say something to me but is too nervous to speak. The pizza's cold.

"Go on, Dom, spit it out."

He leans forward before speaking. "Can't they monitor those things?"

"What?"

"The phone. They can listen in."

"If they've got my frequency, yeah, but no-one really says anything, do they? They just say their name and I say how long."

"So you got some on you now?"

"Course. It's my business, innit?"

"Aren't you worried about getting a pull?"

"No." I finish the pizza and take a hit on the beer. Already I'm getting a lift from it. "I'm not as sensitive as you, am I Dom? You're jumpy."

"You said my name."

I just look at him for a moment, not sure what he's getting at.

"Huh?"

"My name, you said my fucking name."

"When?"

"On the phone, just then."

"Oh, yeah, so what?"

"Well that ties me in with what you're doing. Look, thanks for the pizza . . ." He stands up from the table and drops his serviette on the plate. "And the beer as well, but you're pissing me off today Charles."

"Dom . . ."

"You don't think, do you? Far as you're concerned 's just a game. First you're trashing a car on the high street, getting me running my ass off, then mentioning me now on a deal . . ."

"It was only Clark."

"I don't wanna fucking know who it was." He looks angry now. "I'll give you a ring."

He stomps off. I sit there sipping my beer.

Why is Dominic so tetchy? I wanted to have a brotherly chat with him, try and patch it up so I can talk with him about things like meeting Bond, what he's got planned for the future, all that stuff. My brother just keeps drifting further away from me.

I finish the beer and grab the bike. Then I'm on the Common, flying across the green and heading for Clark's. I can't worry about Dominic, got enough going on myself. I'm not going to start living in fear of everything like he does. This is the first time I've had some control on my life, I'm making it work. I know it was unusual for me to go for the car but I don't need to put up with that crap. Having a bit of money, being in demand with my circle, it's my time.

When I get down to Balham I'm thinking about Bond. She's a very effective distraction. That's another side of my life I've been neglecting. I'm too old to be sex-fresh. She was the one who suggested a date, so she must be into the idea. I didn't get her number though and I don't want to speak to Lenny. I'm trying to work out a means to contact her when the phone goes again. I pull on to the pavement and click it on.

"Clayton."

"Yes, man. Thought you were supposed to be ringing."

"Wanted to check you could come round tomorrow."

"Safe."

He's bound to have her number if he was out with her in Brixton that night.

"Kinda hectic today but I'll be round at the manager's place in the mornin'. Got a meeting. You can make it?"

"Where?"

It's an office in Battersea, not far from me.

"I can be there first thing."

"Call it eleven."

"See you there then."

Relief. I can set up a date with her tomorrow if Clayton comes over with her number. Otherwise it'll have to be Lenny. I'm not going to get blocked just because I don't see eye to eye with the guy. Everything feels right about Bond. It's all flashing through my head as I sweep up to Clark's place. Must admit I'm nervous but you have to face these things in life. I can't think of another girl I'd rather break it with.

Clark opens the door and he's in a suit, a charcoal two-piece.

"You going to a funeral?"

He smiles as he checks a thin black tie to see if it's hanging right, then backs into the room. "Going for a talk with the bank man."

I walk into the kitchen, wheeling the bike next to me, feeling scruffy in his presence.

"Sure. I have to say . . . you look good, Clark. Not my usual opener, is it?"

"Yeah well . . ."

He's rushing round the kitchen, shutting the window over the table, checking that the stove is off and picking up a folder that he tucks under his arm. The change from his appearance at Beautiful People is so stark I can say nothing. He looks full of energy, purposeful.

"What's going on, Clark? What you up to?"

"Off to the bank."

"I thought you were winding me up."

"Nah, got an appointment to see the man there."

"For what?"

"Do us an eighth, C."

"In the money?"

"Got a float."

"So tell all."

I twist the cover off the handlebars then tug the wrap out.

"Doing a course, need a grant for it."

He can see from my face what the next question will be.

"My folks 've been good since Indigo left. They've said they'll watch the kid an' everything, long as I go into some kinda training."

"I saw her the other night."

"Don't want to know, Charles."

"She was – "

"Said I didn't want to know what the bitch is up to. I haven't heard shit from her, she hasn't checked on the baby, nothing, so fuck her."

He hasn't stopped rushing round the room. Now he comes over to me and makes a gesture for me to hurry up untangling the creased bank bags.

"Need a smoke before I see the guy."

"What you doing then, this course?"

"Bruce put me on to it, just a computer thing – database, spreadsheets, real thorough introduction . . ."

"You never touched a computer."

"Nah, but I need something that'll earn fast, boy. This is tied in with this company, yeah. They'll take me on when I get through with it."

"You got a job with them?"

"When I get the basics, yeah, I go on to train there but with a salary. He's set it up for me. Hurry up there, man."

"I thought Bruce was through with it."

"Yeah, he's pissed off with it but he's in with the management there and stuff. He's turned out really well for them, even if he does go off and do his university thing."

"Huh?"

"A degree. Look Charles, we can meet for a beer, yeah, have a chat, but I'm rushin' here, yeah?"

"Alright . . ." I pull out one of the eighth bags and pass it over. "When all this happen?"

"After the other night I knew I had to get going. I'm not standing still while the bitch runs round with that man there . . . nah, sir. I sat in the flat for a day or two, just fucked, way down, yeah, then I got in touch with the folks and they were great. After that was sorted I checked Bruce 'cause I knew he was working out really well with his company . . ."

I almost feel guilty listening to him. Where was I when he hit bottom? I should have come round the next day after the club right. And when he wanted advice it was Bruce who helped him out. I thought Clark wouldn't touch selling but I should have asked.

"He was cool, fixed it up."

I wonder if there was some connection with Bruce being shifty with me the other night, not relaxing till

he got talking with Spence. If he was helping Clark out
. . . was Clark dissing me to Bruce? Clark is skinning
up, spraying tobacco and bits of herb everywhere as
he hurries. He keeps talking, excited with the change
in his life.

"Yeah, should have done it ages ago, Charles. Just
been fucking wasting here, you know." He takes my
Clipper and lights it up, sucks deep so the stick burns
down an inch. "Ahh. Needed that, serious." He blows
out a massive plume of smoke and passes it over. "I
hear you mixing with that friend a Lenny."

Now he's beaming at me, the smoke rushing
through his system. He looks sharp, clean-shaven,
stands tall in the middle of the room. He blows the
last smoke from his lungs.

"You shouldn't listen to gossip, boy."

"Oh yeah, so it not true then?"

"Well . . ."

"I knew it. Charles going for the high class."

"Don't take the piss."

"Well make sure you take precaution there."

"Man, know what I'm doing, you know?"

"Oh yeah?" He gives me a mischievous glance then
lifts a foot on to one of the kitchen chairs and fixes his
lace. Clark might have guessed I'm fresh. He knows
me well enough to read me like that but I'm not sure. I
decide to bluff it.

"Yeah, know the score, course I do."

"Come on, Charles . . . don't try it on . . ."

"You what?" I'm trying to look stern but can feel a
blush starting on my cheeks.

"Ahh, give yourself away there, I knew it . . ." He

breaks out into a laugh. "First timer boy, can't fool me. Can't fool a kidder. No disgrace, enjoy it . . ."

I can feel the heat of embarrassment, toke hard on the joint. "Well . . ."

"Ah, relax Charles. Look, I gotta move, yeah. Bell me later and we'll go out." He opens the door and stands waiting. I ham the blow back into the handle-bars.

"Just don't . . ."

"Safe. C'mon, man."

We start down the metal staircase. I keep toking until he reaches out and takes it. He's puffing away as we get out on to the street. Clark has never been worried about open smoking. I feel humbled. Not only has he got his act together but he's hit me with the 'wise old man' stuff, making me feel like a kid. The confidence from earlier is forgotten. How can I shift from feeling on top to this in a matter of minutes. Do the others know?

"Relax, Charles. Get it together with this girl, every-one saying she criss."

"Yeah."

I've always been so cool about girls, acting like I was getting it easy, I thought. Now I feel terrible – guts are churning, weak legs, ashamed that my friend has sex graduated and I haven't. Why does it always go wrong as soon as I get close to involvement with a female. It must be a chemical imbalance in me but it's not like I'm gay or anything. Just thinking 'bout Bond gets me limping.

"It'll be chill."

We're down on the high street. A new Jag cruises past.

"Shit, man, what a machine? Criss. Really like what they've done with it." Clark has forgotten about my embarrassment already. He's full of the day's promise, a new life. I feel sick. "Anyway, bank's further down the high street, yeah. I check you later."

He slaps my shoulder and marches off confidently. In his suit he stands out in the crowd and I follow his back until it disappears along the curve in the road. I saddle up and start for the Common.

Any businessman has to take the knocks. By the time I got over to Clapham I was feeling better. It's only an ego thing with women and I know it'll be fixed soon. As for his new-found vitality I can't really be envious. My plan is working perfectly, the accounts are healthy. No, I'm happy for him. He's moving into something new and I hope he can stick it.

I move down the high street. The shops are starting to close and it's getting dark. Already the bars are filling up and the night is dragging the drinkers away from their desks. The traffic is still thick so I take the pavement. I go past the spot where I licked the car and the memory charges me. The tingle from the joint is working its way through my body. I feel mellow, think I'll cruise back and just watch some TV, maybe check Trev and see if he fancies a beer. My stomach twists and I think about food, grab a burger perhaps, but then I see the blue-and-white tape stretching across the side-road, the police standing there in the cold.

I pause on my bike and take it in. This is going on in my neighbourhood, I have to live with it everyday. Maybe it's not as bad as the States has got but things take time to filter through from over there. It'll be coming. It's only a symptom of the whole thing, the hard edge that still gets press because blood and guts are news. They always have been. But there's a new attitude underneath that, the everyday changes that have happened recently. That's the deal. You have to get by, keep pushing all the time.

I can't afford to get down or lose my vision – you don't plot then you drop. I push off on the bike, get some horn as I cut up a bus then I'm heading for home.

I chain the bike and push into the hall. I can hear my parents talking in the kitchen.

"Charles, that you?"

"Who else you expecting?"

"Alright, no need to lose your temper."

The kitchen is hot and bright. Father stands up from his chair as I come through. I feel as though I've interrupted something important, broken up their conversation. They look uncomfortable.

"What's going on?"

"Nothing. We're going to have dinner, d'you want to join us?"

"I'll take it upstairs, got a few things to do."

My father leans back against the refrigerator. "Haven't seen much of you lately."

"Yeah. 'Cause I'm on holiday, enjoying it whilst it lasts."

That's the extent of our conversation. He picks up a local newspaper and starts thumbing through it.

"Give me a shout when it's ready."

"Fine."

As I take the stairs I hear the chairs shuffle at the table. They've gone back to their talking.

I can just about pick up Cool FM on my radio. After a quick account check I slouch across the bed and flick through some magazines, listen to the beats. I know there'll be a shout when it's time to eat. They're probably discussing what to get me for my birthday or something. After the blow-up over the car I expect some CD-Rom gear or something, even though I'm not so interested in that stuff. Computers are just a tool, not a way of life, but I'm making sure of my own present so whatever I get on top of that I'll be happy with.

There's a break in the music then it kicks back in with a dance track. They've beefed up the rhythm with the pure adrenalin of jungle. I kick my shoes off and lie back on the bed, still a bit charged. Everything's sweet. All I need now is the date with Bond and I can put that into motion in the morning. I'm coming back to ground level, feeling chill. After dinner I'll have a single skinner out of the window and sail off into rest. I feel on track again.

Nine

Tuesday

Clayton's manager has an office down in Battersea Church Street. The area is so close to the river it's almost got the Chelsea charm – some flash restaurants, a couple of bars with pine floors and chrome fittings, even a little art shop. It's a joke really, because on either side of the area there are the usual estates and broken-down shops, but in their tiny enclave the workers can kid themselves they're in the West End.

I check the address he gave me. By the side of a newsagent there is a thin corridor with a door at the end. I check the bells: "Shark Attack Management' is the top one. I push the button. The electric mechanism sounds and I push in. I have to leave the bike just inside the hallway because there is a block of steep stairs immediately in front of me. It's hard trying to be smart. The carpet is a deep cream, soft under my trainers, tall plants are wedged in the window ledges. I can hear some music above me, a seventies thing.

On the first landing there is an open doorway and I get a flash of a desk, some computer terminals, piles of paper and all the usual office gear. Then a girl sweeps round the edge of the door and smiles at me. She's young, attractive, around my age, with her hair cut short, club casuals.

"Next floor for the music office."

"Thanks."

I take the stairs and come up to a shut door. It swings open just as I raise my fist to pound on it.

"Good morning, Charles. Good to see you again."

Theo is standing in the doorway. He wears a suit, the city look, with shiny black leather shoes. A cigarette dangles from his fingers.

"Didn't expect to see you here. How's things?"

"Fine, plodding on with the routine."

I can smell coffee from the room behind him. Music is pouring out into the stairwell. From what I've seen of the office – the girl downstairs called in to take a memo whenever you want, the plush decor and the obviously relaxed atmosphere – I can't see his job as 'plodding'.

"Looks like you've got it easy to me."

"It always looks better when you're not doing it yourself . . ."

He waves me past him and I walk into a large white room with leather sofas, mirrors and coloured discs on the walls. Clayton is talking with a young guy on one of the sofas. They look up and nod hello then go back to their chat. The music is very loud now. Theo shuts the door behind me.

"Yeah, I may get out next year, go travelling for a while."

"Sounds good."

"Want a coffee?"

"Thanks. White, no sugar."

Now Clayton stands up and walks round the sofa. We shake.

"Alright, Charles. This is Steve."

The fresh-faced guy he was talking to comes over and gives me a firm handshake. He doesn't let go until he's finished talking.

"Hi, Hi Charles. Just the man we've been waiting for. Really do with a bit of puff. Have a coffee."

He talks quickly, with no sincerity to his voice, like he's talking to a moron. I don't like him. It's a split-second judgement but I'm happy with it. He's in a shirt and tie, neat grey trousers and some brogues. I can smell his aftershave. Cheap. He's all smiles, eyes boring into mine, but I'm not sufficiently important to him for him to make much effort at it. As soon as he drops my hand he turns to Theo and takes him by the arm.

"Now let's run through this proposal with your in-put, Theo." His facial expression shifts to one of interested concern as he leads him over to the sofa. I smile at Clayton. He needs no explanation.

"Yeah, I know. Wanker." He takes over with the coffee making and we stand and chat a few yards away from where they sit. The music's volume means neither pair can hear the other. "He's a bastard, I know, but that's why he's a good manager. You know the lawyer?"

"Yeah, he's alright."

"Oh yeah? That's not the vibe I got from him. These two are one and the same boy. Steve wanted him in special, so I wouldn't trust him to watch my car boy, I tell you."

"No, he's cool, he's not sly or nothing."

"Well Steve is. You like the track?"

"Oh, this you?"

The beat is thudding round the room. I can just pick up the fast drum under the music but it's more subdued than I remember from the gig. Sounds almost commercial now the way they're mixing the jungle in.

"Not what I was . . ."

"Yeah I know . . . soft, yeah? 'Ambient jungle' Steve calls it."

I don't want to insult him but the band was a lot harder at the show. They had something fresh and the track playing in the office could be any seventies rip-off, jazz–rock crap.

Clayton gives me a big smile and leans in close. "It's a fuckin' double cross, man. We did two versions of the same track in the studio, gave Steve the soft one. If he gets us something then we drop the real one back in and tell him to piss off and take it if he doesn't like it. Should hear the other track – 's wicked, harder than anything."

"I don't get you."

Clayton looks pleased with himself. "Look! Reason the lawyer's here is 'cause we might have a small label interested, right. They sent Steve a contract."

"Huh?"

"A record deal, jus' a little one. We only got Steve in as stepping stone, you dig, but you have to play these fuckers at their own game. No-one trusts them anymore anyway. So he was getting us gigs and we were gonna bring the track out ourselves but if we get backing . . . anyway, don't get the idea we're selling out or nothing, just being sneaky as they are. You have to."

I stare back at the sofa. Steve is almost whispering to Theo now.

"Didn't realise it was so bent . . ."

"Bent? Telling you, Charles, I've been doing this long enough to know. They're not bent, they're fuckin' crooked, boy!"

I join in on the laughing now. He goes on.

"Serious. Only way for a band to survive is to sign up with them though." He hands me a coffee. "Fucker's been trying to speak patois with me all morning, thinks I'm eating off his palm, boy. Fuck him."

The sophistication of the office atmosphere has shifted to the same mood as the street. Maybe in certain areas of business it's just as cut-throat. I've always thought that was the case but only by seeing it close-up can I really understand it. Steve's just a respectable mugger. They finish their talk on the sofa and walk over.

"So Charles, why don't you fix us all up with a

spliff?" In his shirt and tie, with the fresh face of a right-wing politician, it feels like a polite order. Without waiting for a reply he goes on. "I'll send Sandra out for some sandwiches and we can have a quick rester."

Even the words he uses I find irritating. His voice has the old-style twang of the yuppie. He picks up a phone and talks to his secretary.

"I'll roll one if you want."

"Nah, it's alright, C. I'll do it."

I go over to the sofa and sit down. There is a glass coffee table there with some magazines and an ashtray. The track was finished and I can hear cars out in the street.

"Got any more music?"

"Sure."

Theo wanders over, still looking at the papers in his hand and triggers a CD player on a table in the corner of the room. It's a dance track. I pull my kit out and lay it out in a space on the glass. Clayton sits down next to me.

"Wanna roll a long one?"

"Uh?"

"King size, man."

"Only got normal papers."

"Nah, I mean like this."

He pulls six papers out of their thin card packet and lies them flat on the table. The top rim is three papers long. Two support it and the last one lies across the seams.

"Never be able to roll that."

"You have to be a craftsman, that's all. Give me some room."

His fingers are delicate as he takes the first pair and joins them at the edge. He only used a tiny part of the glued rim and holds them right for a few seconds so they bind. Then he fixes the third. It makes a rectangle at least ten inches long.

"It's fucking massive, Clayton."

"That is quite ambitious." Theo has become interested in the assembly at work. He leans over from the other sofa.

"Keep clear, man. Biggest problem is perspiration drops."

I check his brow and see he is breaking into a sweat. He fixes the two support papers halfway down the rectangle then licks the last paper and uses it to hold them firm. Next he folds the new paper so it bends at the glue.

"Don't want too much paper, spoil the taste." He takes my Clipper and lights the edge of it, which now stands up at a right angle.

"It'll burn the whole thing."

"Nah."

It glows and the paper slowly disintegrates up to the base but stops before damaging the main papers.

"The glue stops it."

He takes two cigarettes from my pack, licks the thin, glued seam and tears them open, but does not lie them out on the joint. Instead, he makes a little pile on the table. Then he flicks my bank bag open and takes a generous pinch of the drug.

"You don't mind?"

"Be my guest. I can't wait to see this."

He mixes the grass in with the tobacco, pulling the

thicker bits out, checking for seeds and tiny twigs. "All this shit in tobacco, man. You not supposed to look, so they put it in." There is a little pile of tobacco he has rejected. The main pyramid he picks up in the cup of his palm and starts to stir with his forefinger. "The Spanish method, man. Learnt it on the road."

"Yeah, they mix it first, don't they?"

"More even burn that way."

He takes little pinches and starts to lay the mixture out in a long line. By this time I'm leaning in too and there's a little huddle round the operation. "Now it get tricky." Clayton pinches the end in either hand and sweeps the tube up into the air. Then he stretches his first fingers up so they meet behind the papers. With a roll of his thumbs the tubes slowly closes and he licks the glue in a long, easy sweep of his tongue.

"There you go."

It's perfect, like a conductor's baton. He picks up one of the cigarette filters and carefully fits it in the end. Then he prods the mix until there is enough room for a filter. He rips the top of my papers packet, tubes it and slides it in. Then he takes a tiny bit of the cigarette twirl left on the stub and rams it into the filter. "I don't like those nasty bit a tobacco when you pull hard. Now, a punch for the smoking end." He shakes the other end until the mix builds up in a bulb, then gives the papers a little twist so they taper off. This he nips off between his teeth. Finally he rolls the huge tube between his palms to ensure an even spread of the mix. He holds it aloft.

I have never seen a larger, more perfect joint. There isn't a crease in it.

"Master blaster."

"It'll burn hot."

"Bollocks."

He reaches down for my Clipper and fires it up, watching so the ember is a full circle and not burning down the side. A mushroom cloud of smoke wafts into the air.

"Sweet. Almost a pity to burn it though, innit?"

After three tugs he passes it to me. It is strange to hold – heavy, smoking way out beyond my nose. The smoke runs cold into my lungs. I can hardly taste it but within seconds the familiar rush is seeping down to my legs, my stomach tightens and my arm muscles relax. I get the easy feel. I pass it over to Theo. He says nothing for two pulls then sits back in the sofa and crosses his legs. "That ... is a humdinger of a joint, my friend."

"What's that?"

Steve appears with a girl carrying a tray of sandwiches. She looks a bit like the girl downstairs – young, attractive, enthusiastic somehow. Being fresh and cheery about everything must be one of the job requirements. Her eyes light up when she sees the joint.

"Wow!"

"There's plenty for everyone." Theo offers her the joint.

She looks at Steve but he doesn't complain so she reaches out for it and takes a pull. "Impressive, lads."

Steve takes it from her and takes a little drag. "Nice, Charles. I might take a bit off you."

"That's the idea."

"Free sampler, yeah?"

He takes a longer pull and starts coughing. Sandra has to go and get him a glass of water.

Clayton takes an eighth, Steve a sixteenth. Theo goes back to his papers when they start buying but I know he's getting an ounce for the party so I don't ask. Maybe he doesn't want the others to know about it. that's cool. Steve makes some signs that he wants to talk about the band and then I'm heading out, shaking hands. Steve is quite nauseous with his sugary goodbye. Just as I'm about to take the stairs I remember Bond and have to go back and hassle Clayton.

"Jump in my grave, boy."

"Well, you didn't get anywhere, did you? An' I seen her a couple of times . . . thought I'd call her."

"Yeah, yeah, no problem. I was only joking. Fact is, Charles, I'll have to check I've got it then ring it through to you later. I haven't got my book on me."

"To big to cart around, yeah?"

"Don't push it. I'll call you, alright?"

"Sweet."

Then I'm down the stairs and out by the bike. It's bright on the street, sun pouring down and my eyes feel tight. Freddy told me the bush pulls the muscles back around your eyes, that's why they feel tired. This in mind, I dive in the newsagent and buy the cheapest pair of shades I can find. Out in the street I slide them on then pull my baseball cap back on my head. Just before I push into the street I check myself in a shop window. With the leather and some black jeans, the cap and the shades. I look fly.

Clayton called me on the mobile a few hours later.

It had been a slow afternoon, just one drop for a friend of Spence. I was over on Battersea High, by the bike shop, thinking of calling in on Trev after picking up a new rear light for the Fox. It's been cutting in and out. I don't want a pull because I've screwed up on the lights.

"Here the number you wanted, boy."

"Thanks, man. How'd it go this afternoon?"

"Easy. The two sharks wanted to cut our percentage down to nothing but I got something decent, anyway. These things cost, you know."

"Yeah sorry. Didn't know you only had the mobile number. So . . ."

He gives me the number and rings off. I think about ringing her straight away but don't want to do it out on the street. That puts it off for a while as well. I hate ringing up for dates.

"What's with the glasses, man? You look all delinquent."

"Just functional, Trev."

"Oh yeah? Your folks been asking about the state of your eyes then?"

"Nah."

"You getting to be a proper smoker, Charles." We're standing in his hallway and his sister rushes past. "Come on, we'll go up to my room."

The flat's layout is exactly the same as mine and Trev has a bedroom like my own. The only difference is the decor and the debris. My room is white walls, cream carpet, magazines and tapes littered everywhere. Trev has a nasty yellow paint on his walls and a brown carpet. His room looks like a huge wardrobe with all the clothes scattered about. They cover everything. He has a small desk where a computer monitor is flickering. A tape is playing, some soul track.

"You need a cleaner."

"Yeah, I gotta do something 'bout that. Right now, before I get some grief from my mother." He starts rummaging, shoving the clothes back into some drawers. A few of the them he hangs up in a wardrobe. "Check out the machine."

I lift a T-shirt off the chair by his desk and sit down. The monitor is showing some kind of 3-D puzzle. Dozens of small tiles are covered in strange shapes and symbols.

"What's this?"

"It's sneaky, man. You have to solve each level then . . . look, I show you." He leans over and take the mouse. By dragging the shapes to similar patterns he makes them disappear from the screen. Some of the connections take him a moment to solve but he clears the picture quickly.

"There are logic things on some of them, you have to get that first. Here." The screen fades and then turns blue. There is a selection box: 'Choose Marilyn or Hank!'. Trev clicks the Marilyn box. "See, the machine ain't sexist. Hanks's for girls."

A figure takes shape and then gets clearer until I see the outline of a woman. It hits picture quality and I peer at a girl in elaborate cream underwear. She is sitting on the end of a bed in a small room with no other furniture. She drops her head, slides a hand down one leg and unfastens the clip on her stocking.

She slowly peels it off, lifts the bare limb into the air and then the image focuses in on her smile. The picture flicks to an overhead shot of lying flat on the bed. An American drawl whispers from the side of the monitor. A girl's laughter accompanies it. "Marilyn has seven more items of clothing to remove. Please continue."

Then the screen goes back to another tile puzzle.

"Trev, you pervert."

"Nah, it helps stimulate me to go on to the next level, that's all. This is soft, boy, some of the programs are disgusting – animals and shit."

"You played it through to the end yet?"

"Nah, getting her to slip the bra off is hard. The game gets tougher. Apparently, you can get the two of them together in the later stages. Talking of which, how's your great love affair going?"

"I'm gonna call her."

"You got her number?"

"Course."

"Jus' ring her then."

"Yeah, I will."

"Do it now, what's stopping you?"

Trev has a phone in his room. He picks it up and holds the receiver out to me.

"Yeah, later. I'm not worried about this, you know."

"Call her then. When you done that, we can see how far we get with Marilyn." He's enjoying the wind up, laughing.

"I will, jus' relax, Trev. You know me. When something needs doing . . . I jus' do it. I'm . . . decisive like that."

"The numbers?"

"Get out the room then an' I'll do it."

"Alright. Don't go giving me any of the 'not in' bull-shit though."

"Trev, get out man."

"I'm gone, see me now."

He shuts the door behind him.

I don't pause. It rings four times then there's a click.

"Through to Bond. Entertain me after the tone."

"Hi. It's Charles ... Tuesday afternoon and I was thinking, after the ... seeing you the other night, that ..."

"Hello, Charles." She was monitoring the call. I feel stupid, wonder why I'm calling, but when I listen to her voice I remember. "Go on." I can hear her giggling.

There's only one way to stop the embarrassment. "You want to meet up?"

"Doing what?"

"A drink maybe. Tomorrow, that's Wednesday."

"Really? Alright. Where?"

Now she's agreed I feel more awkward than before. There were a few things I was going to suggest – meeting for a drink over the river somewhere, maybe a club or a film. With a rush of nerves I realise that I wasn't properly prepared. These ideas all seem parti-cularly crass now, like only a maniac would come up with them. I can't stop thinking about everything else but the date, like where she's sitting in her house, if she's on her own or with a bunch of friends. I can't concentrate. The seconds are flashing buy. She breaks in.

"I know a place by the river."

"Let's do that then."

"Do you want to pick me up?"

I can't imagine Bond riding two-up on the Fox. Tension. A large drop of sweat lands on my jeans.

"No, I'll meet you there if that's alright."

"Eight, in the Prince Regent, St. Catherine's Dock. You know it?"

"Yeah, I think so." I know the dock she mentioned over by Tower Bridge or somewhere. You have to own a yacht to fit in with the crowd.

"See you there then. Thanks for calling."

"Yeah."

I sit there staring at the computer monitor. I feel as though I've come through some gruelling experience, like visiting the dentist or taking an exam. And this is supposed to be fun? I've never had to go out on a limb for a date, things have just 'happened', like getting smashed at a party and realising you're necking some girl, don't even know who she is. Then that drifts into more dates until it's dump time. It's always been like that before. This was more significant, like I'm going in deep. Trev creeps in through the door behind me.

"How'd it go?"

"She said yes."

"There you go. Congratulations, Charles. I envy you, boy. Let's get back to Marilyn."

"Nah, I need a drink."

"It's only six or something, we can go in for an hour or something."

"Six already? Shit."

"Skin up and get into the game. I need some help."

I'm thinking about real flesh, not the sad computer graphic. Bond's voice has affected me. She's stormed into my thinking again. Trev looks at me.

"Charles man, you got it bad."

"Drink."

"Chill out, will ya? I'm broke anyway. Been spending, boy. I've had two months advance on the job already."

"I'll buy."

"Where you want to go?" He's messing with the tiles again.

"Anywhere."

"Boy, she got you shell-shock. Could go down the Moon if you want."

"I don't care."

"Shit, can't get this last sequence."

"Come on, Trev, I need sustenance."

"Alright."

He turns the machine off and stands up. Then he looks me up and down. I feel drained, scruffy – but underneath I'm excited. I've got a date with Bond. There's so much to consider, things I don't even know about yet.

He interrupts my thoughts of her. "There is one thing."

"Yeah."

"Well, where you going with her?"

"Over to the city, a dock over there."

"Right, well that settles it."

"I don't get you."

"You and I are taking a little trip tomorrow."

"Yeah?"

"You need an outfit, boy. Better go shopping with someone who knows."

"No way."

"Gotta dress to impress, boy. Special with someone like her."

I sit there for a moment. I can't believe it but I'm taking his suggestion seriously.

"Shit, man, I don't know what's going through my head but alright. Maybe you're right. Now though, we drink."

We walk out of the room laughing.

The Moon is in full swing even though it's only seven. There's no comparison with the atmosphere in the afternoon. The music is pumping – dance stuff, druggy, open grooves. Everyone's shouting to be heard and the air is full of smoke. There are a few office types in suits, girls in leggings and short skirts. But most of the crowd is the benefit crew that hangs out in Clapham. People have got it wrong when they write the area off as all money, the Range Rover crew. It's mostly little groups in easy gear, denims, leathers, club T-shirts. No-one's over thirty. Trev and I slump at the bar and sip on our Brooklyns.

"How's the empire bit going then?"

"Working out, Trev. Hard work though."

"Sure, smoking and selling, I can imagine."

"Nah, there's a lot of biking involved."

"You gonna stick it then?"

"Till I want to, yeah. So what you think I should get tomorrow?"

We talk and drink. After an hour I'm getting blasted. The bar is rammed now, people crammed into the main room and spilling into the back.

"You know they got a room upstairs?"

"No. You wanna try it?"

"Yeah, can't breathe here."

We work our way to the back and Trev takes some steps. He takes a right and we come out into a large room, blood red walls and soft lighting.

"Loads a room up here."

There's a crowd round a little bar but most of the tables are free. One large group in the corner is making a lot of noise, drowning out the music, so we sit opposite them by a huge fireplace.

"I've got about enough to get us a round."

"Cheers, Trev. Very kind of you."

He wanders over to the bar. As he joins the mass I notice a guy getting up from the group on the other side of the room. I see the hat and let out a sigh.

"Easy, Charles."

"Hello, Deacon."

He's in a black Raiders jacket, done up tight, and some black jeans. Even though it's dark outside he's wearing shades – little round, black discs. All I can see is his wide smile.

"Fancy running into you here."

"This is one of my regulars."

"Yeah? Well, you change yo' mind?"

"Bout what?"

"What I was saying to you in the club there."

"No."

"Cool. You carrying?" He has pulled a chair up and

straddles it. He lifts the hat off his head and lies it on the table. His head is shaved.

"Don't see how it matters to you . . . but 'No' is the answer to that."

"Not very friendly, Charles . . ." His voice can change tone in an instant. At first he was sounding relaxed, now it's thin and sharp. "Thing is, it is some a my concern."

"Oh yeah?"

I lean back in my chair and take a long pull on my beer, finish the bottle. I study him. I'm no fighter but I could probably take the guy. He's not very big, more lithe and wiry than real muscle. He takes out some cigarettes.

"No thanks."

He lights one with my Clipper.

" 'Cause you been . . . well, extending your network, yeah?"

"You said it was out of your market."

Now I'm feeling angry. All I've seen so far is this guy talking big. He has a mad, business-like tone to his voice, like he's selling insurance or something. After talking with Freddy and thinking it through I'm in no mood to sit there now and listen to the guy, pretending I'm impressed. I've lost interest, got too many other things on my mind.

"I sell weed too, you know. But now I got my boy going round there finding you been there first."

"Competition, Deacon. Way of the world. Anyway, I didn't think you were bothered about that."

He can tell I'm not paying him much attention. The muscles round his lips draw tight.

"Don't mess me about, Charles. You're selling across the river now and I know what gonna happen. I got eyes all over town, boy. People you with now gonna get you into trading big, boy, serious – and that I can't allow."

"Oh, fuck you."

Now I do it. I lean forward and stare into his shades. I don't know what he's getting at but it's winding me up. He's in no position to preach.

"What you saying, man? You just gonna sit here and hassle me? I told you, I'm not interested in that."

"I know what you're doing, Charles." He lifts the cigarette so it is only a few inches from my face. "Watch." He twists it in his hand so the ember is next to his little finger. He pushes the cigarette so it touches the skin. I can smell it burning. He holds it there for a long time, long enough for me to feel sick, then he stubs the ember out on the table.

"That's the difference between you an' I. I'm a no-fuck dealer from the street. Years of it, in my face. I sold outside pubs from when I was fourteen, calling out to people, hustling them. So it's something for me to be so . . . gentlemanly. You're nothing but a kid who doesn't even see what's going on around you."

I just stare at the fading ember on the table top. Trevor is back from the bar with two bottles. Deacon sticks his hand out to shake. He's smiling, the voice has changed again.

"I'm Deacon."

"Trevor."

I feel cold, find it hard to say anything. Deacon speaks first.

"Anyway, catch you later then." He stands up from the chair and drops the hat back on his head, then turns and walks back to his table.

"What goes on then?" Trev taps me on my shoulder and I come back to life.

"Nothing. He's trying to scare me off a bit, that's all."

"Yeah? I seen him around here before. Don't look so dangerous to me."

"Says he's got a team working for him."

"Well, time to stop maybe. 'Sides, it's no big deal for you, is it?"

"I don't know. Think I'll get out when I'm ready, Trev."

I expect him to go on with the conversation but instead he stares at me. He looks bored. "So, what we gonna get for you tomorrow? Charles gets a makeover."

We talk for a while but when the beer runs out I want to head back and we wander up to the cab office before closing time. I keep thinking about Deacon and the cigarette show. For a cheap trick it's made quite an impact. What with that and the prospect of meeting Bond it's an effort to get to sleep.

Ten

Wednesday

I was up on Battersea High Street when Theo called. Trev was chatting away next to me, excited by the prospect of spending my money. We're heading for the Junction.

"You still OK about the party then?"

"Of course. I wouldn't miss it."

"It should be a good one. I'm taking Friday off as a holiday so any wreckage won't be a problem. Yeah, sorry about the other day, it's hard when I've got my work hat on you know, that's all."

He's the only person I know who doesn't mind chatting on the mobile. The expense doesn't bother him. I picture him in his office, calling New York and Hong Kong every ten minutes. I'm huddled up in the doorway of a wine bar, trying to block the traffic noise.

"Forget it."

"And there are a few things I want to talk about with you."

"Yeah?"

"A business proposition. Of a kind, anyway."

"Well, I'll see you on Thursday, we can talk then."

"Excellent. It starts around ten. And . . ."

"I remember. Alright, thanks for calling, Theo . . ."

He rings off but I carry on speaking. Trev is listening in. "Five thou yeah, no, six. That's not a problem, anytime. Fine." I holster the phone and smile at Trev.

"Business, Trev. Your phone doing me a lot of good."

When I woke up this morning I had a moment of real, intense panic. Maybe it's because I've been smoking a lot lately and the drug is triggering the anxiety area in my brain, but when I pulled the curtains back in my room and stared down at the cars lined up in the little enclosure we have for the block the first thing I noticed was a blue saloon car. It was the same as the car that was parked over at Waterloo, watching me. Now I know there are thousands of the same make and model in the capital but it stirred up all my paranoia and I freaked, yanked the curtains shut and quivered. I stood in the middle of my room, waiting for the sound of the front door being air-blasted off its hinges. Then there would be heavy steps coming up to my room, shouts and yells, then the door crashes open. For a second I really thought it was about to happen. I went over to the drawers where I keep my stash and thought about how to destroy it. There was too much to flush away. I could try eating it but there were mounds of the stuff and I pictured the police charging in – me standing there, chomping merrily away, with the bags in both hands and waiting for the huge stone to descend. At this point I went back to the window and took another look. The car was still there. I couldn't see if there was anyone sitting in it because of the angle from my window but now it just looked like any other blue saloon. It had lost its significance.

When I had first seen it there was a strange echo in my mind, like seeing a face you know but you can't remember the name, a gut feeling of some connection that you're not fully aware of. That's when I realised it was the bush playing games with me. I've heard all sorts of stories about dope paranoia, anxiety attacks, but had always rejected them as bullshit. After my freak this morning I had to accept that I've been smoking a lot and there must be residual affects from it, lingering chemicals in the blood that can cause these things. Freddy told me that over a period of years the drug collects in fatty tissue around the brain. That's why old smokers can get blasted on a few tokes. There are lots of things people don't know about herb because they've never really done any research into it (no profit if it's illegal, I guess), so I started to rationalise that I had suffered a dope-related panic attack. I felt better after that.

The crazy thing is, that if I had woken up and got dressed and gone out as normal then I'm sure I would have been worrying about other things. The run-in with Deacon was on my mind all through the night. I had Bond to think about. But because of my five-second shake experience I blocked it all out, felt chill. I even sat down and had a quick single skinner to re-assure myself that everything was alright. I felt mellow after that, stretched out on the bed and smiled. Deacon was nothing to worry about. If things do get bad with him I can always quit or take him on. I'm not scared of him, even when he pulls dumb stunts like burning his finger in front of me. Any asshole can do that. The business is sweet. As for Bond, she must be into me if she accepted the date invite. I shall let Nature take its course with that one.

So by the time I'm walking down Battersea with Trev, everything is in order. I feel relaxed and on top of it. I've got the shades and the cap on, strutting along in my black jeans and eager to get an outfit. Trev can see it. After all, it's me with three hundred in the wallet. I can't help making the joke about the five or six thousand. I'm in a light mood. When I get off the phone he gives me an envious look and we pace off. He doesn't say anything for a few minutes. When he talks his voice has the anger of an upset child.

"The rent's due on the phone."

"Been a week already?"

"Yeah."

"Can change a fifty?" I hold a note up.

He stops on the pavement. We're on Falcon Road, only a few minutes from CJ. "You taking the piss?"

"No."

"Just give me thirty and I'll leave you to it. Fuck you and your shopping."

"Oh, come on, Trev. Easy. Don't get jealous on me."

"Who jealous?"

"So why the moaning?"

"I hear you making deals on *my* phone and you haven't even remembered to give me the rent for it. You gettin' selfish, Charles."

"Give me a break, Trev. Here . . ."

There is a newsagent behind us and I walk in and buy a pack of cigarettes with the fifty. The guy behind the counter takes a long time to check the note, holding it up and creasing it and I'm worried Trev may have stormed off by the time I get out.

He's still there.

"Have a cigarette and calm down, will ya? I need your help on this."

"Yeah, yeah."

"Best dressed man in Battersea standing next to me."

"Just don't make me ask for things I'm due, alright?"

"I respect that. I'm sorry. Here." I give him the thirty. He makes a little show of checking it's all there then pockets it. "Alright?"

"Yeah. Don't forget I'm poor, that all. No big money man like you."

"I'm sorry, really. Come on, we can get a sandwich or something first, yeah?"

He is silent for a moment, making up his mind what

he wants to do, deciding whether he's still angry with me. Then he gives me a big smile. "Wanna share a pizza?"

"Yeah, fancy that. I'll buy."

"We'll split it."

It's only when he's riled that he minds taking a freebie. I've been buying nearly all the drinks for the last week but that doesn't bother me. If I didn't buy he'd have to stay in.

"Right, we'll split. Couple a quid each, safe."

We head up to the railway bridge and he lightens up, starts talking again. I make a note of not winding him up about the phone again. Funny how my friends seem to be getting so sensitive about all this.

When we get to the pizza place, Trev orders something. I don't really care what it is. Pizza tastes the same to me whatever you put on it. We're sitting by the glass front which looks out on to the street.

"See Ben there?"

I can see him walking by on the other side of the street. He's got his shoulders back, standing tall, a cigarette dangling from his lips, care-free and confident as ever.

Trev leans round the door. "Hey, Ben!"

He looks around for the voice but it takes him a moment to spot us. Then he heads across the street, stepping in front of a car and lifting a hand to halt it.

"Alright Trev, Charles. Doing lunch then, are you?"

Ben is always smiling, laughing, despite the fact I'm always hearing about him getting into trouble, running up debts – some heavy stuff a while ago. He had money of his own back then. Since I've known him though he's always broke.

Trev touches fists with him. "Yeah. What's been happening?"

"You hear about the killing, over Clapham?"

"We were there, boy."

"What, you saw it?"

"Nah, we were coming out of that place. Pharaoh's yeah, an' it was all going off."

"Getting some mix up here. I mean today, like an hour ago."

I come over to the doorway. "There's been another one?"

"Yeah. Middle of the fucking afternoon, practic'ly a drive-by . . ."

"Nah."

"I tell you. Some guy in a garage get gun down and they just cut out in a car like it nothin'."

"Shit. It's getting like a war."

"Is a war. I seen some a it. Gotta stay on your toes, boy." He makes a little gesture, imitating a boxer and we all laugh. The uniform behind the counter mutters to us.

"Hawaiian?"

"Oh yeah, that's mine."

We move out of the shop, splitting the pizza between the three of us. Ben takes huge mouthfuls of the soft dough, as though he hasn't eaten for a day or two.

"Money tight."

I know he could be earning a lot in my trade. I've heard he used to deal but have never asked him why he packed it in. Although Ben is always laughing he's not the sort of person you can hassle. I don't think he'd appreciate my questioning.

"Yeah, another dead. An' you wouldn't think this that kinda place, looking around I mean, would you?"

Trev sweeps out with his arm to indicate the busy pedestrian area we have entered. It's full of rushing shoppers, kids laughing, old people sitting next to walled-in flower beds and all the comfy sights of a high street. Ben grabs another piece of the steaming pizza and shoves one side of the triangle into his mouth. He carries on talking even though his cheeks bulge with food.

"You look under the surface an' it not so clean an' wholesome, boy. There a whole section a people who part a this but they earn from drug an' other thing. Not like Charles here, who jus' sell a bit week to him friend. But people thinking only a the money, trying to survive. City a jungle, you know."

"There is pressure, yeah, but it's a long way from wild."

"Wild it is. You feel different if you get shot today. Him only your age, you know . . ."

I finish my portion and wipe my lips with the back of my hand. Then I interrupt him as he is about to go on.

"I agree with you. This shit with guns is way out of control, an' it's not just the news people kicking up a storm, it is actually happening. We're living with it every day."

"Exactly."

Trev gives me a sneaky look. "So you gonna get one?"

"You what?"

"Spence can get you one, can't he?"

"Don't talk crap, Trevor."

"You're the one saying it affects all of us. I bet Deacon's got one."

"So what? Anyway, he wouldn't have one, not him."

"He's just the sort of nutter who would have."

Ben breaks in. "Course. Gun is common, man."

"I'm talking about bush though, Trev." We stop on the pavement and I drop my voice. They lean in to hear me. "I'm only talking 'bout weed . . . not fucking crack or anything. That's what the shooting's about."

"Wouldn't be so sure a that."

"Money is money."

"Nah . . . it's crack that's bad for it. 'Cause there's so much money in it. I mean, you can't get a fucking new Merc selling bush, an' there's plenty of them cruising by up on Acre Lane."

"Plenty in fucking Clapham too."

"An' where you think they got the money for that? Guys Ben's age this is."

"I know. There is money in rock, serious money."

We stop the conversation for a second. I was in such a good mood before this talk I decide to break back to it. I know what I think and I'm right. Guns have got nothing to do with me.

"Thought we was out to look for a jacket an' stuff anyway."

"Yeah, well there a place just across the lights."

Ben looks up another street that leads off from the lights. "I better be going, got a few people to see."

"Well, see you for a drink sometime."

"Bell me, yeah? Later."

He walks off into the crowd.

"Time to transfer you into loverboy then."

"Easy, Trev."

"Only kidding. I'll just show you a couple of things I saw last week, that's all."

"Let's do it then. I got to be over there in a few hours."

We crossed the lights and I followed Trevor into a shop.

I have to get the tube over to Tower Hill. No matter what anyone tells you, the tube system stinks if you live in south London. I can either hike over to the northern line in Clapham or get a train from Battersea to Victoria, then sit on the District Line as it follows the Embankment's lazy curve. The route east on the tube is depressing. The stations are run down, dirty and the trains themselves should have been taken out of service years ago. It's not too bad if you're going to the West End but as I'm going far east I take a train into Victoria. At least the District is clean. They must have more money to spend on the trains north of the river. Want to keep the commuters happy.

It takes me nearly an hour to get there. I pass the journey checking the constant flow of new passengers. The tube is a huge flirt game. If you're sitting opposite a girl it's hard not to stare at her. There's nowhere else to look, and anyway there's something about the fleeting glimpses of other people as you connect for a bit of their journey which I find interesting. I try to work out where they come from, what they do for a living, if they're happy with their life. It's all body language on the tube.

A wino gets on at St Pauls and I have to move carriage the stench is so bad. Two builders get on and they smell of the pub already, going home for dinner – pie and peas probably, weak tea. A city type is reading a computer magazine: sad. Three women get on who look like they've either just left a cheap nightclub or an office party. A miserable guy in cowboy boots sits next to them and they all start talking in some strange language. There are a lot of whores coming over from Eastern Europe and I guess they've spent the day with a procession of fat businessmen in a King's Cross hotel. A student crashes through the doors at the last moment and drops into a seat. He takes out a fat book and hides behind it. People come and go, off and on, changing at every station. Every time I take a long ride on the tube I remember how many people there are in this town, how many I'll never know or come across to speak with and understand a little.

There are two ways to react to this. You can take the view that because you'll never know them they don't affect your life, are unimportant. Like the guy said in a movie, staring down from the top of a ferris wheel at the crowd below, 'Look at them, just like ants, what would it matter if some of them were to disappear?' They exist but do not really exist for me. I will never know more than one millionth of them. The other side is more the Freddy philosophy. I've been talking with him quite a bit lately. He thinks that every one of these people plays a tiny role in each other's life, that we're all connected like one huge heart beating together, each one of us vital.

I'm not sure what to make of it. I just like to sit and watch. That kind of thinking makes my head hurt and I'm not convinced it really matters anyway, understanding these things. The best thing to do is to *pretend* you care about everyone else but really just get on with looking after yourself. That's the way to play it. That's what everyone else is doing. That's what the nineties are all about.

I arrive at Tower Hill and walk past the castle where Queeny keeps all her jewels. Then I cut past a large building and down to the river by the side of the bridge. This part of town is all business – big office blocks, banks, the factories on the other side of the water, hotels, and bars that shut when all the workers have gone home at eight. I walk round to the dock.

It's more a marina than a dock. I think of docks in terms of industry – cranes and rusty boats, tired men with sacks on their backs. But you only see that stuff in books. All the docks in London are dead, turned into yuppie playgrounds. This place is huge, walled in by tall buildings with their river-view apartments. The water runs in and is channeled round through a system of small mooring ponds to a lock on the other side that goes back into the river. It's all very flash. Old-style gas-light lamps line the walkways, plants are everywhere and lots of glass looks into the bars, coffee shops and insanely expensive restaurants that cater to the visitors. And they are here. There are families in matching blue-and-white suits, the little berets, all the sailor gear. There are businessmen with tired girlfriends who probably make more than they do.

There are yachts. Here, by Tower Bridge in the heart of the Smoke there are yachts moored – huge, Florida-cruising, shark-fishing, 'gin and tonic on the bridge darling' yachts. Some of them are smaller sailing boats but I walk past one that takes up at least sixty paces of the quay. For a moment I wonder what it would be like out on the ocean in one of these things, but I can't see myself as the nautical type. I like earth beneath my feet.

I see the pub across the marina, a big wooden ranch-house type being with light pouring out of it. I have to follow the wall all around the watery square to get there. I push my way in. It's packed with suits and I can't see Bond anywhere. I order a Brooklyn and light a cigarette.

These sort of bars were a lot more popular back in the boom of the late-eighties when everyone thought Britain was the new gold rush. I don't remember much of those times. My bar drinking only started a couple of years ago. However, Dominic was around for it and he's told me what it was like. The whole city was full of money, everyone was making. He has always maintained that the blunt material philosophy back then played a part in his crack-up.

I stare at the drinkers. They are mostly men in their thirties, wearing suits that are off the peg but still cost five hundred up. A lot of them are smoking and the air round the bar is full of the tobacco cloud. I reflect that stress levels must have risen in the present economic age – not so many people are trying to quit.

As I watch them shouting to one another, waving their arms and getting drunk, I notice one man take some stairs in the opposite corner of the room. I make a mental note that this must be the way to the bathroom. A moment later two men come in through the locked-back entry door and walk straight over to the stairs. This puzzles me. It's not until a large group of women who I haven't seen before emerge from the stairs that I realise there must be another floor. Cursing myself, I rush over to the stairs and go up to the next room.

It's a large balcony area with simple wooden furniture. I can see out across the whole dock from up here. On my approach I had not noticed the veranda. This was due to the wooden slats that surround it. They make it hard to see the figures standing around, chatting. I ditch my cigarette and light another, then sit down on a wooden bench that affords me a view of the dock, making sure the boards are dry first. I don't want to trash the trousers.

Trev had no real intention of helping me buy some gear. Once we started in the shops he was off in the changing rooms, flicking through shirts in the sale piles, making talk with the assistants if they were female. I wandered around the shop with the same feeling of mounting confusion as always. It's not that I'm a weird shape or anything. I'm five-nine and slim. The problem is the choice. Once I get started I find it impossible to make decisions between clothes – one shirt or the other, what colour, all that stuff. It seems unimportant to me. As long as I don't feel scruffy and the clothes are functional then I'm happy. Occasionally I think it would be interesting to experiment, feel like I'm missing out on something, but I don't really worry about style. I've known too many people who dress well that turn out to be morons. It's like you can have one or the other – style and hip dress, or a brain. They rarely seem to go together in my view. Einstein didn't worry if his tie was too wide, did he? Maybe I just think this way because I'm not stylish – it's a defence mechanism. Anyway, I have very little tolerance for shopping. So I wanted Trev along for his boundless enthusiasm for clothes. This was no help for most of the afternoon. As I said, he wasn't interested in helping. But just as I was about to drop it and head for home he came over and pulled me across to another shop. At the back there was a small display and he pointed out one of the mannequins.

"There you go."

"The leather?"

"Yeah, with the Go Vicinity jeans and some boots."

"Aw man, it's a bit rave, innit?"

"Nah, it's criss. You never look better."

The jacket was more of a coat, coming down to just above my knees. It was black leather, soft and smooth to the touch, with a vanilla cotton lining.

"How much is it?"

"Two eighty."

"What?" This was a wild figure to pay for a coat, as far as I could tell.

"It'll last you, C. Anyway, can get it for less if you pay cash."

"Can spend nothing if I just wear this one." I finger the ancient brown jacket I'm wearing.

"It's to reflect your new status, boy. Can't go round wearing that old thing."

The new leather does look criss. However, spending like this brings you into the circular pattern when you don't save anything. You start spending what you earn and I've been fighting that since I decided on the car.

"Nah."

"Girl think you something in a new coat."

"If she only thinks about that then what am I seeing her for? Nah, she can take it as I am."

I have some standards. I'm happy with what I am, what I will become. One day a purchase like this will mean nothing but today I'm still moving towards that. I flick through some more leathers and find a jacket similar to the one I'm wearing. I check the label. It's one-seventy.

"This is cool."

"Not so good with the jeans."

"I'll just get some new boots. Fuck the jeans."

So I paid ninety for the shoes and got the jacket for one-fifty. Trev looked unhappy that I hadn't followed his advice but when we got back to my place I tried the lot on and he had to admit it looked good. I even wore the cap.

"Yeah, you still look like you, for better or worse."

"Thanks."

I see her crossing the bridge over to the bar. She walks fast, head back. In the light from the period lamps I see she's in a little tunic and a tiny black skirt with leggings down to some high-heeled ankle boots. It's a very different style to the hippie gear I've seen her in before. Then she vanishes and I take the last swig on the Brooklyn for strength. As I turn to watch the steps she appears. Without hesitating she strides over.

"Get me an Irish whiskey, will you?"

She leans over and kisses my cheek. I can smell her scent, feel the soft down on my face.

"Hello, Bond. No don't worry, I haven't been waiting long."

She says nothing but sits at the bench and takes one of my cigarettes. I stand up and head for the bar, happy I've reprimanded her, established myself. When I get back I place the glass in front of her. She looks up lazily.

"Make another crack like that and I say good night. I've had a shitty day and the last thing I need is a hard time from you."

"Sorry."

"Good. How are you?"

"I'm fine."

"Have you got anything to smoke?"

"I have, yeah?"

"Then be a darling and roll one up. I'm feeling completely stressed. Wired." As she talks to me she looks round the bar, checking the other drinkers, not concentrating on me. I can't think of anything to say to her. My kit is in the jacket pocket and I slide it out under the table. I try to sound easy when I speak.

"Direct, aren't you?"

"I thought you liked that."

She has finished her drink and I watch her reach out for my bottle.

"Don't do that."

She picks it up, sticks the glass rim between her lips and tilts her head back. I don't say anything until she puts the bottle back in front of me. It's empty.

"You know how to fuck me off like an expert." She smiles. I go on. I'm angry now. She was late, she's impolite and now she's hit a nerve. "I hate people doing that. If you want a drink then tell me . . . I'll buy you one. I don't like sharing my drink so don't do it, alright?"

"Why's that then? What's the big deal?"

" 'Cause I grew up sharing my drinks. Every fucking day of my life I was sharing a drink, washing down a Coke between three of us or saving little bits at the bottom of the can for a friend, all that shit. Never had a drink each, just sharing all the time. More spit than Sprite. And since I've been drinking alcohol I've seen that a drink's important, it matters. There's a whole social network built around drinking, from the official toast, to the old friends keeping track of the rounds, to this situation where I'm buying you drinks in the name of relations between the sexes . . ."

"Romantic . . ."

"A drink is a gesture, a statement. Me buying you a Brooklyn or a whiskey means something. If you attack it, mock it by stealing bits of my drink, then the whole thing crashes down and then there's no . . . no elegance to the situation."

"I like that. You really believe this, don't you? And I thought you were so straight."

"Are we clear on the drink thing then."

"Sure. I'll have another beer, thank you. I'll drink it all by myself, promise."

She says it with an exaggerated politeness and I stand up, pretend to bow. I take a cigarette with me to the bar. When I get back the conversation is forgotten but I'm glad I had the vocal outburst. One of the things about her that appeals to me is her wildness, the way she is so irreverent, off-hand with everyone. However, I don't want her thinking I'm a door-mat, taking it because she looks good, so it was wise to make the speech. Now I feel at ease with her, the alcohol is taking the sharpness away.

"Here you go."

"Thanks. Any chance of the . . ." She mimes smoking a short roach joint, putting her little hand up to her lips and sucking in air.

"You look like a naughty school kid."

"Well?"

I pick the kit up under the table and twist the finish to a joint. Then I pass it to her over the table.

"Not nervous, are you?"

"Looks better if it's casual."

I fire it with my Clipper. She draws deep and I watch her lips pinch the end as though it tastes like a bitter fruit.

"It's strong."

"Yeah, I seem to be building up a tolerance."

"Oh, well I've been smoking for years and it gets stronger all the time."

I go into my speech about the accumulated effects of dope. She follows my words, gives me little smiles. It feels easy, all my concerns about meeting with her have gone. I relax, the alcohol is helping. After a few minutes of this she puts her beer down and passes me the half-smoked stick.

"So what's the plan for tonight?"

"What would you like to do?"

"I'd like a meal in Chinatown, that grab you?"

"Sure."

I'm sounding casual but I've never eaten there. The fifty notes I brought out with me is feeling pressured. I know you can spend two hundred on a meal in town. Sitting there with the stick hammering my lungs, sipping at the Brooklyn, I start to feel nervous again. The barman gave me a curious glance last time I went down, thoughtful of my age. I've got the size to carry it off but I thought we'd just drink. If I wander off to an expense-account restaurant with her it could be a chiller. I might be washing dishes all night. I suddenly feel very young.

"Then some friends of mine are having a party down in Fulham. I said I might drop in. Don't know what it'll be like but we could have a look. 'Less you have other plans."

"No, I left it up to you really. Let's get into town."

"Alright."

Got to keep confident. I stand up and my legs are weak but I stride round to her side of the table. The jacket feels good, that brand-new feel. It's cured well enough so the scent is warm leather, not the stink of the tannery you get from the cheaper options.

"Head back to the tube then?"

"Aren't we getting a cab?" She has the unhappy look of a five-year-old who's lost something. I can see the danger in that look, could make some guys do anything for her – but I like it. Her eyes have a soft glow, maybe from the THC that's flooding her bloodstream. I make the spliff almost one hundred percent.

"A cab, yeah, if we can get one."

"That won't be a problem."

We start down the stairs. She takes my hand and it shocks me. I feel her press into my shoulder. It's such a simple and natural movement but my heart flips, I have to breathe hard. We cross the dock like this but then she turns us into a car park that leads up to a main road. It's dark here. I can see head-lights flying past on the other side of the square. Tall buildings full of glass tower into the night sky. We are surrounded by the shapes of cars, silent Mercs and BM's.

"There's a rank up here."

Then her hand is on the back of my neck, she swings me round and pulls me in, tugs my head down. Her lips brush against mine and her tongue darts into my mouth for a second. She pulls away and smiles at me.

"Just getting a taste. Come on, I can see one."

She starts running and I don't get a chance to say anything to her about the kiss. Then I get excited thinking about the rest of the evening, the form of her body I felt as she pressed tight against me. I'm getting the tingle, feeling the rush of alcohol and bush as my blood speeds up. When I catch up with her she's chatting with a fat cabby. She pulls me into the back and then I've got more time, all the time I want. I shut my eyes and kiss her until the cabbie's yelling at me, telling me we're there. All I can taste and smell is her. She breathes quickly, almost panting, and pushes past me. I stumble out of the back after her.

Eleven

The Date

Chinatown is deep in the heart of the city, stuck in a triangle between Leicester Square, Soho and Piccadilly. When I come into town I usually roam the more touristic areas, wander past the shops and buskers, ice-cream salons, burger joints, cinemas, all the bright lights and artificial glamour of town. I never walk round Chinatown. It's only really one street, nearly all restaurants or exotic grocery shops, and I haven't wanted to eat here before. I might have a Chinese take-out but that's it. Trev loves the food but I'd always go for other things.

The cab costs me eight pounds and I hand him a tenner he grunts and drives off. I sigh but my thoughts are more on Bond. The night's only beginning and it's already taken a turn for lunacy. I'm feeling fully trashed from the joint. She scampers over to one of the doorways, next to a telephone box with a tiny pink pagoda on the roof. I stare at it for a second – it reminds me of the huge one they built down in Battersea Park. People are filing past me, all oriental. They stick to the area. She vanishes into a side door and I follow. The street is noisy, bright lights everywhere, goofy American tourists taking pictures of the locals.

Walking into the restaurant I think it is one small room. Some elderly couples stare up at me. Then a small girl in a white shirt nods at me and I start up some stairs behind her. We go through a glass door and out into a massive room full of people. It stretches back at least two hundred yards, high ceiling with yellow and red hangings on the walls. Each table has a little candle floating in liquid in the centre. The serving staff are rushing between the tables, shouting at one another in sharp, thin voices. I am brought to a small table against the wall and sit down. I light a cigarette. Bond is hidden behind a massive menu. She lowers it and smiles at me.

"Shall I order for you?"

"I think I'll have a look, if that's alright."

I lean across for a kiss but she backs away. The atmosphere has changed again. In the cab she was smothering me. I thought that was the breakthrough and was going with it but now she is back to the tease.

I say nothing but stare at the menu. I'm more interested in the right-side numerals than I am in the lists of strange ingredients. It's around nine pounds a dish.

I've only eaten out twice at these prices in my whole life. The first was for Dominic's university acceptance, the second for my father's birthday when his brother came over and bought the whole family a meal. I feel wasteful paying this much for food. I'm thinking of my wallet when my foot gets nudged under the table. I look over at Bond.

"You coming on again now then?"

"Aw relax."

She has a teenager's smile on her face. My feelings for her are changing every moment. She gets sophisticated, dry and mature then instantly flips back to the girly kid act. I've seen plenty of that with the girls I've been out with before and it wasn't what I wanted from her. The footsie has irritated me, hence the rebuke, but she cuts it short with a hard look and an invitation.

"You see anything you want to eat?"

It's such a simple flirt tactic I ignore it.

"No, why don't you order for me."

"I will."

Before she can raise a hand there is a waiter next to her. She orders the food by name not number. When he goes I say nothing for a while, just smoke.

"I like the way you kiss."

"But you don't want one now."

"When we get to the party we can kiss, if you still want to."

She waits for a response but gets none.

"This is a restaurant. I *like* to eat in these places. Don't be a bore, Charles."

"Sure."

Something arrives on the table, a selection of bowls and small pots. It's half a duck I think but all the meat has been shredded as though it's been mauled by a large animal. She lifts a lid and offers me a pancake.

"Thanks."

There is rice with bits of pork and shrimp, some sauce which I guess is plum, a plate of weird vegetables, some tangled noodle stuff and some chicken in a thick, black syrup. Two beers arrive and I take a big gulp of mine. It's got a sour, yeasty flavour. Suddenly my hunger is roused and I attack the food. She eats delicately with chopsticks. I just scoop with the spoon. I'm really not sure how this evening is going to turn out so I'm determined to enjoy the meal at least. At this price I have to.

We talk about music, Lenny, the band's concert and other light things about going out in Battersea. She doesn't give anything away about where she lives or if she works but I don't push it. I'm feeling more relaxed now. The food is interesting (if a little fatty for my liking) and I order beers as they run dry, which seems to be every few minutes. I'm past caring. I'm drifting with the course of the evening, just enjoying the flavours in my mouth, lighting up a cigarette as we finish eating. Bond freaked me earlier in the cab but I'm not going to be some gooey-eyed kid about it. If nothing happens then that's cool. Our conversation wanders into the vague attacks and embraces of people who don't know each other very well, who are getting drunk, out on a date and not sure if they like each other. She leans back in her chair and blows a cloud of smoke into the air above her.

"Lenny told me you're a tradesman."

"In a manner of speaking, yeah. You could say that."

"So what do you trade in?"

"Narcotics."

"Oh, very cool."

"I'm sure Lenny told you that as well, didn't he?"

"Maybe."

"Fact you're in pretty close with the guy, aren't you?"

"We're just friends. I've known him a long time."

"Yeah, well, may as well tell you I don't really like the guy."

"Why tell me that?"

"'Cause it's the truth."

"Well the truth's boring most of the time. I don't care about what you think of Lenny."

"What you mean' the truth's boring?"

"I prefer fantasy. The truth usually means something sad or cruel or unjust or plain dull. I'm sick of truth."

"Why d'you agree to come out on this date, Bond?"

"Had some idea you might be interesting. I'm bored most of the time, have a very short attention span, you see."

"So, I'm boring you?"

"Not right now. You were when you gave me all those dirty stares . . ."

"When was that?"

"When you staggered over to the table and wanted me to kiss you."

"I wasn't staggering."

"Really? Looked like it to me."

"Then you can't see too well."

"Oh, my, what a witty remark. Surely you can get nastier than that." Her words are accompanied by smiles or snarls, as though she is still pondering whether to like or detest me.

I break back into the talk. "This party a busy thing?"

"You still want to come?"

"May as well have a look."

"You're strange, Charles. You don't seem to care much, do you, but then sometimes you look all excited. You lack consistency."

This mirrored my thoughts of her a moment ago. I hear my voice rise.

"Bullshit. You're the one that's confused."

"Sorry?"

"You don't know if you're into me or not, do you?"

"That's just one of my games, Charles. You have to allow a girl a changeable mind."

"Another beer?"

"Thank you. I was almost on the point of taking a sip of yours. That would have been terrible, wouldn't it?"

At this I almost smile. Her joke is a relief. I'm not used to the sparring. The girls I've been out with before have become clear 'types' after an hour or two. They either dote on my words or stare away lazily, feigning disinterest. Some of them laugh at everything I say or find it hard to relax but they all opt for one choice, their basic personality. That's the difference with Bond. Her character is jumping all over the place, shifting, adapting to every new sentence. When she says something crass I know there are a dozen other thoughts flying around her head I could never guess. If she nudges my foot under the table I can't tell if she's serious or trying to provoke me – and succeeding. When she leans back and flicks the block of her hair she catches my eye, knows what I'm thinking. I feel transparent in her presence, whereas she is impossible to read. All I know (despite my determination to play it cool and leave now if I want to) is that her appeal does not change and I want to see what happens at the party. She said I could kiss her as much as I want. When I start thinking like this I have to stop and run it through my head. Two hours ago the prospect of the kiss was a wild dream. Now I'm casually weighing up the possibilities of taking it further, maybe to total dick immersion even. I see how the act of kissing has changed my attitude to her. The first stage has been reached so my longing moves on to the next challenge. I've forgotten what she tasted like. She looks so good, is checking her tunic and rising from the table. It's a scarlet cloth, tight to her body. The skirt appears but stops after a few inches and the fabric of her leggings coats her legs like paint it's so tight.

"Shall we skip dessert?"

Another opportunity for innuendo. I leave it. "Yeah. Are we getting another cab?"

"Of course."

I hang behind when the waiter arrives. I flick the bill

open. It's two figures, a four and an eight. My throat tightens.

"How much is it?"

"Forty eight. Bond . . ."

Washing dishes? Running? I can't ask her to run. Leave my keys as a deposit and race back to Battersea? Will they accept some blow as part payment? It's Thai stick so maybe they'd go for it – their part of the world after all. I'm sweating. The waiter looks like he's seen it all a thousand times, keeps a large knife concealed on his person which he will produce any second. I have never felt so embarrassed.

"You pay twenty-two then. I've paid four more for the taxi I owed you, yeah?"

She drops a slip of paper and a plastic card in the middle of the table then pushes her flat palm out to me. Two small white balls are resting on her skin.

"I went to get us some mints. Want one?"

"Thanks."

"You better get the tip as well. I've no cash."

"Of course."

The kiss of relief is better than her tight little lips. We walk out of the room and down to the street. All I can whisper to myself: 'Thank fuck for the nineties woman'. They split the bills. Some of them do anyway. Bond slips her hand into mine as we walk up to Shaftesbury Avenue.

The party is down in Chelsea, not far from Theo and Julia's pad. I stumble out of the car with Bond wrapped around me like a koala bear. She's ravaged me on the way down here. We stopped at an off-licence and she bought a bottle of vodka. I got two bottles of wine and some cigarettes with the last of my money. So now we clank over to the door, bottles banging everywhere. There is a low hum coming from the house. It's a brick terrace, three floors, a tiny garden. All the curtains are pulled tight but enough light creeps out for me to be able to see the house is well kept – the stonework is painted a chalk white, two colourful flower jars flank the front door and the windows are clean. I notice these little things. How much someone spends on something like a window cleaner can be an important character tip. When a guy in his thirties wearing a shirt and chino jeans opens the door I'm not remotely surprised. I don't like the way he grabs Bond and gives her a huge kiss but this too I can accept. This is the respectable greeting for the moneyed Chelsea gang, pretending they're hip Europeans even though a mile away across the river it's kebabs and pints of cheap lager. His voice is flat and nasal.

"Hello, come on in and grab a glass of something." He takes my hand and squeezes it in his fleshy, moist mitt. I stare past him.

The hall is done out in regency tones, deep navy blue and a rusty red. The carpet you could drown in it's so deep. I can see the kitchen at the end of the tall corridor, full of people dressed like him. Bond smiles at me when the guy turns his back on us and heads for the kitchen.

"Your sort of thing?"

She obviously thinks I'm incapable of enjoying a brush with the money gang. What she can't see is that this house and the way it's decorated – champagne in the afternoons, a polite wine party – is all in my plan. This is no big deal for me, all in the future. I have to admit I find the guy who answered the door a bit of a geek but so what? There are dicks in every group of people.

"I'm chill, whatever."

"Mix me a vodka then, will you?"

We sink into the kitchen and I lose her in the crowded space. There are at least thirty people in here. I get pushed up against a brilliant white wall of a fridge and swing the door open, looking for a mixer. The people round me are all well-groomed, in the same sort of gear as the geek. Lots of them are smoking but they drink cautiously. At this stage I think they're trying to keep their wits because the conversation is savage. I can hear a thin, critical tone in the voices. It's not friendly. This said, I catch glimpses of Bond floating from one group to another, smiling, socialising, kissing cheeks, getting the odd dirty look from another girl. Music is seeping through from another room, awful chart stuff.

I wrench the top off the vodka and slam it down into two tumblers I've found in one of the overhead cupboards. The thick, greasy liquid fills the glass. Then I swing the coffin-sized fridge door open and a waft of icy air rushes over me. I can tell the group nearest me are wondering who the hell I am. I'm ten years younger than any of them and that makes me feel good. I find a bottle of orange juice in the fridge and splash it out into the glasses. It's the expensive kind naturally – there are bits of orange pulp floating in the alcohol. Finally I locate some ice-cubes and crash them into the tumblers. There's liquid everywhere.

I want to make an entrance so I hunch over to block out peeping eyes, whip out the kit from the leather and roll a clumsy spliff – break a whole head into it. Now there's bits of tobacco and bush, vodka spills, crushed ice, papers, cigarettes and the Clipper littered over the work surface next to the fridge. I fire it up and spin round into the room. The spliff is rammed into my mouth – man, what a reek – leaving a trail of smoke behind me and I've got the deadly vodka and orange mix in either hand. I make it over to where Bond has her back to me, talking to two huge rugby types. All around the room I can tell they're talking, pointing at me with their wine glasses and stares. I stand behind Bond for a second but get sick of waiting. The bush is going straight into my eyes and it burns. I lift my foot and with the toe of my new ankle boot I gently tap her ass. She flicks her head round, eyes full of fire.

"Got your drink, innit?"

By the time the party filters through to other rooms in the house I'm trashed. Bond is ripping through the vodka, keeping up with me on the spliff. We crash from one group of people to another, lounge in the armchairs, squeeze into sofas, turn the music up, spill ash trays and generally freak everyone out. It soon became clear that she is enjoying the novelty of her date. Her friends are alarmed by my smoking, the way I'm mixing the wine I had bought with the vodka, swigging it from a pint glass. I try talking to some of them but don't get very far. This is partly due to the massive gap in interests between us but mainly because of my drugged state. If I was straight then I'm sure it would be easy but the Thai is turning me, twisting my world. I watch events from behind the glass wall of stone, separate from the reality of this Fulham townhouse. There is a rumble in my ears like I can hear the world spinning beneath me, the clouds scraping past above. My flesh is cold, clammy. I am incredibly wrecked.

The times before when I've got this blasted I ended up feeling sick and heading for bed, waiting for the stone to fade away. That's happened at a couple of parties in the past. But Bond is firing me up with little touches, glances, strokes on my face as she drifts over from her friends. The grass is so clean it carries me along, lifts me. I want more. There are none of the sickness symptoms – the nausea, the tight stomach and leather throat. It's a pure stone, changing my thoughts, playing with my perceptions but not making me feel ill. I storm round the house after her, spliff roasting my fingers and the hot blast of vodka in my throat. The faces are flicking on and off in the dark around me. I hear their whining, the arrogance of their accent.

"Who's Bond invited?"

"Think he's had a bit too much, don't you? – whoever he is. Should we call his father – hur, hur?"

"He just offered me some of that . . . joint."

"The jazz cigarette you mean, Gretchen. Oh dear . . . not very with it, are you?"

"Look at him now."

I'm spinning in the room. Paintings, fireplace, thick carpet, faces, mean-looking, ugly girls and fat, office-lunch-belly guys staring me out. It's OK Charles, don't fight it, it's over your head, you're on the stone, no stopping it, you'll wake up in bed so don't worry, just chill. I take another pull, deeper in. I want to go down, sink into it. Never felt so trashed. Where's Bond? Shit, the music's weird, shaking me – want to show her what I am. She's by my side.

"You look like you're enjoying yourself."

Her friends are round her, they are siding against me. Getting so out of my head was the answer, I thought, breaking into their circle, relax and chat, but it's not working like that. There are more people now – they're warming up, getting drunk, must have piled out of some club, one of the girls slips out of her shirt and they start dancing in a little group, a circle of rich girls dancing for the fat boys. Stoned, very stoned – where's Bond? They wear little tops like she did when I saw her last time, when was that? Head getting tight. Blasted.

Now she's coming over with another girl – I recognise her. It's the friend from Pharaohs, long blond hair, some kind of tiny dress. I'm wobbling, try to smile. I hear them whisper.

"Think your friend's alright?"

"Of course."

"Well, a strange choice of date I think – for you anyway."

My lips are not confident enough to reply.

Bond gives her friend a snarl. "Charles and I are going upstairs."

"You checked with Tony? He may not be happy about . . ."

"Fuck Tony. Come on, Charles."

She leads me out of the room like I'm a child. My head is pounding. I start up the stairs behind her.

"Where are we going?"

She pauses at the top and spins round to face me. I can hear voices below. Bond stares past my shoulder, down to where her friends are standing. "Thought this was what you wanted."

She kisses me, fold her arms around my waist. I'm trying to focus on the wall behind her, so out of it I'm scared of falling backwards down the stairs.

"Let's go."

Then we're in the bedroom. It's like a Knightsbridge showroom – pastel colours, lots of books, more cream carpet. I let out a howl. There's a mock four-poster bed in the middle of the room.

"Come on then, Charles."

Bond is beside the bed, stripping. I stand and watch.

"Get undressed!"

I know she's only doing it to shock her friends, maybe she doesn't even care about that. It's so easy for her, perhaps she's as smashed as I am. Why did I get so trashed? Now the evening is moving to the peak I was dreaming about, worrying about, and I can hardly move I'm so wrecked. I feel cheated. I watch her slip into the bed, naked, a glimpse of her leg as it sweeps under the duvet cover. I'm watching a film – frame by frame the scene flicks by – click, click, step by step – Bond's smile – flashing a cigarette as I stumble over to the bed – the room spinning, shouts and sounds from below. I rip the duvet off the bed and stare down at her. It's a wild body, a celluloid snap from the cover of a magazine. I gulp. She is motionless, one arm behind her head on the pillow, the other balancing the cigarette by her mouth.

"What's the matter?"

"Nothing."

I can just about take my clothes off, stumble backwards to yank the boots off then I crash down beside her. She giggles and pulls me close, moulds me.

It's a mess. In the blur I try and push into her, feeling none of the nervousness or concern I thought I would. I feel angry with myself, irritated with her. She guides me but I feel nothing. I smell her body, a heavy, oppressive odour, finding it hard to breathe. I'm numb with the alcohol and blow but still I get the familiar wave of the come and I fall on top of her. Bond just looks up at me. She puts the cigarette between her lips and flares it up.

"Already?"

Not like that. There has to be more. I grab her body, cover her with my hands, brush the stick from her mouth. I want another try to make it important. Already I'm in her again, she lets out a rush of air as I pound down on her, sweat flying everywhere – fuck – fast again and no feeling, not sure where I am. She moans and twists, breaks free and then I'm wondering what to do. Her ass is up in the air in front of me – this is like a mud fight. She guides me in again and it's tussle rustle all over the bed. I can't come, feeling gone – all I want – and so I increase the speed – warped stone head trying to get tactical. She grabs my hand and pulls it on to her, then I'm rubbing her like I'm a boy scout or something, trying to start a fire.

The door crashes open and the geek screams.

"Fuck . . . Bond."

"Get out."

It goes on. I'm not there, I'm floating off by the ceiling or somewhere, just my body is fighting the good fight. Bond starts to move again and then there's a wild wrestling moment with her bucking around the bed – I can't hold on. We're both covered in sweat. She turns again and I think I'm going to fall off the bed but she hangs on and now I'm in her and her hands are wrapping round my neck. I can't breathe.

"Do it, Charles."

I want to come, it's all I want, but my dick feels like it's fallen into a tumble dryer – can't feel anything. I'm going to fake it, I have to – this is ripping me up, making muscles ache I never knew were part of the operation. My stomach is icy. I start panting. Come on Charles, make it good. I increase my panting. Where am I inside her? The dope is taking over, making me think clearly somehow.

"Yeah, yeah."

I fall on top of her again. She starts stroking my hair, post-fuck intimacy. I feel awkward, still a block in her. I try to deflate, think of anything to get it off my mind. I pull out of her.

"Baby . . ."

Then I'm on my back and past caring. I want to sleep. Bond slides off the bed and starts dressing. I

fumble for her cigarettes on the side table, flash one
into life. The room skips into a spin. I force it to stop.

"Fuck."

"Precisely. Let's get down again."

"I have to split. Get home. Really."

"You can get a taxi then, come on." She throws my
boots on to the bed. "Tony's going to be pissed off
with me, so you get a taxi, alright?"

She watches me as I dress. I'm in a coma. Even so, I
know there's no money for a taxi.

"Charles . . ." She comes over to me and kisses my
cheek. "Do call me, OK?"

"Yeah."

Then she escorts me down to the front door and
kisses me on the porch. I stumble into the street and
turn to wave but the door is already shut. Then it's
just me and the odd car flying past on the long walk
home.

When I cross the bridge I stare down at the river
and think about it all – the night, the date. Even
though I'm stoned and drunk and freaked because it
was so clumsy with her, so 'normal' for her, I still have
a feeling growing in me. I've crashed through into
adulthood – a rush of confidence seizes me. The circumstances do not matter, the frenzy and confusion
mean nothing. What is important is that I've done it.
When some guy makes a crack about a woman, when I
flick through a skin magazine, the next date I go on,
it's all changed because I'm no longer an innocent. I'm
a graduate now.

On the walk back I start to think about her body,

the sex. Somehow the details seem clearer in my memory than they did when they were happening. By the time I'm home it's become a triumph and I crash out full of a sense of achievement. I can feel her touch all over me.

Twelve

Thursday

I woke in a trance, head busting with a hangover that would kill an elephant. The only thing I could think of doing to get everything straight in my head was to look at the accounts, so I'm sitting on my bed, the radio's blasting and I'm covered in bank notes and my filing system. It's not good. I've been cutting into the savings. However, it's an effort to worry about it. My mind keeps flashing back to Bond. I want to call her but know that would be a mistake. The night has taken its toll on me but I'm full of nervous energy, fired up. My body feels stronger, like the freshness you get from exercise.

So much happened, so many feelings. I want to speak with her. She wants to see me again, she told me. Covered in the light-coloured banknotes I'm buzzing: money and sex. I can see how one devours the other. With the clothes and the expenses, the way I've been smoking, the profits are melting, but I don't seem to care. This is dangerous. The reasons why I was making money are clear and now they're being stripped away.

I force myself to think without my mind wandering back to Bond. I have to get the ounce for the party tonight. If Freddy's out that could be a problem. Should have done it days ago but I've smoked nearly a half in the last two days. Crazy. I start to work out a new schedule but Bond creeps in again. Something has changed. If I stop selling then it's back to being a schoolkid – but does that matter? Would she still go for that or is she hung up on the idea of me having draw and some cash? I feel confused. I let a girl in, I knew this would happen. My values are under threat.

I leap off the bed and stash the files and cash. Then I pull on some jeans and a denim shirt. I reach down for the boots. One of them has some dry powder on the toe. I can't remember how it got there. Was I sick on the way back crossing the bridge? The walk back is a mystery. I pull the jacket on and reach into the pockets to check for the kit. It's all there, even the Clipper and that's a miracle – that it survived the thousand lights of the party. My hand rummages and comes up against something slimy, plastic. I pull out a handful of tissue, torn foil and a mound of dick rubber. I almost retch. She must have stashed it in my pocket last night but I can't see it in my memory, don't even remember using them. I was so blitzed. I dump the remains in my waste-paper bin, think again and pull them out, wrap them in some writing paper and bury them under the rubbish. I walk over to the mobile and whip it off the charger, stick it in my jeans. Then I grab the cap and the shades, walk out to the stairs.

"What's this then?" My mother is out on the landing, beaming at me.

"I'm going out."

She fingers the edge of the jacket.

"Oh, it's Trev's. I'm trying it out, might buy it off him."

"With what?"

"My savings."

"I see. Heard you come in last night, rather late."

"It was a party."

"You know we don't mind you being out late . . ."

"And?"

"Nothing, just look after yourself, that's all."

"Yeah, I'll see you later, then . . ."

"Charles, Dominic's coming round tomorrow. Will you be here?" She sounds casual.

"What for?"

"Will you be here?"

"Yeah, sure."

"We thought it would be good for the family to get together."

"That's what I thought a long time ago."

"I know. But it takes me a while to ... decide on things, you understand."

"I'll be here, don't worry. I haven't seen him for a while myself."

"Yes, that's what he said. I spoke with him on the phone again last night. Anyway ..."

"OK."

"I take it you'll be late again tonight?"

"There's a good chance yeah, another party."

"Your social life has really picked up."

"It's the holidays. Everyone's going."

"Then I'll probably see you tomorrow."

"I'll be here."

I start for the stairs. She's walking off towards the bathroom.

"Like the sunglasses."

I head on down to the Fox.

The park is full of people, tents and parked cars. There must be some kind of event on. I cut round the river side and glide past the pagoda. Dominic seems to be gaining favour, drifting back in. Now he's got an invite, that's a real breakthrough. I knew my mother would soften. If I've got time I'll go round and see him this afternoon. The prospect of my brother making it up with them is a good feeling on top of everything else: Bond lifts me, the thought of the party tonight, everything is slotting into place. I'm doing an ounce for Theo so that should drag me back into money land. I get out of the park and pull up at Freddy's.

The last time I saw him he was making an effort to dress up for his date. Today's he back in the usual gear – tired jeans and a rough shirt, ancient boots. The room is a mess, like he had a big session the night before.

"Enter."

He leads me over to the sofa. I pull out the cash.

"Better take two ounces."

"Business good then?"

"Moving, yeah?"

He sits next to me and reaches down to the floor. Amongst all the trash there is a large block covered in newspaper. I can see the print, it's a foreign lettering system.

"What's that?"

"I'm out of bush, Charles, but . . ."

"Oh man, that all you got? People aren't so into resin."

"But this is not like anything you've smoked, you have my personal guarantee."

"All I know is I got to give a guy something and he's expecting a certain type of . . ."

"He'll love it, don't worry."

I look up at the dealer. He's fumbling with the edges of the parcel. His eyes are all over the place.

"You stoned?"

"Absoletum . . . obsoletum."

"Huh?"

"Latin, Charles." He breaks into laughter.

I've never seen him so trashed before, not even when he was on the acid. The cloud that was forming in my head about the change in gear starts to evaporate.

"You wrecked from this stuff?" I point to the parcel he's still struggling with.

"Shit yes, can't even open it. Here."

He passes me the bundle. It's heavy. I peel back one edge of the paper to reveal grey slab. It's about two inches thick.

"Woh."

"Yeah, that's a weight. You have to smash it, 's rock hard."

He takes it from me and puts it back on the floor. Fiddling again in the trash he pulls out a little hammer and proceeds to whack the edge of the slab. Bits fly everywhere.

"Easy, man."

"Relax. There's at least an ounce on the carpet already."

Then he picks up a chunk about the same size as a cigarette pack.

"Got a lighter?"

"Yeah?" I pass him the Clipper.

"So hard you have to burn it to do anything." He flares the lighter and burns a corner. I can smell a sharp, heavy incense coming off it. "Better than oil, man. This is double zero, real head-frying batch as well."

With his first finger and thumb he breaks a pea-sized chunk off and drops it in a paper. "Here, roll that up. On trial. You might need to burn it in silver first." He passes me a household sized silver-foil roll then wanders over to his music stack. I tear off a strip of the foil and fold the pea into it, twist it tight then heat it with the Clipper. He comes back and music crashes in.

"What's this?"

"Hammond organ stuff. It straights me right out. I got the whole day ahead of me, only had one bong."

It's a hard blues thing, lots of saxaphone and guitar.

"Sounds a bit sloppy to me."

"This is before the days of sampler's Charles. Lots of hiss."

"Hmm." I lick the spliff up and fire it. Then I sink back into the sofa. The joint has a bush taste even though it's resin. I hog it for a while.

"You keep smoking. I'm gonna clean up a bit." He lurches to his feet.

"Hey, Freddy."

"Yeah."

"What's a 'bong'?"

A smile spreads across his face. "Shit, Charles, you know how to make a guy feel old."

"I never seen one. Seen pipes, heard of them – but never actually . . . seen one." The same maniac's grin that is on his face is pushing my own lips apart. My hearing's gone weird, the music's rushing in. I can feel my skin getting hot.

"You want to get trashed?"

"Well, I'm in a good mood an' this – " I wave the joint – "is interesting. You know sometimes it feels right kinda, getting wrecked I mean? In itself, nothin' else."

"Oh I know that feeling. In that case."

He goes into the kitchen and comes back with a stand-up water pipe. It's at least two and a half feet tall, a dirty red colour.

I'll fill it for you." He kneels on the floor with the

bong between his legs. After breaking another pea-sized lump from the slab he heats it and breaks it into a little silver cup that is sticking out of the side of the tube on a long stem.

"I can see this stuff going down fast." Already I'm feeling blasted. I am at one with the sofa. But it's true that I'm in a good mood, the blow will push it further.

Freddy starts to heat the pea with my Clipper, keeping his mouth over the top end of the tube. The tube starts to fill with thick blue-grey smoke. I watch eagerly. I can hear him sucking gently and for a moment I'm worried about his saliva. Freddy is not the safest member of the human race to exchange spit with. Then again, I've shared plenty of joints with him. I watch from the sofa. When the grains in the silver cup are all dead he leans back with his palm covering the top of the tube. He blows out a plume of smoke.

"Man, this'll send you right to Tangiers."

"Yeah, Freddy, come on and pass it."

I can take it. The last week has hardened me, even after the blast from last night. He waves for me to join him and I shuffle over.

"Just take it all and keep it in as long as you can."

I blow out, approach the tube and circle the top with my lips. In one mighty effort I inhale the smoke. I can feel it rush down my throat, sweet and dry. It's cool, but after a second with my mouth clenched tight I can feel my throat hairs tickling. My face gets very hot and my eyes water. After a few seconds I lean back and exhale. The smoke comes out thick and fills the space of the room.

"Not bad."

I make it back to the sofa. The first thing to go is my legs. They're walking off somewhere, leaving me behind. Then I get the full lift, the THC rushes round my bloodstream, filling me with the stone.

"Man."

"You dig? He, *he*."

Freddy stands in front of me, offers me a cigarette. A trembling hand reaches out. It looks a long way from my body. He lights the stick and I get it to my mouth. The smoke tastes like a spliff. My body is set. The sofa is a warm, comfy home. Freddy sits next to me and starts building a spliff.

"People say dope doesn't get you there are talking bullshit. Double zero is fucking shut-down boy."

"Yeah. I agree with you." My words are mumbled, difficult to get out.

"You just chill, Charles."

We sit there listening to the sixties music, chatting.

After an hour I decide that some fresh air might be a good idea. I try to get serious. Our conversation is broken by laughter, me rubbing my forehead trying to activate my brain.

"Same price?"

"What?"

"The double stuff."

"Double zero?"

"Yeah."

"No, it's not the same. Sorry."

"Well . . ."

"Oh, well, alright."

"You what?"

"Here." He puts his hand out and I put a note into it. "More." I put another note down and he nods his head. This is repeated until I lose count but I know it's about twenty over. I must make the adjustments but mathematics is the last thing on my mind. With his fist of money he staggers off to the mantlepiece and grabs the scales. I watch him weighing out. It takes him a long time.

"Fucking trashed, man."

"Open the curtains."

"It's dark out there, innit?"

"No . . . what time is it then?"

"Round seven I think."

"You joking?"

"Nah. Here." He hands me a bulging bank bag of the resin. "You going then?"

"S'pose I should. Got a party on."

"Have a good time."

"Oh, I will."

I can't believe it's so late. I wanted to call Bond, check my brother. I get to my feet and make for the door.

"Hey, Charles."

"Yeah?"

"Don't operate any heavy machinery, will you?"

I'm out in the street and I'm boxed. Cars whiz past in slow motion. My movements are constricted, like I'm wading through maple syrup. Theo is going to love this. I start trying to think – punch up Bond's number on the mobile. Should I ring now? She might be going out and I should ring now – but I'm trashed, can hardly stand up. She won't be able to tell. I trigger her code. It rings as I stare up at the sky. The clouds are taking on the orange glow from streetlight gas being warmed. Odd, I think, this coloured sky. The answer-machine cuts in. I don't leave a message. I shouldn't be making any calls on Trev's line but this is urgent. I'll try her at regular intervals. I saddle up and head for home, wobbling through the park on the Fox.

Trev is coming out on to the street as I pull up outside my block.

"Thought you'd be out all night."

He's smiling, dressed up and ready to go out. I can't tell him about the party – it was a private invite and I'm talking business with Theo.

"No, just been out for a bit."

"Getting wasted?"

"Yeah, yeah."

"You doing anything tonight?"

"Not really, thought I'd take it easy, you know – night in, I think."

"Don't fancy a beer?"

"Uh-uh, not tonight, boy."

"I'm meeting up with Clark and Bruce over at the Moon. Clark said he was gonna bell you."

"I didn't hear from him, no."

"He got the training thing. Good news, innit?"

"Yeah." It's a strain chatting with Trev. I want to get inside, have a shower, eat something, then rest up until the party.

"We'll be down there anyway."

"Safe."

"How'd the date go?"

"Uh, it was rather good actually."

"Let's have the story then."

"Nah, you have to wait. I better get in, Trev." I want to tell him about it but there's no time – head's all foggy and needs a recharge. I decide to leave him with a taster. "It was good, everything I was hoping for."

"Oh yeah?"

"Truth. But I tell you later, yeah?"

"Alright. Maybe see you down there, otherwise give us a call."

"Sweet."

I wave him off and stumble into the flat.

Thirteen

The Party

I can hear music out in the street. Always a good sign. I hammer on the door and Julia sticks her head out and smiles at me. She looks drunk, sloppy lips, lazy eyes.

"Come in, Charles. Good to see you again."

She gives me a kiss on the cheek as I pass her in the hall. I can feel her body through a thin, kid's-style dress she's wearing. Even though she looks plastered – and I believe women are at their least attractive when they're drunk – a series of sex images flick through my mind. The collision with Bond has awakened me more to sex than I had thought possible. It's been a fairly constant flow in my thinking for the last few years' but now I'm aware of the potential the calling has doubled. Julia looks at me as though she knows what I'm thinking, takes my arm and guides me into the main room. It's a wall of bodies in front of me. Music fills the air. The room's dark, just a red glow in one of the corners and some light coming from the kitchen.

"Want a drink?"

"Cheers."

I'm feeling straight, clear-headed. Back in the flat I stood under the shower, gradually adjusting the temperature until the water was cold, letting it bring me back from the stone. After dressing I went downstairs and raided the fridge, nuked a chicken Kiev and had two cups of strong coffee. I got a mini-cab over.

Julia worms her way back from the kitchen with a glass of red liquid. "Theo had a go at making some punch."

I take a sip. "Bit pokey."

"I topped it up with two bottles of tequila."

"Oh."

I'm finding it very hard not to stare at her breasts. Their shape is perfectly defined by the cotton of the dress, like she's rammed two oranges down the front. I wish I'd been able to get hold of Bond but it was the answer-machine every time I rang. I want a repeat but it'll have to wait. I have to see Theo, then I'll get into the party. I can call her tomorrow.

"So what you been doing with yourself?"

She's swaying a little, taking gulps of her drink.

We're hemmed in by the crowd, pushed together. I'm looking round the room, trying to find a face I know.

"This 'n that. Pretty busy, isn't it?"

"Oh, there's loads more people coming. This is the advance party." She laughs at her own tiny joke. I offer her a cigarette and light it for her. The music switches from the common seventies jazz stuff to a reggae track, then breaks into rock. I have to shout now it's so loud.

"I know this band – the music I mean." It's Radical. I can hear the jungle beat under the guitars, cutting them out altogether now and again, the vocal rushing in.

"Theo's got lots of bands hanging round. I can't keep up."

I stare at her. Her face is tilted slightly. She looks as though she might break into tears, like a sad little girl lost amongst adults.

"What's wrong?"

"Nothing. I'll find Theo for you, come on."

She takes me by the arm again and we move through the crowd. She stops to speak with someone every few yards, introduces me. They're all older than me, well dressed but not stiff with it, more like club-types. This must be Theo's gang of easy professionals. Most of them are smoking cigarettes, talking loud, drinking the punch from paper cups. I feel relaxed, in control, glad I'm not still stoned from the afternoon.

"He's over there."

Theo is sitting on the sofa, deep in conversation with a young black guy. When he sees me he looks up and nods.

"Alright, Daddy C?" He sounds friendly this time, not the stern politeness of the office.

"Yeah, how you doing?"

"Good. You got a drink? Yeah. You arrived in the nick of time, boy . . ." He motions to the guy on the sofa. "He's got some sweet bush apparently, but I was holding out till you got here. The party's dry."

I stare at the other seller. His head is shaven, black eyes, a scruffy denim jacket and jeans. He stands up.

I speak directly to Theo. "Thought it was all arranged. I got it on me."

"No problem. I didn't think he'd have any, that's all. Have to keep my options open."

"Of course. But it's not bush, better than that."

"Oh yeah?"

The dealer speaks. "This bush I got can beat anything else, boy."

"Yeah, well try some a this then." I dip a hand into my leather and slide out a spliff, hold it up to Theo. "I was going to smoke it on the way over but I got a cab."

This is a lie. I've brought some weighed-out bags with me but after the water-pipe experience I decided not to get too wasted, so I've kept my own supply down to a minimum. I rolled up three joints in an attempt to ration myself. I fire the joint and push it in between Theo's smiling lips.

"May as well sit down." I fall back on the sofa and take a hit on my glass.

After a few tokes Theo is all smiles.

"I'll take the ounce."

" 'S a bit more money."

He goes for his wallet but I stop him.

"Let's go in another room, yeah?"

"You getting shaky, Charles?"

"Just being sensible."

"All the people in this room are gonna be smoking this in a few minutes anyway."

"They don't need to know where it come from, though, do they?"

"Alright, case proved. Follow me, boys."

"Him too?"

"Yeah, for something else. The blow's just his side-line."

We walk round the crowd and push through a door out in the hallway. It's a small bedroom. I drop the ounce on the bed.

"There you go. It's another . . ." I flick some fingers to show how much. The other guy picks the bag up and has a look. "You want some?"

"Funny man."

He goes round to the other side of the bed, opens his jacket and pulls out a little sack made of soft, black cloth. Theo is counting out some bills.

"I'll take two grams."

"Wise."

The sack pulls apart to reveal lines of small plastic wraps tucked into tiny pockets. There are at least ten packages. He pulls four out.

"You reckon I'll get rid of all of it?"

"Sure. I know a bunch who'll want some. Not here yet."

They talk in an easy tone which indicates this isn't the first time they've met. I can imagine Theo enjoying coke. He must have the money for it. The dealer smiles at me.

"You want some of it?"

"Nah. Wouldn't mind seeing your bush though."

He laughs and pulls out a little metal box, tosses it on to the bed.

"Nothin' to hide."

It's from the same batch as the stuff Freddy was selling – same colour, cut, smell, everything. I hand it back to him. Theo gives me the money. As I count it he lifts a round mirror off the wall and spills some of the bag's contents on to it. Starts to cut the powder, running a razor through the pile and sweeping a smaller clump to one side. He makes two lines. I watch as he rolls a twenty and leans over the mirror, sucks the contents into his nose. He sniffs, taps the nostril and sniffs again.

"Hallelujah. I've found my calling, a back-packer in Bolivia. Man."

The sight makes me feel slightly nauseous. I've seen plenty of snorting before, usually amphetamine, and it always makes me feel uncomfortable. There's something clinical about it, though it's not as bad as pins. When it gets to that you're finished.

It's a strange atmosphere in this little room. Theo is still smoking the room out, acting the money man with a fist of cash. Me and the other guy stare at each other, not quite sure if we're rivals or not. We look down at the mirror at the same time.

"Give the pickney a go."

"Fuck you."

"You want a bit Charles?"

I can hear the thud of the party outside.

"Sure." I've never touched it before but I don't want

to look a dick in front of these two. "Why not? it's a party, innit?"

I've turned it down in the past and thought the users were suckers. Now I feel differently towards it, even though the sight of Theo a minute ago turned my stomach. I've got some status now, things have changed. I should try it. It's only desperate people that get badly into it, a guy like me can enjoy the benefits of adult activities and not blow it. Besides, Theo's got his act together and he clearly takes it big time. It's not the drug that messes with you, it's the way it positions you in society. If you're on top then there's no problem. There are plenty of junky doctors and accountants – doesn't change their lives at all.

I step over to the mirror, roll one of the notes Theo gave me into a tight tube, and stoop. I ram the stuff into my head, pull it deep down into my lungs like I did with the water-pipe, then I stand tall and stare at the guy across the bed. The back of my throat is stinging.

"Yaah. No battery acid sprinkled in there, I hope. You having a go on some?"

My body feels massive, like the top of my head is caressing the ceiling. It's a wild rush, like adrenalin but without the insecurity, the chaos. It's reassuring. I want to run out of the room and rip it in the party, cane the bar and the wraps I brought, kick it up. The dealer smiles at me.

"No, I'll stick with smoking for a while."

Theo slaps me on the back and steers me out of the room and back into the throng. I'm breathing very quickly, buzzing. The music has gone crazy – some strange jazz bouncing off the walls, broken piano chords, a funk bass line with chippy guitar on top, a screech of trumpet. The faces in the crowd are beaming, yellow flesh moist with the heat and drink. Theo lurches over to one group. Some guy shakes my hand, looks familiar for a second, but then I'm turning to another group and a girl's trying to dance, spilling wine all over her dress, dropping the glass, way past caring. A guy wraps his arms round her from behind and lifts her into the air, swings her into the mass.

We crash into the kitchen and I dip a mug into the punch, drop the thick orange liquid down my throat and charge back to the crowd. The mood's changed, livened up. I'm still on the powder burn but it's mellowing. I feel it replaced by an easy confidence, the sense that things are going well, my life is flawless. Theo clicks his fingers in front of my face.

"This resin's wicked, Charles. Buzzing on it already. You want me to ask around for you, check with some of my friends?"

"Sure, I've got some more on me. You do that."

Now I'm left in the middle of the room as Theo sees a friend walking in. Julia is suddenly by my side. She starts to speak but has to stop and start again, so drunk the words are running away from her.

"Ah . . . you got some to smoke Charles, a joint?"

"Yeah." I whip out the second joint from my jacket pocket and fire it up, pass it straight over to her. "You alright?"

"Me . . . just fine. I have to watch the party king in action, not let it get to me."

Her eyes are staring after Theo. They don't seem

like a couple tonight. She looks miserable, drunk – skulking around watching her partner whilst he is all over the room, shaking hands, kissing girls on the cheek and laughing. I don't want to get in the middle of anything so I leave her with the joint and spiral off towards the sofa. I'm feeling too good to suffer a lover's tiff. I sink down into the leather, next to two girls in jeans and boots. The music is loud. I try to speak with them but the conversation is lost. The powder is filtered from my blood now. I feel a little tense, muscles strained.

For a second I consider finding the dealer and taking a bag off him, getting up again, but I'm straight enough to see the trap. It's the same bullshit I've heard from friends, doing a line at fifteen minute intervals and then the money evaporates in no time. Dumb. It was just an exploratory move on my part. I've got too much sense – will power – to get into it. Anyway, it wasn't so great that it makes instant addicts like crack does. One sniff on that and you just want more for ever if there's nothing better going on in your life. I lean back in the sofa and relax, pull out the final spliff and light it. I'll sit here in all the may-hem of the party and feel good that I can control my desires, get chill on the double zero. Maybe I'll get talking to the girls. One of them has the bright eyes, the invitation.

As I smoke and lean in to talk, the figures before me in the room are shuffling, some dancing, some heading for the kitchen to get more punch. There are little groups in the corners, whispered come-ons and carefully staggered journeys out to the landing or bathroom so two people can pretend they are alone, pretend to be having a secret romance. It's all the standard party stuff except the crowd is older than I am used to. The games are the same though. Some drink too much, others flirt. I watch it all and smile, consider some opening lines to the girl next to me with the movie-star eyes. I look up and there's a guy shaking my shoulder. He's smashed, tottering on his feet. He wears the shirt and trousers of an office suit – must have stashed the jacket in the hall. A forgotten cigarette burns in one hand, in the other he has a paper cup with drip-lines all over it.

"Theo shaid you might be able to shawt me out with shomething."

"Maybe. Man, you pissed bad, aren't you?"

"Yesh, had a good day. What do I get for ten pounds then?"

He tries to tug a wallet out of his pocket with the two fingers that aren't holding the punch cup. Liquid spills down his leg. His face is fat, bloated like he's been running out in the cold.

"Take twenty. Ten gets you nothing."

"Can't you give me . . . jusht a pinch."

"Not gonna start doing that in here, no. You must have twenty, don't be mean."

"Alright . . . one shecond." With great difficulty he stoops and manages to put the cup down. Then he takes the wallet out and flicks it open. "Schtake a cheque, do you?"

"Huh?"

"Switch?"

I just stare at him. His wallet has a bundle of cards poking out. I can see a thick rim of bank notes.

"Give me some cash, man. I'm not carrying my card machine tonight."

"Thought, swas schtandard proshedure with you people."

"Well, there are still some fields of commerce that haven't been reached by technology. Cash, or I stash."

"Fine."

He hands me a crisp twenty, fresh from a cash machine. I rummage in my leather and drag out the smallest wrap, stash the money in the other pocket next to Theo's.

"Here you go."

"Many thanks. Could you roll one for me. I'm not very good at it."

I'm about to lose my temper with the guy. He's obviously wealthy and therefore able. His voice is educated and plummy despite the alcohol interference. Just as I open my mouth my eyes flick past him and stare at a girl who has just entered the room. It takes me a moment to be sure.

"Hey, Bond, over here. Sorry, mister – 'scuse."

Then I'm in the crowd and heading over to where I just saw her by the wall.

Fourteen

I make it over to the kitchen where the bright light from a strip tube dazzles my eyes after the gloom of the party. Bond is being offered a cup of punch by Theo. He leans over and kisses her cheek. The room is full of people – two guys with Theo in smart casuals, the powderman, a group of girls with the Chelsea glow and couples chatting, making awkward pick-ups. Bond is wearing a mini-skirt, leggings and a blood-red top that hugs her figure. She laughs at Theo then stares over at me.

"Hi, Charles."

She waves me over and I give her a kiss. I am for the lips but she turns her head at the last second and I hit her cheek. I catch a look of reproach from her eyes, warning me not to come on as boyfriend, then she is smiling again, the party queen. I manage to whisper a few words to her under the music pouring from the other room.

"How are you? I tried ringing. Never thought you'd know Theo."

"We're old friends. Don't forget you're new on the beach, Charles."

"I want to talk with you."

She turns back to the others. I say nothing, feeling humbled. She is the centre of attention her and I watch as the gang surround her.

"Hey." Theo leads the group over to a gas cooker and fiddles with some blackened knives in the flame. "Fancy a knife, Charles."

He's acting the big-time dealer, spilling the chunk of blow out on to the work surface. It surprises me. It's the first time I've seen him anxious to impress. My heart sinks as I see Bond's eyes light up with admiration for the host.

"Yeah, let's all have a knife."

I hate seeing people trying to act big. If you're going to do that you have to make sure you can back it up. I went round to Freddy's place once and he was juggling with ounces, didn't give a fuck. These big balls of dope were up in the air, four or five of them, and Freddy was laughing like it was nothing. He was more interested in the juggling than the blow, even threw one over in my direction which I just caught and examined. It was clammy, like clay.

"Pass me the bottle someone."

One of the city types reaches to the work top and comes over with a two-litre drinks bottle. The bottom third has been sawn off. Theo starts trying to break chunks off the ounce. He curses.

"You have to heat it first." I say it very calmly and it cuts through the talk around the stove.

"Why don't you do it then, Charles?"

I step over to the side and heat an edge of the grey lump with my Clipper. It crumbles and I shape five small balls, lay them out in a line. Then I wrap the cuffs of the leather round my hands and pick the knives up from out of the flame where they have been resting. They glow red with the heat.

"Who's first?"

One of the guys steps forward. I tilt one knife down to the surface and touch one of the balls with the flat side. It sticks. Then I bring it back to where the guy stands holding the bottle to his mouth. I clench the knives together so the dope sizzles with the heat and a dense cloud of smoke fills the bottle. The guy starts sucking, then coughing. He steps back and bangs his chest. I get a rush of smoke in my face. The others step forward. I do them all. This was the first time I'd given knives but I was an expert. I gave Theo the largest and stuck the hot steel up into the open end of the bottle so he got a lot of heat. He had to gulp some tap water to stop the hacking. Then Bond bent her perfect head down towards the knives, placed the bottle rim between her lips and turned her eyes up to me. She took all the smoke and kept it in without a cough. I did my own, holding the bottle in my mouth and crossing the knives by watching through the plastic.

"Man, what a charge."

"Need a cigarette."

Theo and his friends grouped round the stove for another blast but I managed to work between them and Bond.

"Can we talk then?"

"Charles, relax will you. You look really wound up about something."

"After the other night I thought we could get together again."

"Maybe we can. I don't know. You're not my only male friend though, remember that."

She keeps smiling, like she's talking to an idiot. I take out a cigarette, try to keep my cool.

"I thought everything was sorted, Bond."

"What are you being so pushy about? If it happens again then good, but we only fucked, Charles."

"That quite a big deal to me actually."

"So I heard."

"What d'you mean by that?"

Now my stomach tenses. All I want is to lead her off to one of the bedrooms, make it right again. She just smiles at me.

"Bond? Stop fucking around."

Again she ignores me, looks over my shoulder. I spin round and see Lenny walking through the crowd, pushing his way into the kitchen. He comes over, picks her up in a hug. I pull hard on my cigarette.

"Alright, Charles? Thought Theo might have asked you along."

"Hi, Lenny. Alright?"

Bond steps in close to him. So, Lenny might have told her I was inexperienced but how the fuck would he know? Why are these people so close? I start seeing some of the connections. It must have been Lenny who gave my number to Theo.

"How's business?"

"Fine."

Bond wraps around him in a tight hug, rustling his hair with her nose and then breaking free, laughing.

"Charles wants a commitment."

"From you? He'll be lucky."

The cigarette smoke is drifting up into my eyes, making me blink in pain. I can't think of anything to say. She sounds very casual, unconcerned, and I suddenly see that it really was nothing to her.

Theo smiles at me. "Listen, Charles, half the men in this room have been trying to get a 'commitment' out of Bond for years. You were lucky to get what you did . . ."

Bond gives him a joke punch in the ribs and laughs.

"Bastard. I just pick and choose."

"From all the sweeties, yeah."

I'm dazed, can't think. Watching them play out the brother–sister routine is making me feel sick. I taste bile through the cigarette smoke.

"Hello, Bond baby."

It's the dealer, stealing up behind her. He kisses her and puts an arm round her waist, lifts his hand so the top rolls up and he touches flesh.

"Sly, watch your paws, man." She's giggling, enjoying the attention. She talks with Sly like he's another old friend.

Lenny has a wide smile on his lips, bloodshot eyes. "Come on, Bond, I got something on me. We can chill in one of the other rooms."

I stand in the kitchen, staring at the girl, the lust in the men's faces round her. For minutes I've been silent, motionless in the chaos of the party. From nowhere I feel a surge of rage. I don't know if it's the hot-knife or the coke's last whisper, Theo's arrogance, Lenny sharing her sex secrets about me, the dealer rubbing up against her ass in front of me – but anyway, I stop caring. My shame is gone. I'm not someone you can ignore. I step up to her, push into Sly in his battered denims.

"Get your hand off her, you fuck."

He knows I want her and smiles at me, grips her waist, slides a hand up to her breast. I should leave, this is a mistake. Reasons scream at me again: get out, forget the girl, get away from here. There are other things at stake here though. I can't just accept the laughter between them when she told Lenny I was fresh and it confirmed his suspicion – the ugly laughter afterwards. I'm angry. Am I going to walk out or face this guy Sly? He was pushing it earlier, thinks he's something just because he's selling powder. I'm better than this group of people. They're sick, no truth, nothing real between them.

Bond tries to stop it. She can see what's coming.

"Charles, settle down. When you get a bit older you'll see it's not so clear cut, what you want, it's not so simple . . ."

Her attempt to calm me has the opposite effect.

Although we're about the same age, Sly gives me a twisted grin and hugs her waist even tighter. He thinks I'm still a kid.

"You heard me?"

I move closer. He breaks free from her. Bond looks scared.

"Charles, what you doing?"

I push him but there's no weight behind my fist, not close enough. He backs up against the stove and I follow. As he raises an arm to protect himself I step in again, throw a tight punch and clip him on the side of the head. My hand hurts. There are screams from behind me. He rushes into me, almost lifting me off my feet, and we crash into some people on the other side of the room. Lots of noise now. The cigarette burns my lip and I spit it out. He's still got me pinned, tries to get a leg free to kick. I chop a fist down on to his neck and his grip loosens. He leans back and kicks me but I feel no pain now, crash into him again. This time I catch him with a fist on his nose, slide the hand down to his chest and get a grip on the denim. Than I yank him closer, lift a knee into his stomach, pound the side of his head with my right until the skin splits. He's yelling now. His legs go and he crashes back against the floor cupboards. I try to connect my foot with his head but he rolls to one side and makes it to his feet again. He stumbles into the party.

"Fuck, Charles, leave it – he's going."

I break free from Theo's arms. There's no strength there.

"Fuck you."

I rush after him and the kitchen people follow after

me. He's half-way across the room but his legs are stiff and I catch him before he reaches the hall. There are dancers all around us. At first they think it's nothing when I start wrestling with the guy. We roll around the room.

I'm not giving up on this one. After turning into stone in the kitchen I want the release the fight is giving me. I feel a pain in my foot. Sly is stomping on it. He's wearing Cats and it feels like my toes are breaking. I find his face in the mesh of bodies and stick my hand into it, trying to get his eyes, but I hit his mouth, rip my hand out as fast as I can and feel the flesh tear as his cheek gives. Then the side of my head is burning. He's got my ear between his teeth and I know I'll lose it unless I'm quick – feel the cartilage snapping.

"Fucker!"

I form a hammer fist with my left and snake it round to his head, whack it into the side of his neck, then further round so I hit his throat, bang into the apple. He drops.

I kick him free.

"You fucking animal, get out! Get off him!

Bond is at the side of the clearing, screaming over the music. I shake my head, trying to wake up. The pain is coming on now. I look down at Sly and he rolls clear again, ends up with his back to a wall. I watch as he pushes himself up with his feet, sliding up the wall. He's staring at me, wants my eyes to look into his and not at the knife that rests in his left hand. It's a short stub of steel, a kitchen knife maybe. I can see it's got a wooden handle. He's trying to get up but hasn't the strength. I step over to him. His arm goes straight out from his body as he prepares to sweep round with it and get me in the leg but I'm too quick. I lift my boot a few inches off the floor and flick it down on to his wrist. Hard. I can't hear it break (the music is still thudding) but I can see it. At the end of his denim cuff his shirt is pulled back, maybe because the kitchen was hot or something. Through the skin, just above the ball of bone at the end of his hand, I see a black spurt and the smashed bone of his wrist peeks out an inch. His face contracts so all the muscles are pulling it into a scream. The he passes out.

The crowd are all around me but I push through, make it out to the hall. The music dies behind me and I can hear the shouting start up. I thud into the wall, leave a stain of blood on the cream paper. My ear feels wet and hot. My eyes are closing black and white – can't see, feel weak, don't know if I can make it. My hands are clenched in pain, battered when I hit him. I see a shape in the hall, over by the door, blocking it. I can't force my way out – feel sick, don't even know why I did it. I want to sit down, go to sleep, forget everything. There are voices behind me in the hall, sounds of people. I make a last stumble towards the figure.

"Charles?"

It's Julia. She leans on the wall, head on her chest. I can see spots of sick on her dress. She's crying, eyes all screwed up, make-up smeared.

"Theo's a bastard."

"Yeah? Julia . . ."

"Doesn't give a shit about me, none of them do."

Shouting getting closer now. Must get out, they'll kill me. My hands won't work though – can't get round her anyway.

"Julia, let me out will you. Please."

"Fucks around, doesn't care, all . . . thinks about are his other . . . bitches."

"Yeah, I'm sorry – the door, Julia."

"You want to go?"

"Please, if you could just open it for me."

"I understand. Can I come with you?"

"No, you stay here and make it up with Theo, huh?"

"That's finished. Got those bitches round tonight and that's the last thing I'm going to take – no, over."

"Great, you tell him but can you . . .?"

She steps aside and pulls the door open for me. I fall through and land on the pavement, roll into the street. The air wakes me up a bit and I get over to a parked car, hide on the other side against the tyre when the party vigilantes finally make it past the dejected hostess and rush through to the street. They split into groups and make off down the street but I'm still there when they get back a few minutes later, their interest gone and their thirst renewed.

"Must have had a car."

"Well, it was as much the other guy's fight anyway. His fault, I mean."

I'm covered in blood and dirt, can smell the drain I'm lying next to. I check my pockets. The money and stash are still there.

"He's in deep shit anyway."

"Truth."

I crawl away from the car and start across the

square. After a few minutes I'm strong enough to stand and I start pacing my way back to the river. There are no clouds and it's very cold. Up above, the stars are brighter than I've seen them for a very long time.

It took me over an hour to get to Spence. He was the only person I knew I could get out of bed without disturbing parents or a girlfriend. He also knows how to fix cuts and I had a few. More than that, Spence is a friend, trustworthy. I was alone on the streets walking back to Clapham. In a city this big it always surprises me how dead it gets after midnight. I tried to flag a cab but the driver pulled off when I got up close, so I guessed Spence would be a bit shaken when he saw me, bloody and beaten. Instead he looked easy, said nothing, pulled me into the living room and sat me down on his sofa. Then he went through to his back rooms and came back with a small aid kit – bandages, disinfectant, all that stuff.

"You got a smoke?"

"Yeah."

"Might ease the pain."

He sits down and rolls one up. It's the first time I've been in his flat when he isn't playing music.

"You need stitching really, kiddo."

"Nah, fuck that. I'm not sitting in a cubicle for three hours waiting around for a sleepy doctor."

"Alright, I got some steri-strip – that might hold you together . . . but the ear . . ." He turns my head in his hands and I let out a groan of pain. "That should see a hospital."

"Tape it."

"If I do that then I have to cover it in iodine first and that's gonna hurt."

"No more than it does already."

He stands up and examines me through the joint smoke.

"Fucking mess, Charles. What you doing walking into this? More Ben's style or mine even." Spence broke his nose playing football once and for two weeks he let us all think it was a fight that caused it. He's been cut a lot of times. He goes on. "I been drinking, you know, can't be held responsible for this. Thought you were coming down the pub anyway."

"Wish I had."

"So what happened?"

"Not like you to ask questions."

"This is me fixing you up. Least I deserve is the gossip."

To Spence it is a normal event, something to laugh about later. Now that I'm inside and safe I feel the shock hitting me. I've never been through this, never even been to casualty with a cut before. I try asking myself what happened but I can't get a clear picture in my head.

"Some guy pissed me off."

"In a big way."

"Yeah, and there was a . . . shit, it was a party and I just lost it, got mad with Bond . . ."

"Ah, the true root of all evil . . ."

"An' got in a fight with this guy because of her . . ."

"Money is pure in comparison."

"Bitch. This guy . . . Fuck!" I cry out in pain. He is

splashing a dark purple liquid on the side of my head – pours some into a cloth and dabs at my ear. "Man, that hurts."

He searches me for other cuts, finds one on my hand, across the knuckle.

"Anywhere else?"

"Nah. Got my foot though."

"Cut your foot?"

"Crushed it."

"Better take your boot off."

He tokes on the joint as I slide it off.

"You were saying?"

"I think it's bad. He was a seller."

"Yeah?"

Spence stares down at my bare foot. The flesh around the toes is grey, bloodless.

"Not good."

"Why?"

"Don't know, 's a funny colour. You better have a drink."

" 'Bout time."

"I'm right down on Scotch, have to be Pernod."

"I hate Pernod."

"So write an' tell me next time before you get in the fight."

"Sorry."

He pours me a tumbler of the clear liquid.

"All of it."

I down it, pinch my face up against the taste of aniseed. "Rank."

"Have another.'

"I drank a lot at the party, Spence."

"Drink! You'll thank me in a minute."

I swallow. He kneels at my leg and picks the damaged foot up in both hands.

"Shout if you want." He runs his thumbs along each thin bone that stretches out under the skin. The pain is intense. I let out a howl. "They're all straight. Might be a hair fracture though, but you'll be OK."

"Great." Tears in my eyes.

"Think I'll have a shot. Had this girl round the other night and she said all she liked was Pernod so I got a bottle in, ordered it from a mate of mine . . ."

"Ferry booze?"

"Yeah. Anyway, she comes round and straight off she drinks one glass and can't stand it, almost spat it out in her lap . . ."

"Charming."

"Truth was she's never had it before, has she? Just thought it sounded good, sophisticated. So I'm stuck with it."

"How'd the date go?"

"I rushed it a bit and she ran out. Same problem every time. I pull it out an' . . ."

"What?"

"No sense waiting is there?"

"Not very subtle."

"Forget it. I asked her friend out. So, what happened with you? You look a bit better now at least."

"Yeah, thanks Spence."

I start pulling my boot back on.

"I told you, it was a fight – crazy of me, I just . . . lost it, you know."

"Course, happens with me all the time. Thought you were a businessman though."

"No, it was . . . out of character, I guess."

"Who was the guy then?"

"Some black guy called Sly."

"Yeah? I know him."

I look up at my friend, trying to see if he's kidding me or not. He raises his glass and drinks. Then he takes a last toke and passes it to me. He speaks.

"He hurt as bad as you?"

"Worse."

"What worse?"

"Kicked his arm into little bits."

"Shit." He reaches out for the joint.

"Just roll another one, I've only had one toke."

"Yeah, you should enjoy it . . ."

He fills our glasses then sits down and starts to roll. He's like a little animal the way he skins up, a rodent fiddling with the papers.

"So what d'you say about this guy?"

"He's one of Deacon's runners, inee? You couldn't a picked a better way of pissing him off."

"Shit."

"Yeah, too right. I quite like Sly actually. Pity, all sorts of trouble gonna start up now."

"Don't Spence, I'm not in the mood. The guy pulled a knife on me."

"Don't mean nothing. You beat on him then Deacon comes after you. He's been watching you, hasn't he?"

"Only so I don't push in on him."

"Well, I think you just done that. An' it not just you. All of us are gonna feel it."

Fifteen

Friday

I wake up with Spence shaking my shoulder. He's holding a mug of tea out to me.

"You look better than you did last night anyway."

"Feel it." I slump forward so I'm sitting on the sofa, toss the covers off me. I'm still fully clothes and my legs feel hot and cramped in the jeans. "You got a shower?"

"Yeah."

He brings me a towel.

"Second door down the hall."

It's a grimy little room, cracked tiles and a stained

shower curtain but I climb in and blast myself until I wake up. This is the first time I've ventured out of his living room. There's a dirty mirror above the sink and I check my injuries. The ear looks swollen but I can sweep my hair around to hide it. My foot has gone back to a normal bruise colour and I can move all the toes. Other than that there are a few cuts but I don't look too rough. At my age the recovery is rapid. I go back to the living room where Spence is on the phone. He's put some music on, some up-beat reggae, and the room is full of light from the front window, seeping through the light curtains.

"What time is it?"

"One minute, yeah . . .?"

He goes on talking into the phone and I pull my boots on, finish drying my hair. The fight has become a memory and I can think about it clearly now. I keep wondering about Bond. Even though she was shrieking maybe I can still rescue it, talk it through with her. Then I remember Lenny's sick grin and her words, sexing it with all the guys around her. I had such a different picture of what was going to happen the next time I met her, another world away from the party, where we could get it down to a relationship. It shocks me that I was so stupid to believe in it. All my instincts had told me to leave it but the night with her was so good. I think about that night for a while.

Then there's Sly and the crippled arm coming into my thoughts. I lean back on the sofa and light a cigarette, slurp the tea. In the space of a few hours I've managed to switch the situation completely. I've got problems now.

"It's just after two."

"Shit. There was something I have to . . . today I . . ."

"You should be alright for today."

He drops the phone in the cradle and swivels round to his system, turns the music up a little. What he said registers with me and disturbs the feeling that I have some other arrangement, have forgotten something. I turn to him.

"You mean the fight?"

"Yeah. Think it might be wise to take some precautions though."

"I can't think straight right now, Spence."

"Listen, this room is nice and cosy and safe . . . but out there you got things going on. Deacon is gonna be mightily pissed off."

"So what do I do?"

"Get out or sort it out."

"I think a trip to Rio is a little excessive, don't you?"

"You haven't even got a passport have you?"

"Get real, Spence. No, I'll just keep my head down for a while. It wasn't all my fault."

"Oh, you're appealing for reason from the guy . . . right, very likely. It won't be so easy. You should go to him then."

"No way."

"Go to see him and pay him something or whatever. Sort it. No, I shouldn't even say that." Spence takes one of my cigarettes. He looks cool but thoughtful. "What I should say is, it isn't my problem so get the fuck out of my house."

"Spence! Take it easy with me. My head hurts."

"I'm not surprised, Charles. This is way past your

regular field of experience. Take it from someone who knows . . ." He taps the side of his nose with the cigarette and I break into laughter. "No fucking joke. You don't know this game at all. I think you'll be cool with the police . . ."

"Shit. I hadn't . . ."

"Well don't worry about it too much, I don't think they'll get called in. You've moved into the other scale of justice now, which in a way is worse 'cause you're so dumb in that respect. No, this is far more savage, what you're into now. You've only seen the good side. Deacon's been round for a long time and I've heard stories about him. This isn't a party trick with the guy. If he finds you, then he'll fuck you up bad and you can't do shit about it. You know nothing, remember?"

"Easy."

"Bit of dealing don't teach you about criminals. It's a different mentality altogether. I . . ."

"Huh?"

"I can get you a gun maybe."

"What? Excuse me, Spence, I have an appointment with reality."

"One-fifty I reckon. You must have that much. Only to wave about a bit if something goes off."

"Don't be fucking stupid."

"Serious. You feel more into it when he jumps out of a car and pastes you."

"That's not going to happen."

"Well I know for a fact – a fact, boy – that the guy has one. He keeps it round his house."

"You know where he lives?"

"Nah. I know people who been round there though and he gets it out to shit them a bit you know – bit of a crazy bastard – for kicks. Now I'm not saying he'd use it, that's something totally different, but I know he keeps it for show."

"So you're saying I should carry one then?"

"Don't sound so fucking shocked, Charles. Gun ain't nothing these days. I know people who carry them. It's more a status symbol than anything though, just to stop people messing with you."

"No, that's another level for me. I just sell herb."

"He told you not to fuck with him, you go and fuck with him, so what does he do? Least is scare you a bit."

"Maybe I will go see him. I have to think about it."

"Well, I can get one for you I think. An' if you're going round there you might need a few friends so let me know."

"Thanks, Spence."

"Sure, you'll return the favour."

He still looks relaxed, his legs crossed in the chair and the cigarette held just by his mouth. His face is set, hard and I can see the toughness in my friend. When he says the favour will come back on me I have a feeling he means it. He goes on speaking after a moment's silence.

"You have been acting a bit stuck up lately, C – but that doesn't mean your friends ditch you. You can probably count on Trev as well."

"I should get going."

I don't want to think about this now, it's scaring me. Nonetheless I feel reassured by his words, the knowledge I can rely on him, maybe Trev too.

"Well keep an eye out. I'll be around if you want to ring."

"Think it's alright to go home?"

"Don't see what choice you got."

He stands and hands me my leather from the hallway. I walk slowly to the front door.

"Watch yourself."

"See you."

Then I'm out. I light another cigarette and start down the street, working out what it is I was supposed to do today other than freak about getting shot by some maniac. It's Dominic's lunch. I step it up down to the Common.

When I get to the North Side I'm regretting not ringing for a mini-cab from Spence's flat. My foot is throbbing. I could ring from a call box but I've got no change (just a wad of notes) and anyway the phones are usually broken or stink of piss. I hate call boxes. So I decide to head for Clapham Common and hold a cab from there.

I cross the road and start across the Green and that's when I see it. Circling round the perimeter road is a blue saloon car, two guys in it. I pause for a second and change my route so I'm further from the road. It can't be Deacon, not so soon. It's the car from before I'm sure and the same fear grips me. I know I can't afford to panic and it could just be my nerves. I'm feeling frazzled from the events last night and the walk from Spence's has tired me out. I must keep moving. I make it on to the Pavement and bend round to the cab firm, past a shabby off-licence and a couple of winos who are arguing over a can of beer. All the time I can hear the car purring up behind me like a predator. I walk faster, pass the corridor of the cab place, go out on to the High Street and round the corner, then dive into the cinema bar. There's always a few people here and I can see who it is if they follow me in. Through the glass doors at the end of the room I watch the car cruise past, stop and park. Now I'm freaking. They wouldn't do anything in here. I order a coffee and sit down at one of the tables, light up a cigarette.

I've never seen a movie here. It doesn't show the kind of films I like, specialises in obscure art stuff. The bar is full of couples, girls mainly, about twenty people. I feel better in the crowd and pick up a flyer that is tucked under the ashtray, start reading to look occupied if anyone comes in. There's some soft jazz playing above the din of conversation but I hear the door slam, look up and see a big bull of a guy in his thirties. He stares at me. Then he walks directly towards me and my muscles tense, ready for whatever he pulls. He steps past my table and sits down next to a young girl. She starts stroking his hair and kissing him, looks angry with the way I'm staring at his back. I turn away and drain the coffee cup, stand up and leave. I'm late as it is – must be nearly three. I can't keep having panic attacks that I'm being followed like this. I haven't even smoked anything today, maybe that would settle me down. I go out into the street and turn towards the river.

It feels like I haven't been home for days. All the familiar sights of my neighbourhood lift my mood. I can see the same old wrecks lined up and down the kerb, the weedy flower-pots, the bits of graffiti that have lasted the elements and the scrubbing brush, the blue and red doors and new brick of my block. I wait at the bottom of the stairs and check I look alright, pull up my jeans and wipe the sweat from my brow. The walk down here took a lot of effort with the busted foot. I've been working out my problems on the way and think I've got it sorted. I'll set up a meeting through Freddy and make a cash payment to calm things down. I can afford it. On top of that I'll guarantee that I'm quitting selling. Spence was right. I only got into this to raise some quick money and I have succeeded in my aim. I may keep trading to a few select friends but there won't be any more Theos or strangers ringing me up. I've even come up with a solution for the Bond problem. I almost surprise myself how well I'm dealing with this, but I've always believed that presence is the best test of a man. There are going to be lots of demanding situations in the future that will require my cool reasoning. I'll ring her, arrange for us to talk. When I explain how I was the guy supplying the dope at the party, how it was me with the status, then she'll have to listen. Considering her behaviour and what I've learnt about her, I don't even know if I'll keep seeing her as a girlfriend but it's important to have another night with her. After that I can finish it, should I wish. Then I'll be back in control again. So it's all resolved. I make peace with Deacon, tone down my selling, chill things with Bond and wait for the birthday and the wheels. I climb the stairs up to my flat, happy with things again.

I close the door behind me. They must have gone out, I can't hear anything. The smell of food from the kitchen reminds me I haven't eaten for a long time. I walk on through.

"Charles, come in here will you?"

It's my father calling from the front room. Maybe he was asleep and I woke him. I step up to the living room door and see him stretched out on the sofa.

"Hi, Dad. Sorry I didn't get here when . . ."

When I walk into the room I see my mother and Dominic standing against the window. They're standing very close to one another, almost touching. I smile, expecting criticism for my lateness.

"You're still here, I . . ."

"Have a seat. Do you want some tea?"

"Hi, Charles." Dominic is beaming at me. He looks well-dressed for a change, like the old days. My mother leans down to the coffee table and offers me a cup.

"No thanks. Good lunch? I thought you must have gone out it was so quiet."

"No, no, we've been talking a lot, that's all."

My father turns to me as I sit next to him on the sofa. "You didn't come in last night, did you?"

"No. I was out late at the party. It went on all night, then we had breakfast and you know, just been up."

"Sounds like you had a good time." His friendliness makes me wary.

"So what have I missed?"

"Well, we had a long talk with your brother."

I scope Dominic again. He's lost his twitches, the nervousness I've got used to in the last six months.

He looks relaxed, as easy-going as he used to be. I check my mother. She looks radiant, as stress-free as he is. The whole atmosphere is one of calm.

"What's going on?"

"Dominic's moving back in. He's going back to his studies and he's moving back in."

They all stare at me to gauge my reaction.

"That's great. Back into the room I'm in now, you mean?"

"No, that's your room – " She's overdoing it, worried I'll feel pushed out – "and you can stay in it. Dominic can have your old room."

For a moment I can think of nothing to say. In the midst of all the confusion of the last few hours I feel startled by the news. Then I stand up and go over to the coffee table, pick up the cup she had offered me.

"Welcome home, Dom. Good to have you back."

"Thanks, Charles."

That breaks the tension for my mother.

"Isn't it wonderful? We've been getting on so well today and when we saw where he was living, I mean it was the best thing, wasn't it? – I don't know, before it was difficult somehow but . . ."

My father stops it. "Yes, darling. Now Charles, can you pass me . . . ah, thanks." I hand him the tray from the coffee table.

"How soon then – you moving in?"

"Tonight. If that's OK?" He glances at my mother and she smiles back.

"Great. Well I'll get changed and come down in a bit. I've been in these clothes for a while."

"See you in a while."

"I'll come up in a minute, Charles."

"Give me a knock first, will you."

"Yeah."

I pace out of the room and up the stairs.

"When did this happen then?"

"Over the last week or so."

"Didn't get the urge to tell me then?"

"You haven't exactly been around much lately, have you?"

Already the confidence is creeping back into his voice. He's no longer the sad, failed elder brother in a bedsit.

"I've got a lot going on at the moment, Dom."

"How do you feel about me coming back?"

I had time to change but he came in before I could do the accounts. I lie back on the bed and stare up at him.

"I feel fine about it. If you can patch it up then . . . it's good." I had always thought he might come back. With his absence it was easy to think about it, to miss him, to feel the family was incomplete. Now it's happened I'm not sure how it will be with him back. The expression on my mother's face confirmed her happiness, and that I have to go along with, but maybe I was getting used to the space. The times we've met lately he's been judgemental, disapproving. I don't want him watching over me. Dominic can see this in my face.

"I won't step in on anything you're doing. Feel free to carry on with it, the selling."

"Thanks."

"Might even take some off you myself from time to time. Do I get a discount?"

The attempt at humour doesn't impress me.

"You've been out for a long time, Dom, it's good to have you back – but don't get all . . . chummy with me please. There have been some changes for me in the last few weeks. As for the selling though, I'm getting out, kaput. In fact, I'm in deep shit . . ."

Now I've got the attention. It was him with all the news. I want him to know what I'm involved in, how his return is a side issue. I tell him everything except the details of the fight, allow him to think I was attacked. I don't want him thinking I got violent or anything. He starts blustering immediately.

"Shit, Charles, you have to go see the guy. Man. Go see Freddy tonight, yeah? – that's probably your best idea."

"Yes Dom, I know."

"You got any money?"

"A bundle."

He pauses, obviously surprised, then carries on with the voice of concern. I play it cool, lounging on the bed.

"You can talk with him, pay Deacon and get out. God, I hope you can settle it before . . ."

"Relax, Dom." I'm thinking about Bond. I've already sorted the Deacon thing in my head.

"I'll help you."

"That's very kind but I think you should concentrate on sorting out your own life. What are you doing anyway?"

"I've got my study place back – well, kind of. I'll be

through in another year." This brings an old and distasteful memory back to me. A long time ago I used to envy him. He could be making it in a year or two, back on the top again. I've got used to his sulks, apathy and laziness. It's easy to forget Dominic is gifted, has some scary IQ. "But I'm not going to burn out this time. Maybe I'll move into some environmental research or a similar field. My horizons have broadened."

"Really?"

"I mean it. This year has taught me a lot. Anyway I think you should get moving . . ."

"Yes, Dom, if I had a chance to think perhaps . . . some time alone."

"Don't you want me to come with you?" He doesn't have to offer. He could go back downstairs and bask in parental adoration, not worry about me.

"Thanks . . . but no. I've been seeing a lot of Freddy lately, you know?"

"Yeah, of course."

"Got to know him. I'll go over in an hour or two. Thanks anyway, yeah."

"Alright. Let me know though."

"Sure."

He moves out of my room and I can hear him going down the stairs. I roll off the bed and check the money drawer. It's undisturbed.

My room is a mess so I spend half an hour tidying up. It helps me think. Every time I think of calling Bond I get nervy, wonder about my interest in her. It's as though there are two sides to my thinking. Part of me

has her down as a bitch – the sick laughter with
Lenny, being felt up by all the guys, clearly not caring
about me. One the other hand I want to see her, feel
that I can forgive her and that if it's off then I want to
be the one who decides. I can see the contradiction of
my mood but it feels logical, this desire to see her.
When I get close to writing her off I remember the
night we spent in the crazy four-poster, her toned
body mixing with mine. That thought alone is suffi-
cient to agitate me. There are so many women
though, now I feel as though they are available. I must
be attractive. I've been denying myself that pleasure,
that's all. But Bond comes back as the one I think of,
not any of the other girls I have known, passed in the
street and wondered about, watched in the tube carriage. She's real that's the difference. I know it
happened with her.

I listen to my stereo for a while, flick through some
magazines: 'street culture, drugs, who uses them'.
What the fuck do they know? Magazines are for
people on the outside. Then I check the accounts
again. How much should I offer Deacon? I'll have to
check with Freddy, he should know what amount will
calm things. I can't pay too much, that would invali-
date everything I've done, achieved, in the last week
or so. I keep turning to the mobile, wondering if I
should call her. Then I pick it off the charger, turn it
on, but I can't dial, just stare at it. This is madness.
I've never been this indecisive. Only fools can't make
their minds up.

It rings.

"Shit."

I push the signal button and yank the wire out.

"Yeah?"

"Trev. You alright?"

"Yeah I'm fine, Trev. You spoke with Spence then?"

You can rely on Spence to pass the word.

"Not only him. I heard it from another guy. Boy, you gone deep this time."

"Maybe."

"Come round, I can't stay on."

"I've got to see someone but I'll be back in an hour. Why don't you come round here? Dom's back. If I'm not here have a chat with him until I show?"

"What do you mean back? There for good?"

"Yeah."

"Didn't expect that. I'll come round in an hour then."

"Do that. See you."

I ring off.

I know I'm not going to call Bond before seeing Freddy so I put it back on the charger. I'll think it through on my way across the park. I lift myself up and check the mirror. Apart from looking tired there are no signs of the fight or the strain I'm feeling. I stuff a little bank bag and a tenner into the leather and head for the door. Down in the hallway I can hear them all talking. Even my father's joined in now. I wheel the Fox up to the front door from where I left it in the kitchen, softly click the latch and go out on to the landing. Then I pull the baseball cap down and hike the bike down the stairs. It's getting dark. I can see the gloom of the park at the end of the street.

Sixteen

They're closing the park but I sneak through. I should be able to cross round the river side on the way back, there's a small gap in the railings. It's not quite dark but the street lights have come on. A line of traffic comes down from the bridge so I get on to the pavement then duck round to Freddy's house. The lights are on but I ring the bell three times and there's no answer. It's the first time he's not been in when I've gone round and I can't help taking it as a bad omen. Not wishing to dwell on this I jump back on the Fox and head back to the main street. I'll have to check him in the morning. Maybe it's best if I have some rest tonight, work out my plans for the next day or two. There's a lot to arrange. I should ring Bond before it get's too late.

I speed down the pavement towards the park gate, glanced at the bored drivers in the long line of stationary cars on their way down to Battersea and their journey home. The park gate might be shut but I can squeeze through the railings up at the river side. It's good to be back on the Fox. The gears slip in so I can peddle with ease, the breaks are tight and I'm picking up speed. I push between two cars and follow the middle of the road for a few yards, waiting for a gap in the other lane of traffic. Then there's a crash and I'm in the air – don't know what's happening, staring up at the sky.

My hand hurts. I can see bits of grit under the skin, then there's a film of blood, black in the fading light. I scraped my arm when I hit the road. I lift my eyes from the ground. A car pulls up just ahead of me and the door opens.

"You alright?" A young woman talking to me. She's wearing a dress and very thick glasses. I can hear her radio blasting.

I can't understand what happened, my headaches. I must have hit the kerb, cart-wheeled. Where's the bike? I check the road behind my and spot in in the middle of the grey span, lying on its side but looking undamaged. When I get on to my feet my foot is hurting again. I must have twisted it. I stumble towards the Fox and then I see them. Up ahead in the traffic jam a car door has swung wide open and a guy gets out. The hazard lights are on – must be a BM3 I think from the light design. I can't make out his features but he's shouting and it's clear enough from his words that he's not happy.

"Got you now, you fucker? Come, man."

He saw me coming and opened his door. I rode straight into the open car door, flipped up over it. It should be me who's angry, it was his fault, but I start thinking again. There's another guy getting out of the other side, circling the car. It has to be some of Deacon's team. They're both black guys, late twenties or older, the driver in a cheap leather, the other guy in a smart jacket. I reach down and grab the bike, turn to the car driver who's stopped in the road by me.

"Help me please."

She looks frightened, leans back into her car.

"Let me in, yeah?"

"I can call the police if you want."

I hear the lock click in her door, the window goes up and it's quiet again. Here in the middle of the road and the two guys are running over. I've got no strength left, struggle to get on the bike, but my hands are numb. My body hurts everywhere, I'm panting with the effort, but I'm not going to lie in the street and wait for them like a crippled animal. I get on the bike and push off.

Get him, man!"

The park railings are flying past me. I can hear their steps hitting the asphalt as they chase me. I feel groggy, very scared. If I can make it into the park then I'll lose them. The traffic drivers just stare at me – no time to think of them. They'll be locking their doors the moment I creep up to them, scared of getting involved. I stomp down on the pedals to get to the riverside and I'm going faster, can see the gap I'm going to take – the little path that winds through the trees and down past the pagoda, brings me out a few yards from my house. Got to make it – the sound's gone from behind me – if there's a gunshot I'll faint. This is way of control. I duck through the gap and I'm in – have to spin the wheel round for a sharp turn, then I'm in the trees.

It's a hard shape in the dark, hitting my neck, knocking me to the ground. I can't breathe, the bike crashes into a bush, I land in the dirt and can taste the earth.

"Come here."

He was behind one of the trees on the path – just reached out and punched me off the Fox. I start crawling towards the railings – must get out of the park – to the lights of the street and the cars. But a foot lands hard on my ankle.

"Get off, you bastard." My voice is weak. The pain wakes me up a little. The other guy is running over, panting after the run. I stare up at two faces in the sky.

"He looks bad."

"Give him a kick."

I check the face. He has a thin face, strange eyes. I can see they are sickly even in the dark. Then I remember. I start laughing, softly.

"The Clapham boys, shit! Sorry 'bout your car."

The looked puzzled as I break into laughter. I'm happy for a few seconds. The relief that it's nothing to do with Deacon hits me – just the Beamer I kicked back on the high street last week. It seems like nothing, even though they're waiting in the dark to paste me.

"Thought you were someone else. I'm lucky, I tell you."

"He's lost it, the fucker."

"Here . . ." The guy with yellow eyes kicks me hard in the stomach. I double up and retch. It's so long since I've eaten that there is only a little trail of white liquid snaking out across the grass, burning my mouth and nose. I stop laughing, try to control my breathing, cough the vomit out of my system.

"I think he got hurt when we hit him back on the road. Leave him, man. That'll be alright."

"Nah, too easy for the bastard. Let's ditch the bike."

I can't speak. My face is on fire with the sick, my stomach is twisted in pain. I lie there in the dirt, watch them trot over to the Fox. I try to sit up, blow the last bit of sick out of my mouth.

"No, not the bike, man, please not the bike."

They pick it up and carry it over to the river wall.

"No . . . not the bike."

I make it to my feet, my arms wrapped round my gut, (want to be sick again), stagger behind them. I'm up by the wall and they lift the bike high in the air. It sails up in the sky and starts the circular descent. I watch it hit the water. It seems to float for a second but then the black liquid rushes over it and there is nothing.

"Don't touch my fucking car again, alright?"

I slump by the wall, all the power in my body has

gone now. I sink to the ground, feel the cold, damp earth through my jeans.

"Leave him."

"Yeah, we better get back."

I see them walk across the grass and into the dark. It's a long time before I can stand – start the walk home dragging my foot. I taste blood and sick in my mouth. I lost the bike. Can't believe I lost the bile.

I'm not feeling so rough by the time I get back. At least I can breathe properly again and my hand has stopped bleeding. I'm well-practised in the living room slip-by, so I get up the stairs to my room without being observed. Trev and Dominic are sitting on my bed smoking cigarettes.

"Make your selves at home, boys."

"Charles, what happened? You look ragged."

"I ran into those dicks from over Clapham, the car I kicked, yeah? The bastards threw my bike in the river."

"Fuck. You jokin'?"

"How do I look?"

"They get the phone?"

"Don't worry Trev, it's over there on the charger. Thanks for the concern though. Hey make some room, will you?"

I collapse on the bed. They both stand up and start pacing.

"Trevor's been filling me in on the situation."

"Really? You come up with any answers?"

"Just what you were saying already. What did Freddy say?"

"He was out."

"So Charles . . ." I can see Trev wants to talk, he looks excited. I'm tired so I cut him short.

"I need some rest, can't you see that? Why don't we meet up tomorrow?"

"You wanna grab a beer over at the Moon or something?"

"No, it's about the last thing I need right now. Let me get some sleep, huh?"

"Can you front me a sixteenth?"

"Sure." I take out the bag I was carrying in my jacket pocket and throw it to him. "I'll see you tomorrow, yeah."

They shuffle out of my room. I open a window to get the tobacco smoke out.

About an hour later I'm feeling recovered. Showers have taken on a healing status for me lately. I scraped all the dirt out of the cut and smothered it in Germaline, then soaked my legs for a while to relax the muscles. Hunger and the need to get the taste of sick out of my mouth drove me to the kitchen. I made a plate of cold meats, cheese, a slab of butter and some biscuits, retired to my room to devour it. Then I rolled a single skinner and listened to some music, mourned the loss of the Fox. The bike has served me well. It was a blow to see it sink into the Thames, lost. However, it had to go anyway. The car will be here soon and I wouldn't have got more than thirty or forty bar for it second hand. Bikes are cheap once they get scratched up a bit and the Fox had been in plenty of scrapes. I'm still sad to see it go.

I don't know what it is that keeps me going but I'm not going to let the run-in at the park get on top of me. I've been through so much this week and I have to keep pushing, it's the only way. This is how I got started with all this and I'll see it through to the end. Maybe I'm in shock, my body knocked about so much I'm past caring, or maybe I'm just good at dealing with the pressure. I feel determined though, and I start working it out in my head, planning my moves.

It must be nine and I know it's time to ring Bond. If I leave it any later she'll be out. It's going to be difficult but I have to get it done. Can't duck it. I pick the phone off the charger, retrieve her number and dial. It rings twice then the machine clicks in. I only have a moment to decide whether to ditch it or leave a message.

"Hi, Bond, this is Charles. I thought we could . . ."

"What are you doing ringing me?" Her voice has cut through on the line.

"Monitoring your calls again?"

"I'm on my way out. This I have to hear though."

"Yeah, well I am sorry you were mixed up in it."

"What about Sly? We had to get an ambulance and everything."

"I didn't mean – didn't think he'd get hurt that bad . . . not . . . you know?" At the time I wanted to kill the guy.

"I don't know what you want, Charles. I can only say you need professional help."

"Easy, Bond."

I must regain control of the conversation, be strong. Her voice is louder now, mocking.

"That is if you get through with a little talk with Sly's boss."

"That's dealt with."

"What do you want, Charles?"

"I want to talk with you."

"To say what? We had a fuck, yeah, and you think we're married."

"I thought we might be able to meet up."

"No chance. I want to forget you exist. Do not ring me again, you understand?"

"Bond . . ."

"Goodbye, Charles."

The line goes dead.

Saturday

Freddy is cheerful as ever. It's about noon. I slept till late, had a shouted invitation from my father to go into town with Dom and my mother, but I thought I'd grant my brother the joy of a family outing on his own. I heard the door slam then I was in the shower, healing myself. I dressed, had a quick look at the stash of money, worked out how much blow I had to clear, then walked round to see the dealer.

"I'm stopping."

"You do look as though you've been in the wars."

"You sound like my mother."

He's sprawled on the sofa, sucking on a fresh spliff.

"I just washed my teeth. I love it when you've done that, get the minty taste, you know."

"Freddy, this is serious."

He knew all about the ruck of course. I told him the details when I arrived.

"I'm not your social worker, Charles. What d'you want?"

"Talk to him, see if I can buy him off."

"You broke his boy's arm. Least you can expect is the same."

"No. You can't mean that."

I'm still trying to get my head around all this. Two days ago I was happy, selling was great, I had a willing female partner. Safe. Now I'm due a bust arm, want nothing more than to quit selling to fuckers like Theo, and Bond has messed my head completely. I almost cried last night. Only a great show of personal strength kept me going through the night, allows me to press on now.

Freddy smiles at me. "It's likely to happen. You say you're gonna stop? Why?"

"Well, first I thought it might calm him down a bit if I said I wouldn't hassle him with my selling . . ."

"I don't think he was worried about the competition, you just hurt his top-dog pride, all that bullshit."

"Second, I want to get back to my studies soon. I'm going to pursue wealth through a more conventional method . . ."

"No less corrupt though."

"Yeah, save me the lecture alright, Freddy. Please, just go ring the man . . ."

"I'm not sure. He's not renowned for being rational. How much you gonna give him anyway?"

"What d'you think?"

"A grand, could try that for starters."

"Fuck that. That's way too much."

"It's your body."

He lets me think, stares off to the other side of the room. I know my position is lost. I have to stop, can't take a chance on running into Deacon sometime in the future. It has to end now. I can't live under a threat.

"I'll pay a grand."

Maybe I can still scrape enough together for the car. I feel like breaking down – know that my plans are trashed. Five hundred would have been possible, but a grand? That's half my money.

"I don't see what choice you've got unless you want to take him on . . . and that's not very realistic. You're too smart for that, ain't you? Are you really going to stop completely?"

"Yeah. I was wondering if you'd take the ounce back off me actually."

He laughs. "Sorry, Charles, this is strictly a one-way set up. Pity you're quitting though. I thought you were doing rather well."

"I may do little bits but . . . oh, a quarter a week or something, I don't know. Anyway, make the call, will you?"

"Yes, relax. I'll do it right now. So, you might still be interested in the trade, you say . . ."

"Freddy, please."

He walks into the kitchen, picks up his phone and takes it through to the other room at the end of the hallway.

"I'll do my best."

I wait on the sofa, try to chill with the stub of the

joint he handed me before leaving the room. I've never felt so stressed before. My fingers are almost trembling with nerves. All I can think about is getting out, then I'll be sorted. I'll put my head down to some work and take the long way round to money – but you make more doing that eventually. That's were the real wealth is, not with Deacon and Freddy, working the underbelly. He strides back into the room, pulls a doom look but says nothing. Then he smiles.

"Freddy . . . don't fuck around."

"Tomorrow. He's got something on today but he says tomorrow evening is cool."

"The money?"

"I think he'll go for it. I said a grand, he said double it . . ."

"What?"

"But I talked him down to fifteen. You must have made that from what you've been shifting, haven't you?"

"Shit yeah, but . . ."

"There you go. Everything's back to normal."

"You're telling me. I may as well never've got into it."

"Oh, you must have learnt a few things. Besides, it's not over yet."

"I had all that money put away. That's a lot of hard work, man. Fuck."

"Wait and see what happens."

"Yeah. Thanks for making the call, Freddy. You better give me the address."

He passed me part of a ripped-up cigarette packet with some writing on it.

"It's all there. Come back and see me when you're done, yeah?"

"I'll let you know."

"Best of luck, Charles."

"Cheers."

"Hey! Take a few friends with you, yeah?"

I walk back towards my flat. That means I've still got an ounce to clear. The mobile's been off for nearly two days, that's lost trade and people stop ringing if they can't get hold of you. I go through the list of my friends who might be interested in some of the ounce. Spence is always good for an eighth if he's got any money. I could try Clark. I should see him to congratulate him on the job but my own problems are dwarfing that development. I get an urge to call Bond again but try to fight it down. She made her feelings clear, but it's not easy to be logical about her. I don't like the emotions creeping in like this – disturbs my judgement, makes me feel crazy.

It's a colourless day but I'm not going to allow the weather and my mood to disable me. I rush down my street and take their stairs to the flat, grab the blow and march round to Trev's. I've got the mobile tucked in my jeans.

"Alright, Charles?"

"Yeah."

"Come in."

We go up to his room and sit on his bed.

"You want a draw?"

"I already took a sixteenth off you. Don't know when I can pay you for that, do I? Broke, boy."

"That was going to be my next question."

"Sorry."

"It's alright. You know anyone who's searching?"

"No. Could try Ben, or Lenny."

"Fuck Lenny. What's Ben up to? You know where he lives?"

"Yeah, went round to a party there. It's over Wandsworth Common."

"You fancy taking a walk round there? Oh Trev? . . ."

"Yeah?"

"I have to return the mobile to you."

"Thought you might. You moving down in the world, Charles?"

Even though I know he's joking it hurts. It did feel good to have the mobile. I pass it over and he starts checking it.

"I haven't bust it or anything."

"Just looking. Well . . ."

"Yeah?"

"I'd say the sixteenth I took off you covers the portion of this week's rent."

"What? Bullshit."

"It does, think about it. Business, boy."

"I haven't got much choice, have I? In that case you'd better skin up. Works both ways this, you know." We both laugh and it feels good. It reminds me how much I used to enjoy hanging with him.

We start out to see Ben after smoking a couple of spliffs.

He has a basement flat near the station. It's small and dark. I'd go mad in a week living in a place like this.

"Come in, boy. You know I was gonna ring you today?"

"Oh yeah? That's a bit of luck for us both then."

Trev and I sit down on an exhausted sofa, bits of stuffing peeping out through gaps in the cover. Ben sits in an ancient armchair and pulls some trainers on. There is a three-ring gas heater on the wall and one of the ceramic thirds is glowing a deep red. Some old-style reggae plays softly in the background. The walls are painted a dirty white, presumably to try and lighten the place up a little. He's tacked some posters up in places, adverts for past concerts and club nights. Spence told me he used to be a club promoter but went bust or something – got into trouble anyway. That was a while ago though. There are clothes and junk all over the floor. He clears a space and slides an ashtray over. I offer him a cigarette and speak.

"How much you want then?"

"A hundred."

There was no hesitation before his response. I'm confused.

"That much in money, you mean?"

"What else?"

"Well, Ben, you've made my day."

"Should I have asked for more?" He has a hurt expression on his face, tugs hard on the cigarette.

"I don't get you."

"Spence said a hundred should be fair. That's what he said."

"Explain this to me."

"For backing you up. I'm having a few slight money problems at the moment. You could say I'm financially embarrassed."

"Go on."

"I need an air ticket, go see an old friend of mine. You've heard I can take pressure, yeah?"

"Hmm."

"So I'm a gun for hire, boy."

"Gun?"

"No I don't actually mean 'gun' do I? Just mean I'll come along. Spence said he was gonna talk wid you."

"I haven't heard from him. This is interesting though." I turn to look at Trev. "You know about this?"

"No, honest. But if you're paying out a bit of danger money . . ."

"Danger money? Shit, man, everyone turn mercenary. I'm the only one who's in danger."

"Settle down. Charles. Why don't you skin up, that'll ease you."

"I got to sell this to pay the vultures, 'aven't I?"

"Here, I'll roll one." Trev starts picking up some papers from the carpet. He slides one of my cigarettes out.

Ben stares at me. "So what you say then? You on for it?"

"You mean hiring you out? I don't know, don't even know if I'm gonna ask anyone along."

"That doesn't seem very smart – not like you, C."

"So everyone thinks I'm rich, paying for bodyguards."

"You have been earning. I mean if you were broke I wouldn't suggest it."

Trev looks up from the joint. "I don't want any money from you, Charles."

"Thanks, Trev."

"An' Clark might come along."

"Yeah. I should go see him, he's not far off from here, is he? so you don't want any blow, Ben?"

"Like I said, we're talking negative profit situation here."

"Alright, well I'll drop back in a bit, yeah?"

"Sweet."

"See you."

I take the slimy steps up to the road and start walking over to Balham. It'll only take a few minutes to get to Clark. Ben's offer has scared me again, reminded me how others are seeing my situation. Ben's asking for money because he knows there's a risk involved. This was what Spence was talking about, how I end up making the pay-back. I pull the leather round me and walk faster, cross over to the high street from the rows of terraces that stretch between Wandsworth and Balham. Before I get to Clark's street I stop in an off-licence and pick up two Brooklyns. I haven't had a beer with Clark for a long time.

Seventeen

Clark opens the door after I've knocked a few times.

"Was shaving, man."

"Bit late for that, innit?"

"Had a late night. Can't go without a shave though. What you up to?"

"Have a beer."

We sit at the small table at the far end of the kitchen. He wipes bits of foam from his face.

"It's good stuff."

"I might take an eight off you."

"How's the job?"

"It's only training now. I don't start till next week."

"You heard from Indigo?"

"Fuck her. She went round my folks to check the kid yesterday but I haven't seen her. She's moved in with some dick, that's all I know. Skin up, man." He has the same confident air as the last time I saw him. "Truth is, I'm happy we made the break you know. I can get down to something. Way it was going I was heading into what you're doing."

"Huh." I licked the top of the papers and make the fold, twist the end and nip it off between my teeth.

"Suppose you knew I was selling on?"

"Yeah."

"I can't get into that. If I start on that, next thing I know I hit thirty and you can't get out a it. You just go on wanting more money and you get trapped. Take it as a warning, Charles, I seen it." He smiles at me, aware that he sounds patronising. "Sorry, you know the score."

"I'm quitting. I just want to get rid of this last bit then I'm out."

"Yeah."

"Truth. I got to sort some thing out with Deacon first, then . . ."

"Deacon? Yeah, me know him. How you mean?"

"Got in a fight with some guy who works for him. I'm gonna pay him off though, yeah?" I don't want it to sound cocky but I can see Clark is impressed.

"Can understand you don't want him pissed off with you. Guy's crazy."

"Been asking a few people to see if they'd come along with me when I go to see him . . ."

"Man . . . you asking me?"

"I was hoping you'd be . . ."

He thinks for a second, takes the joint from me.

"Fuck, alright. Who else is going?"

"Maybe Trev, Spence. Ben asked me for money, you believe it?"

"You paying?"

"What? You think I should?"

"If you've got it, yeah. Least for a drink or something."

"Yeah, I don't know."

"Anyways, I'll come along. When you going?"

"Tomorrow, round ten in the evening."

"You meeting somewhere first?"

"Hadn't thought about it. He's over in Brixton."

"What about the Prince then?"

"Yeah, alright. Half seven."

"Safe. I'll get your money for the eighth . . ."

He stares at me before standing up from the table. I know him well enough to see he's stalling, suggesting I act with his glance rather than saying something directly to my face. I feel pushed into it but when you're under pressure you're in the weak bargaining position, like selling something when you're broke and the other guy knows you'll take anything you can get.

"Take the eighth for nothing, man."

"Thanks, Charles. That fair?"

"Yeah."

"We all happy?"

"I don't know about happy. I'm running out of cash-ola quick, boy – down to nothing."

"Join the fucking club, Charles. You been selling to us. It jus' comes round in a circle that's all."

"So I come back to nothing then?"

"Ah, stop worrying. Look what I lost and I still happy. Better off, man. It all depends on your perspective."

"Bit deep today, aren't you?"

"Serious, man. Have to treat your friends right, boy. Deacon's a bit of a fucking animal, you know?"

"Yeah."

"So . . . money help. Look, just smoke . . ." He hands me the joint. I can feel the warm flood of the THC hitting my lungs, filling all the empty places. He smiles. "Just smoke an' chill. One day I swear, I just dig up and go – nowhere particular, you get me, jus' somewhere I can go and smoke in peace, out a the big, shitty city, boy. That's where the stress hits you – no lie. I just go, maybe when the kid a bit older, get out. Get away from all the people with a fucking mission, relax and live my life, the way I want to."

"Nice dream, Clark. But freedom costs. You have to make the money first, then split."

"I hope you get there, Charles. Anyway, next we be talking 'bout the universe an' all that crap . . ."

"On the stone express' boy."

"I know, it strong. Don't mean I get all hippy dippy though. Let's have the beer, yeah? What you doing today?"

I feel cool again, at ease with my friend. It was like this when I spoke to Trev earlier. I don't have to explain anything, knowledge of each other makes talk easy. Clark and I sit there for a while just smoking, drinking. It's getting dark by the time I leave for Ben's and I'm trashed. The traffic on the high street fills my head with noise.

Ben and Trev greet me with beams on their faces. Everyone's blitzed. After they manage to get out of their chairs we start walking round to see Spence, smoking on the way. I can hear music outside his flat. He opens the door and walks into the living room.

"Alright, Charles. I was meaning to have a little . . ."

He's trying to be serious. Ben and Trev settle on the sofa and go into a chat.

"I know, Spence. Ben told me you wanted something for backing me up."

"Don't make it sound like that. It's just . . ."

"Yeah, forget it. I told Clark and he's coming along. I've give you fifty each for your trouble, if you want it."

"Fifty?" Despite the fact he was talking with Trev, Ben heard me and his voice cuts in.

"I can't stretch to a hundred. Your choice."

"Money got to come from somewhere. I'm in long as it don't get too lively."

"I won't. I just pay him and go. Financial ruin coming my way but . . ."

"Have a drink." Spence flashes the Pernod.

"Not that stuff. Let's have some a your Scotch."

"That's for emergencies only."

"This counts then, don't it?"

We drink. I tell them the meeting place and leave for home.

When I get in to the flat Dominic's sitting in the kitchen.

"Where are they?"

"Gone out to do some shopping. You want a tea?"

"Nah, I'll have a coffee, I think."

"You sort everything out?"

"Yeah tomorrow."

"I want to come along."

I'm at the fridge, searching for the crumpled tin foil I wrapped some filter coffee in. I find it, stand and walk over to the sink.

"There's no need, Dom."

"If I'm living back here I should come along."

"Very kind but forget it."

I set up the machine and come back to the table. His hands are clasped tightly in front of him. His face is tense, eyes wide open.

"I want to help."

"I don't need it. I said forget it. You want to go upstairs for a smoke?"

"Why not? So who is going with you?"

"Back off, Dom." I go over to the machine and pour myself a cup of the black, oily liquid. "Come on then."

We file up to my room and I shut the door. I sit on the bed whilst he paces.

"Relax, Dom."

"Thing is . . . I know this guy."

"Who?"

"Deacon."

"How come?"

"I used to score off him. I thought it might be of some use to you, to have me along, 'cause he knows my face. We got on."

"You an' him?"

"Yeah, he was alright. Freddy told me he's gone weird in the last year but he used to be cool."

"Not anymore."

I bend down to pick up a magazine. Then I pull the kit out and start rolling. I'm still blissed from the afternoon but I'm not doing anything tonight so I can afford to get trashed. It'll settle my nerves. I break a big lump into the papers and tear a Cut open.

"Mum said she hasn't seen much of you lately."

"No, I've been out a lot. As you might expect in the summer holidays."

"But she said there might be a girl."

"Oh yeah? Well, 'No' is the answer right now. I didn't think she was so observant."

"She was talking a lot about you this afternoon."

"That was always the way with you and her. I suppose you've made it up with her now, back to being the favourite."

"It's not like that, Charles."

"Sure."

"She's frail, you know. Worries all the time."

"Well I'm clear from tomorrow."

"For the best. What are you going to do?"

"I might sell a little, like I said, but I'll go back to my studies . . ."

"The dream?"

"It's no dream."

"You really want to be a lawyer or something like that?"

"I want to be in a position of power so I can . . ."

"I see. That still counts as a dream. It's not very artistic but it's still a 'hope', innit?"

"It's an ambition – no, a reality. Gonna make it a reality."

"Like you sailed through dealing so easy, you mean?"

"What you saying, Dom, 'cause you're winding me up?"

"Nothing. I think it's good to have dreams."

"Here, have a go."

I offer him the joint. His attempts at conversation are frustrating. The next few weeks could be hard work. I lean back to the radio and turn it on. It's on a community channel, reggae stuff. Dominic picks up a magazine, glances at it and starts to talk. I sip my coffee.

"I've got some friends down in Bristol."

"From Uni, you mean?"

"Yeah."

Most of the people I met when he was on the course were jerks but that was years ago. I wasn't even into drinking then. I can't remember much about them except they were loud, talking all the time, developing their egos. He had a girlfriend called Ali. She was the one I liked. She remembered who I was whenever she came round to see him.

"I'm going down there for the weekend, thought you might like to come down with me."

"Why are you asking me along, the kid brother?"

"No reason, thought you might like getting out of town for a few days. I haven't spent much time with you lately, have I . . . ?"

"I get nervous out in the country, Dom. They don't have any drive-throughs."

"Big joke. It's hardly the country, is it – Bristol? Anyway, they offered me the car . . ."

"What, Dad?"

"Yeah."

"Fuck. You spoilt, man."

"He said he'd offered to take you out in it."

"Yeah, who wants to ride in that shit heap?"

Dominic must know my car plan is dying. He could make a dig but he's being kind. "It's just an idea. I'm going anyway and I'd like you to come along. If you can't shift the last of the dope I'll take it along. Sure they'll go for it."

"Is it a party?"

"Not really. A few of them bought a house down there and I never went to see it . . . you know?"

Not only is Dominic being embraced by the family again, he's re-entering his old social world. I realise this must be important to him. He lost his friends when he went to the edge. He wants to build his life again.

"Thanks for asking me along, Dom, but I can't see it really. I'll let you know, yeah?"

"Alright."

"Hey, Dom. You got any scales?"

"Ha, yeah I do actually. They're not great though."

"Give us a hand cutting this up into sixteenth then, will you?"

"Sure, bro. I'll go get them, yeah."

I spent a quiet evening with Dom. The folks came in a few hours after we started bagging the gear but they stayed in the living room, probably talking through the great reunification of the family. We left them to it.

Sunday

It's early. The voice on the radio sounds sleepy, says it's around nine. I take my time waking up, stretch my legs under the covers, wrap the fabric around me. Today I have to try and get rid of the last blow so I worked through my options. If it doesn't work out I can always send some along with Dom. I slide out of bed and pull on my dressing gown. Voices are drifting up from downstairs. I walk out to the landing and take the stairs. The three of them are in the kitchen playing happy family.

"Dawn of the dead."

"Sorry? Lay off the jokes, Dad."

"Afternoon, Charles."

"It's a Sunday."

I eat some cereal and take it all in. My mother moaning about the noise from next door – she wants to go round and complain; my father reading the paper and getting more depressed by the turn of every page, his face looking old and worn out by years in the warehouse; Dominic beaming at me, even throwing a cornflake at me like I'm seven years old again. It confuses me. I like him being back but the change is a shock. I'd got used to the moods of the house, feel uncertain in this new atmosphere. Maybe it's the dealing as well. I can't quite believe I'm stopping. It was going so well. It was giving me more than just the cash. The house was just somewhere I crashed, grabbed the odd meal. With Dominic's return and the vision of college ahead of me I feel tied to the home again. I don't like it.

"I'm going upstairs."

No-one responds. A friend of mine was moaning about his family to me, one time out of many. He told me it's a 'dilution of self' being round your family and I had no idea what he was talking about – but it makes sense now. I feel less important, like I'll only be noticed if I scream or stick the cereal spoon up my ass. Maybe that's why some guys get the urge to be outrageous, just to be noticed. It seems like a simple deduction but I ponder it up in my room as I dress. It's important to listen to people, even if you don't get it straight away. These things can become clear at a later date.

I finish dressing, mess around with the accounts for an hour and head out. There's a call box up on Battersea High and much as I hate them it's too busy to ring from my house. The mobile represented independence, like the Fox, and I miss them both. On the Fox you fly pass the bus stop with the line of sad creeps strung out on the pavement, you miss out on the wino getting in your face, hassling you for an Edge, stinking so bad you give it over just to get away from the smell. The streets look better because you only get a glimpse. When you've got time to check you see the cracks in the picture, the imperfections.

It's a dull walk up to the phone. I pull a piece of paper out of pocket and start checking the names I came up with as potential buyers. It doesn't look good. Even as I sigh over the phone, a police ambles by and gives me a long look. If I was buzzing by on the Fox I'd return the sneer but walking slows everything down. He'd just come over and hassle me, and I'm carrying. My jacket pocket is stuffed with wraps. I go back to the phone. I try Bruce but there's no answer, then Trev's friend but it's the same. Clayton's rings three times then the line is silent.

"Hey Clayton, it's Charles."

"Charles? Oh, yeah, hi man. Sorry, I was expecting someone else."

"How you doing?"

"Terrible. What time is it, man?"

"No, you're supposed to say 'Fine, thank you', not how you really are."

I don't think my humour goes down well with him.

"Nearly eleven, I think – the time, yeah."

"Yeah. So what is it, Charles?"

"Wonder'd if you needed anything."

"A twelve-bore maybe."

"I see."

"No, I could handle a little one."

"Cool."

"You know where I live?"

"Uh-uh."

He gives me the address.

"Ten minutes."

"I'll be here, don't worry. I'll put the kettle on."

Clayton lives just off the Old Town in Clapham, near the Moon. It's a terrace house split into three flats and looks small from the outside, but when he lets me in I walk into a living room that stretches right back to the rear garden wall. It's a huge room. The curtains are drawn and all the lights are on but it's still gloomy. the bulbs are hidden behind wooden slats, like in a wine bar or something. The carpet is cream, as are the walls, and there's no furniture except a huge leather sofa, a cabinet for his system, two massive speakers at the far end and a little glass coffee table. Clayton's guitar is in one of the corners, propped up on a stand.

"But spartan, boy."

"No, look at this."

He goes over to the wall by the system and turns the light switch. The lights dim.

"Man, a love pit."

"When you get to my age you need all the help you can get."

"You're still young."

"Nearly thirty."

"Fuck, that is old."

"Thanks. So you got it?"

"Here." I pull out one of the bags and drop it on the table.

"If it's resin I want a smoke first."

"I should have stuck with herb."

"Of course."

He leans down and slips a CD into one of the black boxes in the cabinet. I start rolling, making it strong to force the sale. Music crashes in.

"Who's this?"

"Fishbone."

"Hmm."

It's a rock riff. Clayton nods his head to it.

"So how come the cold calling?"

"I lost the mobile – well, gave it up. I'm getting out."

"Yeah? Changing career then?"

I want to avoid the subject. "How come you sounded so pissed off?"

"Because . . ." I pass him the smoking joint and he takes a long puff. "Hmm, agreeable. I'll take a six-teenth, I'm bust at the moment."

"Because . . ."

" 'Cause the guy you say was alright, he do us on that contract. The fucking singer goes over to them with all the tapes and the band's fucked. They've offered us a weekly retainer . . ."

"Huh?"

"A wage. It means we're not really a band. If the single does alright then they get all the money. I mean the singer and them. He's gone off on a star trip . . . ah, it's just a mess."

"Sorry to hear it."

"It was that fucker the manager, him and the shark he hired. I tell you, if you're gonna play that game you have to be a ruthless bastard, no other way to survive."

"Maybe."

"Truth. I'm waiting for the rest of the band to get in touch. We're gonna have a council of war."

"To do what?"

"Another lawyer, I don't know yet – try and find a way around it. This should calm things down if they get too heated."

He picks up the bag then digs out some notes for me.

"How's it going with you?"

"Bit tricky. Problem."

"Best of luck with it, boy. You have to keep fighting for it an' it'll work out for you. I gotta get moving anyway, Charles . . ."

"Yeah, me too. Give me a bell if you . . ."

"Safe. Later, yeah?"

I walk up through the Old Town, past the Moon and round to the High Street.

I'm the first one to arrive. In a couple of hours this place will be rammed but right now it's just me and a couple of the Brixton soaks, some groups of fresh-faced preppie types who've just got out of the sports centre and some traders from round the market. I don't like the Prince. It's just off the main road and I used to come here a lot when I was first checking out bars. It was rough then – they didn't care who, how old or what you were, they just wanted to sell beer. There's a little garden out in the back and you can smoke out there – not that I wanted to back then. The music was loud and the crowd was mixed, noisy and young. They had trouble, fights, dealing and the management changed. Bright lights shine down on you wherever you sit and they've installed box cameras, probably on a direct circuit round to the police. Drinking under a camera makes me feel nervous. But the real problem is that the crowd gets no less rowdy, they got worse. The regulars are the worst breed of alcoholics, down so far in the trail of booze, failed and broken along the way, that they've become bitter, vicious. Fights are common. It had a name when they changed the owner and it was too late to make it nice family pub, if such things exist in Brixton. The Effra's not too bad but it's further away from Deacon. I slouch in a corner table, sipping a pint of Stella and smoking a Cut. I've got fifteen hundred in an envelope tucked in my jacket, feel like I'm wearing a flashing light on my head. Clark arrives.

"Wanna beer?"

"I'll get them. What d'you want?"

He comes back with two pints and we start talking. He seems relaxed, chatting away. After a few minutes the others arrive. I buy a round.

"Hey Charles, any news then?"

"No. He said ten."

"Why so early then?"

"Thought we might need a drink."

I had expected a quiet mood but they're all laughing, talking. Trev's dressed to go out, even Spence looks smart.

Eighteen

Deacon lives over by Acre Lane. There are dozens of streets running off this link between Brixton and Clapham. He's on the Brixton side, near the Prince.

At a quarter to ten we file out and start walking up the High Street. None of us are drunk, the drinking was cautious. I walk with Clark at the front, the other three trail just behind. It feels good to have them with me, not only the security of having a team but the fact they're all friends. I can't remember the last time I was out with them all. We cross the High Street and pace past the town hall. Some of the street lights are dead and the beginnings of Acre Lane is dark. There's a lot of trash on the pavements.

"Run down round here, innit?"

"Nah, it's alright. Adds character."

I see his street up ahead and we slow down, stop talking and turn into it, already checking for any shapes in the dark, charging up. There are no people, just rows of parked cars and the terraces. His house is near the top and we stop outside. I can see lights in all the windows. I push a metal gate open and start up the path to the front door.

"He is expecting you?"

"Yeah."

I wait a few yards from the door bell. These terraces are the same all over Brixton. They have a large room at the front, a smaller one in the middle and a kitchen in the back leading on to a small garden. The stairs are on the right as you go in, running off the hallway that stretches down that side of the house. Upstairs you get three rooms. I run through the floor plan in my head, thinking it might be wise to remember the design. Then the door opens in front of me. It's not Deacon. He's only around my age, dressed in black jeans and a baggy T-shirt.

"Jus' you, man."

"Fuck that. They're coming in with me."

I lift my hand and they move up behind me. I expect him to shut the door or cry out but he swings it open. He turns and limps back into the hallway. His legs had been concealed by the door but now I can see they are thin and bent, like a sick child's. This takes away the adrenalin rush I was on as I prepared to crash through the door and burst into the house. I feel foolish.

"He's upstairs."

We stand in the hallway, hemmed together in the narrow corridor. There is no carpet, just bare boards, black and dirty. The walls are scraped, strands of patterned paper clings to them. A bare bulb is the only light. The guy shuts the door behinds us and bolts it, then steps between us.

"Go on then."

I start up the stairs. There is no sound except our footsteps on the old, bare wood.

"Second room."

There is no door. I can see through into the room as I reach the top of the stairs. Deacon is standing in the middle, next to a small table. He's as smart as usual but seeing him in this shell of a house unnerves me. I thought he would have a home as lush as his clothes, fitting with his status. The hat is low on his head so it's hard to see his eyes.

"Bring your buddies?"

I step into the room and Clark follows me. The others wait on the landing. To my right there are some partition doors leading through to another room. They are drawn tight. I can hear music, a radio maybe, a tinny sound through the thin wood. Deacon walks towards the front windows and leans against the wall.

"That's my brother Stan. They say anything, Stan?"

"No."

"That's good. Dis my brother an' I kill you."

I feel tense. Clark is motionless by my side. With

our numbers I should be confident, sense my control, but my fingers are trembling, my feet are icy, blood-less.

"You got the money?"

"Yeah."

"Pay it on then boy."

"We should talk a bit first, don't you think?"

"'Bout what? I spoke to Freddy. You won't have no trouble from me. Can't talk for Sly though."

"I thought he'd be here."

"So you can shake hands, make up? No, he's not here ..." He strikes back to the other side of the room. "Some others are though."

I hear a crash behind me and spin round. The door on the landing has swung open. There are two guys on the stairs, short clubs in their fists. They push into Trev and send him spinning. Ben tries to twist and face them but I see him catch a blow across the cheek. Then Spence is in but he gets shoved towards the top of the stairs, hangs on to the guy's shell suit, and I'm turning to go back and help him.

"Move."

Clark hangs on to my arm and I face Deacon. He's got a lump of metal in his hand – a revolver, ancient.

"Get in."

Stan has a sick grin on his face, shuffles to the thin doors and pushes them open. It's dark, a long space with windows at the end. They are a bright grey with the moonlight.

"I said get in."

We move towards the door. Behind me I can hear the struggle on the stairs – Ben screaming, crashes as they bounce off the walls and try to get into the room

we were in. Now Clark and I are in the other room.
Deacon and his brother behind us.

"Take a seat."

He flicks a switch and my eyes sting for a second
under the glare of the bulb. I can see old furniture, a
single bed mattress in the corner, three armchairs
and a sofa. There are open tins on the floor, grimy
plates and ashtrays.

"What d'you think of my little house then?"

Deacon is beaming, standing tall behind the revolver. I can see Clark is weighing it up, he might leap
at any moment. The muscles are tight under his shirt,
pressing through the fabric.

"Settle down. This thing work, you know."

"I heard it just for show."

"More than that, boy. Sit."

We crumple into the armchairs. I can still hear noise
from the landing but it's fading. It's covered by a
drone from a little radio by the sofa.

"They'll be back in a minute. They my clear-up
men, boy. So, you was thinking I'd be here alone?"

"Yeah."

"Don't know what this place is?"

"No."

My chest is tight, I'm having problems keeping my
breathing regular. All I can look at is the gun, wondering if it's real, if he'd use it. I've never felt so
powerless. All I can do is go along with it. Clark
speaks.

"What is it then? This a joke? He's got the money
so stop fucking around." His voice sounds cocky but I
can hear the tremor in it. He's not scared of the man,
only the situation.

"Big man. This double up as a crack house, that wha' you in." He leans back and laughs. His brother just looks on from the door. "Stan run things fo' me. Nothing like a big ting, you know, just people coming round to smoke it up a bit. Them two guys is always here to help out. But no-one really give a fuck 'bout this place – bother me, ya know. Even though you get wild things happen here."

He steps towards me and I freeze in my seat. The gun lifts and hovers by my face, comes closer, and I try to move my head back, but it moves in, strokes against my cheek. It's so cold it burns.

"Don't think much a it? Well it no matter. The money."

"In my pocket." I reach for it but he slaps the barrel into the side of my head. I can feel the skin split, cry out.

"Stan – get it." He comes over. I can hear his feet scraping on the bare wood. His hand moves into my jacket and pulls the envelope out.

"Got it."

"Now . . ." Deacon takes a step back and his smile changes to a snarl. "I don't give a fuck about penny dealers like you, Charles. You just a kid. But I told you two time not to mess with me and that just what you go an do – cause a lot of shit with that group of people. Good buyers man and you freak 'em out, worry them, yeah. Sly's arm bad, *everyting* wrong wid you. What I'm doing here is just a message. I have to get me respec', boy. I do you then it no sweat wid others. You gonna be walking round – advertisement, you see . . ."

"What ?"

He steps in close again, ignoring Clark. The gun sinks into my waist. As it moves down my body a numbness moves with it, until my whole frame is dead, full of fear. It stops at my leg, pointing directly at my knee, pushing into my jeans.

"I cripple you, boy. You still walk but like my brother, yeah?"

"For what? I'm paying you up, I'm getting out."

"Me know but that not the point. This is a different rule here, college boy. You get hurt here it your own fault 'cause you try an' play wid the men. No-one care if you get hurt 'cause you in drugs now – it always your fault, you see."

"No man, please."

"I tell you it alright to walk, don't worry."

I'm staring straight into his eyes, they're pure black. I can't see anything else in the room but his face. He's going to pull the trigger and blow a hole in my bone, to punish me. I can't move. It's crazy – no sense – none of this is happening. Then his face changes and he must be about to do it. I shut my eyes and scream.

"Charles . . ."

Clark is in the air. I see his fist crash into the side of Deacon's jaw. The bone swings across his face under the impact, snaps and I watch it push against the sagging skin of his cheek. His body bends low but he still stands. He makes no sound but I can hear Stan scream behind me. Clark stands there in shock as Deacon lifts his head, turns his body – everything's moving so slowly. Clark's eyes are full of disbelief. His own hand is trembling with pain from the punch.

Deacon should be out but he still grips the gun, still smiles, lifts his body so he stands taller than Clark. I watch in terror as he opens his mouth to speak and a flood of red washes over lips, spill on to his shirt. He tries to speak but the words are a mumble, then I see him grip the teeth together and this time he speaks with his teeth clenched tight.

"Can't hurt me, ya fuck."

Stan is shuffling over, screaming to his brother, then there's a crash out on the landing – maybe they've fought them off. Deacon looks over to the doors, then turns back. His teeth are bared, covered in blood, pink bubbles of it on his lips. He looks animal. I see him lift the gun.

"Check it, Stan."

His brother pushes out into the other room and makes it to the curtains. He holds the envelope tight in his hand, sweeps the cloth back with it.

"Cars man, D – fucking cars up and down the street." He stands silhouetted in the window, then I see his face and he's terrified. The envelope is pressed against the glass. "Police, fucking po-lice . . ."

Then his body lifts into the air. There is a blast, the window shatters and bits of glass swarm towards us. Stan crashes to the floor in a heap and curls up, his legs drawn up to his chest.

"Fuck."

Then there's more sound on the stairs. Ben and Spence stumble into the room. They hold Trev up by his arms. Deacon watches them enter.

"Fuckers took off when the door went. They're downstairs, man."

I can stand, I can move again. I rush over to Trev and lift his head. One of his eyes is shut with a swelling and there is blood seeping from his nose, one of his ears.

"He got it bad out there. Move it, man."

Deacon pushes into us. There's a shout on the stairs but I can't hear the words. Deacon crashes against the wall and starts to creep up to the partition door. He swings round and levels the gun to my temple.

"You fucker, Charles – set me up."

"No."

"Then they follow you."

This time the gun doesn't have the same power. I stare at him. He's showing signs of pain now from the broken jaw. He looks weak, a mess, blood staining his clothes.

"I didn't know."

"Charles, we have to go."

Clark grabs one of the fat armchairs we were sitting on and picks it up. He's strong, lifts it over his head and charges to the rear window. He hurls it through the glass and it takes most of the window pane with it. His action steels me. I know one of us has to get us out. I ignore Deacon and grab Trevor, drag him towards the window.

"You can't."

"Only way."

"But the garden backs on to another house."

"We crash that one too then." I sound determined, powerful. The others gather round me.

Deacon is still against the other wall, by the partition. I see him dip into a pocket and lift a bag out. He tips it by his head, covering the jaw with powder, then pours some into his mouth. I watch for a second but his spell has lifted now. He looks weak, trying to use the drug to give him strength. I move for the window.

"Come on."

He cries out from the doors, words pressed tight through his teeth. "I'll do you, you fucking welsh. First there a guy in there though."

I can see a shape in the other room, shoulders hunched, leaning low.

"Move."

I push Trev through the window. Clark leaps out after him and I can hear the soft thud as they hit the grass. Then Spence and Ben are through and I'm in the gap, waiting to go.

"Stop."

I flick my head round and there's a figure in the doorway. He's a bull, in a padded jacket, a black metal tube next to his chest. He wears a little cap with lettering printed across it, too dark to read it. Then I see his face come out into the light. It's the guy from the car, the blue car, the same round face from the cinema bar. He fixes his eyes on me and I see another shape behind him. They're moving in. Deacon is by the wall, only inches more into the room but the police can't see him, he's pressed against the wall.

"On the floor now."

I don't move.

"I said . . ."

He steps in and his head is next to the revolver hugging the partition door. Deacon's hat is out of shape, his legs are sagging. I can see the white powder on his face, like a clown. Then there's a shot and my ears are aching, my brain full of the noise. The top of the man's head lifts off with a spurt of blood that covers the door behind him, and he falls to the floor. There is a flash behind him and the walls light up with little puffs of dust and sparks as the other man rakes the room on automatic. In the sweep I see Deacon judder twice and he stumbles into the middle of the floor, lifts his revolver and pumps at the other guy. There is no dive for cover, no roll or stunt. The two men stand facing each other, blasting. Deacon's so charged he takes two more thuds and I can see his back open up. Blood hits my face in a hot rain. The wall around me is pocked with craters. The wood splinters but I sit in the middle, not moving, not hit. Deacon's knees go but he gets a shot to the man's chest. Nothing happens except he staggers and the bullets smash into the ceiling, then he finds his aim again. Deacon's going but he lifts the barrel and aims and there's a crack as he puts a bullet in the guy's forehead, above the proof vest. The skull opens to a neat hole and the guy falls back straight, on top of Stan's crumpled body.

Deacon spins and the gun comes up looking for me but I'm out by then, the air whistling past me for a few seconds before I hit the ground and hands are on me dragging me off to a wall at the back of the garden. The house is full of noise, shouts, crashes. I look up to the window and I'm sure I can see a shape up there, shaking a little but bearing down on me, and my eyes are going to fill with blood as he puts a bullet in my

brain and I scream. Then the room lights up with gun-
fire, three automatics pumping so it's full of shadows
and colours like lightning in a storm.

We make it over the crumbling wall in the back and
we're in another garden. There are lights on in the
kitchen but I can't seen anyone. Trevor's breathing is
loud, I can hear him behind me.

"Need to get him to hospital, man."

"Don't know if I can walk."

"Shut up, Spence. We're all getting out of this."

"You weren't out in the hall, were you?"

There are shouts from the other garden, a siren
goes off.

"Shit, so what now?"

"Follow me."

I'm still buzzing. Someone has to get us out. I pace
across the grass and balance on the window ledge for
a second, swing my leg round and kick into the glass.
My boot goes through, then there's pain from my shin.
I don't look down but throw myself through the window, land in a pile on some black-and-white floor
tiles, covered in glass. The other are behind me at the
window, then there's a body ahead of me. I look up
from the floor. It's a girl in her twenties, wide-eyed,
black hair, jeans and a jumper.

"Can I help you?"

She sounds so formal I almost burst into laughter
but my hands are hurting and I see there's a deep
gash at the base of my thumb. On the other hand I've
got a flap of skin loose just above my wrist.

"Where's the front door?"

"Through there."

She steps aside and I make it to my feet, stagger past her.

"You from all that shooting?"

Clark is helping Trev. Ben and Spence jog through the kitchen and hold the front door open.

"Anyone out there?"

"Nah, but there will be soon."

"Come on then, pick yourself up."

We're out in the street. I check up and down but it's quiet. The girl shuts the door behind us.

"Which way Brixton?"

"You an' Trev have to get to hospital."

"We'll go in a cab. If we get down to Landor Road there's an office there."

"That's fucking dumb. The driver . . ."

"You think we should walk there then?"

"Let's split up anyway."

I lurch down the street, trying to prop Trevor up next to me.

"Here, I'll come with you."

"Leave it, Clark, we'll be alright."

"I'm coming along."

Spence and Ben walk off the other way. I can see Spence is limping. We turn the corner and keep walking. A few minutes later we're at the cab office.

Compared to the one in Clapham this is a war zone. In a little concrete den the controller puts out a message for a car. The office is fortified – I can see the alarm cables running across the ceiling. Trev has passed out and his breathing has become softer. Only Clark is uninjured. I've torn up my T-shirt and wrapped my hands with it but the blood is seeping out by the time the car arrives, making little pools on the linoleum floor.

"St George, casualty."

We mutter in the back as the car drifts through the backstreets. When we get out into Clapham the traffic is building, people are coming out of pubs. A car passes us in the other direction with the siren going. Clark is calm but his voice sounds strained.

"First place they're gonna look, Charles . . ."

"Too bad. I don't think we've got any choice. Trev sounds like he needs a doctor an' I'm not feeling great. Bleeding bad, boy."

"We'll be there in a minute."

"Why don't you get out? We're passing your place."

"Nah."

"Get out, Clark. I can deal with Trev. No sense in risking it, is there? Driver!" We're out on Balham High, winding down to Tooting. "He's getting out here."

Clark just stares at me but I give him a push.

"Fuck off, man." He gets out and we pull back into the line of cars.

The hospital staff took Trev from me, rushed him straight to one of the doctors and told me to wait. They said I'd need stitches. There were a lot of questions. They were pushy. I guess they see this stuff all the time and want to know something about the patient, whether he's going to flip at any second, if he's taken something. I told them we were friends who'd got in a fight over a girl. They looked at me like I was a foolish child, believed my lie.

They came and got me an hour later for the stitching. It was a long wait. I expected police to come

running in at any second and get us down on the floor.
I guess the staff don't have to report anything unless
they think it's important. I had to have a jab in each
hand to kill the pain and one in my ass for tetanus.
Then some guy with very thick glasses and shaky
hands sewed me up. It's basic. They scrape out all the
crap, cover it in iodine, then tie you up. My hands felt
like dead lumps on the end of my arms.

"How's my friend?"

"You broke his nose. He's gonna love you for that.
They cleared it an' his breathing's fine so . . . so don't
worry."

"Keeping him in?"

"He doesn't need it. Besides, you should be looking after him. We're too busy for this sort of crap,
alright?"

"Yeah."

"Call a taxi. He'll be out in a few minutes."

"Thanks."

Back in the waiting hall I have a chance to think. I
light a Cut and lean back in one of the red plastic
chairs that line the room. There's just me and a
couple on the other side. He's put his back out. Sunday is a quiet night, I guess. I think about Deacon, his
threats and talk, how that's ended. Then the two guys
he shot. I wonder if they were both from the car I saw.
It makes me feel stupid, like I'm to blame. Deacon
was only playing his game and he was good at it. I've
been lucky, just a few cuts. They'll pick me up but
there's noting to tie me to the house. I lost the
money. I've lost everything. I start thinking about
Dominic. The flat will be closing down now as they

head for sleep. I'm very tired. The cigarette is the only thing that keeps me going.

Trevor walks through from the attention ward. His face has been put into order, cleaned up, but the skin is stretched and discoloured round the nose and eye. He looks strange in the smart clothes, like a boxer who's dressed up for the press after his bout.

"Charles . . ."

"How you feeling?"

"Alive, which is something. Beg a cigarette."

I light him one and take another out of the pack for myself, grind the butt under my boot.

"Fuck, what you do to your leg?"

My jeans are sticky with blood. I pull the cotton up and there's another cut, deep.

"You better go back in."

"No, let's get home. What you gonna tell 'em?"

"Like I got in a fight I suppose. Hope my nose comes out alright."

"Make you look rugged, boy."

He manages a laugh.

"Hold a cab then."

"Yeah."

We don't speak on the way home. I pay with the last change I have from the drinks in the Prince and walk him up to his flat.

"You want me to come in?"

"No, I'm gonna sleep – like a baby, I hope. Shit, I had a date for tomorrow."

I'll check you in the morning. You still in shock."

He stops at his door and takes me by the arm. With

the bandage across his nose his eyes look far apart, sad. I think he's crying.

"Think we got out of it alright?"

"Don't know. We'll find out, I imagine."

"I'm gonna bell the others, see if they got back."

"Yeah, they were cool, not even cut."

"Should a seen Spence go at those guys, it was fucking wild."

"Wild night. Later, yeah?"

I start down the stairs and hear him pull the door shut.

My house is quiet, dark. I go up to the bathroom and look around for a plaster. Have to stretch two of them across the cut. Getting so many cuts on me I look like I've been stitched back together after a road crash. I stumble back to my room and push in. There's a black shape on the bed. I got tense, hit the light, but he speaks before I make a move.

"You alright? I stayed up for you."

"Yeah, everything's cool."

"You sorted it?"

"I think so. Why don't you go back to your room an' I'll see you for breakfast, tell you then?"

In the bright light he rubs his eyes and smiles.

"Sure. Just thought I'd, you know, look in on you."

"Thanks, Dom."

I undress, turn out the light and sink into bed. The curtains are still open and I can see the slates of the other block, dull in the moonlight. It will take me a long time to fall asleep but when I do I'll black out, there will be no dreams, nothing until the morning sun wakes me up with heat on my face.

Nineteen

I often think back on that night in his house, the room lighting up above me. There's no sound, just the colours, though Clark told me it was deafening, guns screaming in his ears out in the garden. Deacon lost it all, but what did he have anyway? That was the last message. I can see the hall, the tired stairs, the scraped walls, the battered, dusty armchairs surrounded with trash. He lived there with his brother, let people come in to get high in his own home. Whatever money he made wasn't enough to lift him out of that life. He was tied to it. The clothes and the arrogance were a front. Deacon didn't have much from his trade.

It taught me a lot, that run-in with Deacon. There were a lot of ideas I had, things I'd guessed, which were proven. Drugs don't have to be a problem but they represent money and when money comes in then it all changes. Drugs are drugs, all the same, just the profits are different depending on which substance you pick to sell. Society has found ways to control the growth of the underground, the threats it feels. In the States they're killing each other for it, setting up their own power circles whilst the authority looks on and smiles. Here it's different, the trade is still in its infancy, but the control is already in motion. Control of the drug, keeping it underground, that's how they attracted Deacon, gave him a way to earn. Then the trade runs its course and he's dead. They put up the yellow signs with the old-style 'Can You Help' crap and everyone is reminded how terrible drugs are – the dealers, the world outside control. It gives them power. They'd legalise everything but it gives them the power, lets them wield the big stick on the groups of people outside their own framework of thinking. You have to be smart to play that game.

It didn't take me long to work out Freddy was a master at it. I'd been used by the police to tie up the links, bring them to Deacon. They were watching me from the start. Freddy offered me a job a week after it happened. He hadn't been busted. He wanted me to wrap and weigh for him, run the errands, be a helper for two hundred a week. I turned him down. No-one could be sure, but Freddy must have been in on it. I can see him now, doing his deals with police, little chats and smiles. Freddy's not that different from them, not like Deacon. They can understand someone like Freddy – he's helpful, an asset, white, well-spoken. Deacon was on the outside.

I went to Bristol with Dom. There had been so much going on I was spinning for the first few days. I had to sort my head out.

I saw Theo for the jerk he is. He rang me up when I got back but by then I wasn't impressed any more. He wanted to see me, said he'd bust with Julia. Probably screwing Bond, I didn't care. Those people were more confused than me. They'd got to the position that had seemed so good initially, the lawyer or the clerk with the exotic holidays and all the trim, the fat bank balance. But none of them were happy with their lives because of what had happened to them on the way. They lost their soul. Theo was a shark, I had Clayton's word on that – heard all about what he'd rigged on the contract he'd drawn up. He wanted to get out, the bullshit travel idea they all get when they realise how dull the job is. But the money is too tempting. Theo will be with a procession of Julias, a series of Chelsea flats, better paid jobs, but he'll never get out. He's stuck there for ever.

Bond I wrote off as a good introduction to sex. At least it taught me that I could stumble, get involved. It wasn't body talk any more, I saw there was more you have to do to get it right. I wish you could see the brain, check you were compatible that way. Maybe not. That might take all the fun away. I met a girl in Bristol, slept with her on the last night of my stay. Now when I think about her I think what she said to me one night, how she laughs, all that stuff, not just the skin. Of course I think of that as well. I go down there to see her every two weeks. She wants me to move down there but I'm not sure. I'm not rushing.

We got to Bristol and went out into the country. His friends live in a huge farmhouse, the rent's nothing. They all finished their studies and now they're just chilling, trying to forget about the career for a year or two. Some of them had crap manual jobs they could forget about as soon as the day ended. Others did nothing, signed on and smoked roll-ups. It was a bit hippy but this time I wasn't so quick to judge. I'd learnt that you have to wait for the picture to clear before you diss it. They were happy. It was like what Clark was talking about – about getting out of the city, just smoke and be easy. And I saw it wasn't some commune bullshit, it was different from that. They were cool. I'm still not sure though. I love London.

Dom's back and it couldn't be better. My folks are happy again.

Everyone got out of the raided house alright that evening. I see Trev nearly every night now. We drink slow over at the Moon, saving the pound, stretching it till last orders. He's still pretty, the nose set well. Spence is inside. He got taken for something he didn't even do. He says they'll keep him on remand for six months to teach him a lesson. When he's released there's going to be a big party. I'm looking forward to it already. Ben went off somewhere. No-one's seen him for a while. Clark is working now. He's out a lot with women, gone back to being a stud. Indigo went up north with the new dude. Clark told me Bruce has quit from the firm. He's doing an English degree, wants to be a poet. I just smile and nod along with it.

I can see it now, what Dom was always getting at. There is no clear path. I'm not going into the spiritual crap. I just mean you can't be sure how it's going to turn out. I'm driving round in my dad's crate now and I don't care. Anyone diss me then I turn and smile, tell 'em to fuck off. If you live for the car then you only see a very thin slice of the world because you're thinking of status and wealth. You want more all the time, 'cause that's your only creed, so it grows and grows to keep you alive. You see the girl as a fuck and nothing else then what can you expect from it? There has to be more going on in your head than that.

It was a shake-up for me. I'm not saying I saw the light or anything dumb like that. I've just slowed down. I'm easy.

It gets dangerous when you start saying you're a ghetto warrior or a gangster or any of that stuff, trying so hard to be a man. For some that's all they've got, so they have to be proud of it, there's no other choice for them, but that's a hard road to travel. Others pretend to be in that situation but they go home to a nice pad, dinner in the oven. I don't stomach those people anymore. They're not real. I keep with my friends.

I'm still proud, know what I am, but I've seen some of the complexities, the intricacy of what's going on around us. I don't feel like I'm fighting every day. I don't run with any crowd, soaking up the bullshit. Trev says I've smartened up, others think I've gone soft. I don't even get that trashed anymore. That's because there's a lot to do. I'm studying now – so I can put something back into this city some time. Might help a little, who knows?

I'm gonna ask Spence for a sound system for the crate when he gets out – an Alpine or something, maybe a custom. It'll blast the other cars off the road. So watch out when some kid in a wreck pulls up next to you at the lights and you can feel the beat running through the tarmac and shaking your ass. You don't even know what I've seen, don't know what I am.

Best check yourself.